Lost

www.penguin.co.uk

Also by Leona Deakin

Gone

Lost

LEONA DEAKIN

BLACK SWAN

TRANSWORLD PUBLISHERS
61–63 Uxbridge Road, London W5 5SA
www.penguin.co.uk

Transworld is part of the Penguin Random House group of companies
whose addresses can be found at global.penguinrandomhouse.com

Penguin
Random House
UK

First published in Great Britain in 2020 by Black Swan
an imprint of Transworld Publishers

A CIP catalogue record for this book is available from the British Library.

ISBN 9781784164096

Typeset in 12.5/14.75 pt Garamond MT Std by Jouve (UK), Milton Keynes
Printed and bound in Great Britain by Clays Ltd, Elcograf S.p.A.

Penguin Random House is committed to a sustainable
future for our business, our readers and our planet. This book
is made from Forest Stewardship Council® certified paper.

For my little show-off. This one's for you.

'No man has a good enough memory
to be a successful liar.'

Abraham Lincoln

'There is always hope.'

'Girl with Balloon', Banksy

I

As he walked up the stone stairway, Captain Harry Peterson had no idea that time was running out. In less than an hour, a bomb would rip this building apart.

He looked across the lawn. Everyone was peaceful, content. A hundred officers in full uniform were drinking champagne in front of a marquee. The buttons on their cropped jackets were shining in the sunlight. Their conversation, loud with laughter, mixed with music from the Royal Marines Band.

Harry smiled. He'd seen it all before, many times, but he knew he'd never grow tired of the glamour and decadence of a military ball.

Behind the officers' wardroom at Her Majesty's Naval Base, Devonport, a thin man in dark clothes waited patiently. He paced up and down, up and down. He checked the straps of his backpack and the trigger switch in his pocket.

Harry always thought it was a privilege to be in the Royal Navy, but never more so than when he was at Devonport. He smiled as he walked past the two miniature cannons housed on carved wooden lions on his way into the building. He had never wanted to do anything else but this: as a child he'd dreamt of travelling the world on the ships he'd seen in Portsmouth and as a teenager he'd watched films about fighter pilots and tacked a poster of *The Dam Busters* to his bedroom wall. It wasn't that he wanted to fight but he liked the idea of being a hero. Who didn't? He wanted to be a good person.

The man on reception glanced at the rank insignia embroidered on Harry's jacket cuffs. 'Good evening, Captain,' he said.

Harry nodded. He squeezed past the photographer and collected a glass of champagne from a lady dressed in a red-tailed jacket and a gold waistcoat. The biannual balls were themed to separate them from the endless formal dinners and because, as the defender of the seas, the Navy felt it was not only the most senior service, but also the one with the best sense of humour and so *Night at the Circus* had been chosen for this evening's event. Which explained the juggler on the lawn and the man on stilts parading around the concourse.

The room overlooking the lawn had been converted into a complimentary gin bar. Its leather sofas and heavy oak tables had been moved aside and the staff were wearing glittery leotards and feathered headdresses. Harry searched for a familiar face, knowing he was unlikely to find one. He wasn't attached to this base. He'd been invited to attend the ball by Commodore Chris Waite who wanted to sound him out about a job. Harry had no intention of accepting – he didn't want to move back to Plymouth – but it was never a good idea to refuse a courtship flat out. You had to play the game; people in the military had long memories and perhaps he'd be back here one day. But, for now, he needed to be in London and close to his children. He'd missed so much when they were young, and if he didn't take jobs stationed near his ex-wife now, he'd never see them at all.

He nodded to a young lieutenant whose girlfriend was wearing an off-the-shoulder peach dress decorated with diamanté. The dress code had been clear: ankle-length dresses, covered shoulders and minimal bling. No doubt there'd be a coven of military wives discussing the young woman's decision by the end of the evening.

'Lovely dress,' Harry said. He thought he'd put in a good word now, just in case she overheard something different later on. She blushed and thanked him with a delighted giggle.

'Thank you, Sir,' her boyfriend said.

Harry patted the man's shoulder.

The thin man continued to pace up and down outside the officers' wardroom. It wasn't time yet. But he could hear music and the laughter and he hated them for it. He wished he could see their faces when it went off. It was his only regret. But it was a small price to pay.

Harry turned to see Commodore Waite entering the room with his wife, who was wearing a smart black evening gown.

'Evening, Sir,' Harry said, shaking Waite's hand. 'Thank you for the invite.'

Mrs Waite kissed Harry on the cheek. 'When we were

out for dinner last month, you called him Chris all night,' she said. 'But now it's "Sir".'

'That was pleasure, Mrs Waite,' said Harry. 'This is work.' She was the Commodore's second wife and still new enough to the military world to be fascinated by its quirks.

She looked at the gin bar surrounded by well-dressed guests. 'You think *this* is work.'

Harry and Chris exchanged a smile.

'How's it feel to be back? I bet you've missed the old place,' Waite said. It was true that Harry had always had a fondness for Devonport.

'The place, yes. The people . . .' He scrunched up his face.

The Commodore laughed, a loud boom fitting for a man of his status. 'No doubt you'd whip 'em into shape.'

Waite held up his hand to greet a group of officers on the other side of the room. 'I better get over there,' he said. 'Let's catch up later, I want to talk about your next move.'

'Drinks first,' said Mrs Waite, looping her arm through her husband's and navigating them towards the gin bar.

'We better see what they have,' said Waite.

'Everything from black pepper to raspberries, I believe,' Harry replied. He was sticking to his one glass of champagne. He liked to stay in control at work events. He walked to the window and his eyes immediately fell on an elegant redhead in a floor-length dark green gown cinched tightly at the waist with a bronze bow. She was standing in the middle of the lawn. Her hair was tied up so that her face was framed by just a few loose curls. She'd

4

said that there was absolutely no way she'd make it, that work was crazy.

Harry rushed back towards the reception. He loved that she'd decided to surprise him. It's exactly what he'd have done.

At the door, a grey-haired, muscular officer blocked his way.

'Sir,' he said. 'Sub-Lieutenant Philips from Joint Forces Command. May I have a word in private, please?'

Dinner was announced and the other guests started moving out of the building and towards the marquee in typical military compliance.

'Now?' Harry said. He leaned to the side, trying to see Karene through the moving crowd. He wanted to find her, to kiss her.

The man stepped a little closer and spoke in a low voice. 'Yes, Sir,' he said. 'I've come here especially. I need to brief you in person.' The man turned and began walking back to the bar.

Harry knew he couldn't refuse Joint Forces. He was one of them and it would be impolite at best and dangerous at worst. Plus the sub-lieutenant wasn't in dress uniform – just his white shirt and his cap under one arm – so he'd been sent unexpectedly. The brief was clearly urgent.

Moving against the flow, Harry followed the man through the crowd. Commodore and Mrs Waite were lingering at the door of the bar as the final group of officers made their way outside.

The sub-lieutenant strode towards the window on the other side of the room so that they were out of earshot.

'What's so important?' asked Harry. He checked the man's rank and frowned. The epaulettes decorating his shoulders were upside down. That was a rookie mistake. Or perhaps he'd dressed in a hurry.

'This will only take a minute, Sir.'

Harry peered through the window and back out to the lawn. He could see Karene on the concourse looking for him in the crowd. A man on stilts stomped past the window. Karene glanced up and her eyes met Harry's. He raised his hand to wave and she smiled.

And then the room exploded.

2

The blast hit Karene with a violent thrust and she jolted backwards, landing hard on the concrete paving slabs. She instinctively raised her arm across her eyes as glass from the windows rained down on her. She was surrounded by hot air, rushing across her skin, and a thick grey cloud of choking dust. She heard the man on stilts fall, colliding with a table which then collapsed, spraying glassware across the floor.

She could see nothing, hear so little: the world dull and distant as though she was underwater. Should she run? Should she hide? She took a deep breath, trying to stay calm. Her mouth tasted of metal and something somewhere was burning.

She tried to focus. She was surrounded by fog. A figure in the distance was trying to stand. They stumbled and then righted themselves.

'Hey,' she called. 'Hello?' But although her lips were moving, there was no sound at all. She tried again, but the figure moved away from her and was swallowed by the grey.

She crawled towards the man on stilts.

'Are you OK?' she said, pressing her index finger and thumb into an 'OK' sign so that she might at least communicate something.

The man nodded. He sat up. He looked up at the building, just decipherable through the dust, and shook his head.

Karene followed his gaze.

Harry.

She needed to get in there.

She stood up and, staying crouched, ran towards the stone steps.

A strong hand grabbed her by the arm.

'Get down,' shouted the man. He had clumps of grey soot in his hair.

Karene shook her head.

'Hey,' yelled the man, pulling her down to the floor. He pressed his mouth against her ear so that she could hear him more clearly. 'This place is full of military personnel. And none of them are running towards the blast area, are they?'

'Why the hell not?' she shouted. Her voice squeaked each word.

'Because we don't know what that was, if it's finished or if there might be worse still to come. We need to wait.'

Karene looked at the man in disbelief. 'How long will that take?' she shouted, pulling her arm away. 'People might be hurt. They might be bleeding.'

Harry.

She pushed the man aside and continued up the stairs. She could hear someone screaming. She knew that she was out of her depth but what choice did she have?

She stepped inside the reception. It was dark and thick with smoke. Harry had been in a room to the left. She squinted, looking in that direction, hoping her eyes would adjust. The shapes made no sense. She blinked several times. Large slabs of burning wood blocked her path and the mangled remnants of something metal formed a barrier ahead.

A young officer rushed to her side and surveyed the destruction. His uniform was clean, with none of the dust. He must have been further out on the lawn, maybe even in the marquee when the explosion had happened.

'Are you medical?' he asked. His voice sounded muffled and distant.

'I know basic first aid,' she said. 'But that's it.'

'Any idea how many people were in here?'

She shook her head.

The officer nodded. 'We need to get inside. And then triage. Ignore anyone screaming and go to the quiet ones. If you're screaming, you're breathing. OK?'

Karene looked at the young man and wondered how he was so calm, what hell his eyes had seen.

'Check if they can respond. Then airway, breathing . . . Shout if you find a problem. I'll get to you as soon as I can.'

Karene pulled her dress up to her knees and tied a knot in the fabric to lift it from the floor. Then she stepped carefully around and over the debris. Harry had been near a window to the left of the reception. There were no doors before the smashed-up staircase so she kept moving along the corridor and beyond it until she found a door to the left.

She stepped through it. Thin shafts of sunlight broke through the blown windows and Karene made her way towards the light.

'Help,' said a voice. 'Please help.'

A woman was sitting up against the wall.

If you're screaming, you're breathing. That went for talking too.

'I'll be back,' Karene said. 'I promise.'

She kept moving. There were no other shouts, no moans or screams. Which meant that Harry was silent.

She found him on his back by the window. He wasn't moving. She dropped to her knees and did as the young officer had instructed.

'Harry?' she shouted. 'Harry! Can you hear me?'

There was no response. She opened his mouth and checked his airway. It was clear. Then she placed her ear beside his lips. She couldn't hear anything – the ringing in her head was far too loud – but she was sure she felt his breath warm and steady against her cheek. She lifted his wrist and felt for a pulse. It was strong. She checked for injuries but couldn't find anything. There was a thick layer of dust on his face and she gently wiped it away from his nose and mouth. There was also a small graze on his forehead.

She ran her hands through his hair and down the sides of his head, praying that she wouldn't feel any wetness. Then she did the same across his torso, feeling under his jacket and finally checking his arms and legs. He seemed OK. Unconscious, yes, but OK.

'Ma'am, I need you over here.' The young officer's

voice sounded calm but assertive. This was not a request; it was an order.

'You're OK, Harry,' she whispered. 'Help is coming and I'm not going far.' She kissed his head. 'I love you.'

She crawled back to the doorway where the officer was kneeling next to the woman. She was in a sequinned leotard and there was a large wound on her left arm that was pumping blood on to the navy carpet.

'I need you to stem the bleeding,' said the officer. He placed Karene's hand around the woman's bicep, just above the wound. 'Hold her arm up and squeeze here. Harder than that. It'll slow the bleeding.'

The sequinned woman stared wide-eyed at her arm.

'Got it,' Karene said. 'Squeeze tightly.'

'And don't let go until I come back. I need to check the others. Is that your husband?' he asked looking over at Harry.

'Yes,' Karene replied. There was no point disputing relationship statuses in this environment. 'He's unconscious but breathing and his pulse is strong. I can't see any major injuries, just a small wound to his head. He's been lucky.'

The officer watched her carefully and then said, 'It's tempting to focus on the best-case scenario but you need to consider the worst. He's been knocked unconscious so he may have spinal damage or internal injuries. Shout if you see him stir.'

Karene nodded.

Spinal damage. Internal injuries.

Oh God, Harry.

Karene was relieved when she saw the two paramedics move swiftly past her. Clearly the young officer had sent them Harry's way. They would take care of him. He was in safe hands now.

3

Marcus Jameson removed his cycling helmet, hung it over the handlebars and leaned his bike against a large boulder. The spectacular view more than compensated for the steep ascent, and, to be fair, uphill cycling was his favourite. He enjoyed the burn as much as the sense of achievement. He took a large swig of water from his bottle and perched on a smaller boulder to eat the slice of banana loaf he'd bought at a cafe near his campsite.

His weekend in Wales had turned into a week and then a fortnight. He knew he was being driven by denial. He cycled to the point of exhaustion every day so that he'd fall asleep quickly and deep enough to see him through until the morning. Keeping busy also made it easier to ignore his phone; to avoid contact with his sister or, God forbid, Augusta who was still leaving regular messages on his voicemail. You'd think after three months of being ignored she'd have got the message.

He knew he was prone to hermit-like behaviour. He'd been told it often enough during his regular psychological assessments while at MI6. The 'shadow' side of his outgoing, optimistic personality was a loner in denial. He'd been told to watch out for signs he was retreating from reality and, on leaving the service, he'd done just that. He'd focused on keeping himself busy, putting effort into his social life, and he'd found a new purpose working as a private investigator with Dr Augusta Bloom. They had joined forces after he'd heard her speaking on the primary motives behind criminal exploits, and he'd joked that no one was better placed to investigate mysteries than an ex-spy and a criminal psychologist. Using his skills to help people had been satisfying. Until it all fell apart.

He'd spent the first few weeks after Bloom betrayed him hiding in his flat in London. But when it became clear that his sister, Claire, wasn't going to leave him alone, he changed tack. His trips looked like something productive – travelling, exercising – but he knew, deep down, it wasn't constructive at all. He was still alone, still hiding. The problem was he couldn't trust his own judgement any more. It had all started earlier in the year when he'd convinced Bloom to help a teenage girl find her wayward mother. In doing so, he'd inadvertently embroiled them in the scheming mind games of a psychopath who had ultimately tried to kill him. So how could he trust his own judgement any more?

Jameson's phone rang, interrupting the peace of the Welsh valley with Queen's 'Bicycle Race'. He checked the screen. He didn't recognize the number.

'Hello?' he said.

'Marcus Jameson?' It was a woman's voice.

'Uh-huh,' he replied throatily, swallowing a mouthful of banana loaf. 'Who's this?'

'My name is Karene Harper and I need your help. Did you hear about the bomb at Devonport Naval Base?'

'Sure,' Jameson replied. 'It was all over the news.'

'Well, I was there. My partner – Captain Harry Peterson – was injured in the blast.'

Jameson placed his cake on top of its paper bag. 'I'm sorry to hear that.'

'But he never arrived at hospital.'

'What? How do you mean?'

'He was taken away in an ambulance but never arrived anywhere.'

'But that explosion was two days ago. Have you checked all the hospitals?'

'Of course I have.' Her tone was clipped and irritated. 'The police say he likely discharged himself, but he hasn't been in touch with me or with his children.' After a beat of silence, she said, 'You're thinking he's probably dead?'

Jameson hadn't been entirely sure how to phrase that statement and realized his silence may have been abrupt. 'There can be a lot of chaos around these explosions,' he continued. 'It's not always easy to identify . . .'

'He was unconscious but breathing after the blast with no sign of serious injury.'

'That doesn't necessarily—'

'I know,' she interrupted. 'And if he's dead, then that's one thing, but right now I just need to know if you'll help us find him.'

'*Us?*'

The line went quiet for a moment and then he heard a familiar voice.

'I knew you'd screen my call,' said his business partner Augusta Bloom.

Jameson's free hand curled into a fist. 'Oh, that is low.' They'd worked together for five years and that was plenty. He had no interest in working with her again. It had transpired during that last case that Bloom and Seraphine Walker – their unexpected psychopath – were old acquaintances. And they'd both played him. Seraphine had presented herself as Sarah, and he'd fallen hard for the intelligent, charming alter-ego. And Bloom had opted to keep him in the dark, keep him in danger. In the many hours he'd spent pondering her choice, he kept coming back to the same disturbing conclusion. And so he wanted nothing more to do with Bloom.

'Maybe, but I need you,' she said. 'Karene is an old friend and this has military written all over it. You once asked me for a favour and now I need one in return.'

'Yeah and look how that turned out.' That little favour had nearly resulted in his death.

'I don't know how many times I can say I'm sorry, Marcus, but I will continue to do so until you believe me. For now, this is not about me or you; it is about my friend and her missing partner. You know you can get access to the military in a way I cannot. You don't even need to see me if you don't want to. You can work directly with Karene. She's fine with that.'

Jameson clenched his jaw. She was making him sound like a petulant child. 'I'll think about it,' he said.

'You will?'

'Yes.' He hung up.

'Will he help us?' Karene asked. Her voice was softer now, much weaker than it had been on the phone.

'He can't resist a mystery,' said Bloom, handing her friend a box of tissues from the desk. Her words sounded surprisingly convincing considering she didn't really believe them. The events three months earlier had ruptured their relationship to such an extent she wasn't sure it could be mended. She had left him in the dark. He'd seen it as a betrayal. But it had been tactical. He refused to see that she'd had no other choice. Her goal had been to stop Seraphine. Whatever the cost. 'I hope he'll come around,' Bloom said and she really did.

It was late Monday afternoon. Bloom had caught the train to Plymouth where Karene had been staying in a hotel since the ball. They sat in her minimalist bedroom, Bloom on the desk chair and Karene on the small sofa.

'So the last you saw of Harry, he was lying unconscious on the floor?'

Karene shook her head. 'I saw the paramedics with him. I should have gone over; I wanted to but the medic said to stay put. He told me to hold on to this woman's arm until he returned. So I did that. I watched as they took Harry away.'

'And you've checked every hospital?' asked Bloom. 'All of them?'

Karene blew her nose and nodded. 'In a thirty-mile radius.'

Bloom had known Karene Harper since their university days and had never seen her upset or tearful; she was a little taken aback by the emotion. Karene had always been one of those irrepressibly positive types, upbeat and comfortable using humour to bat away the bad times. It had made sense that Karene specialized in mental resilience: she clearly possessed it in abundance. She was the youngest of five siblings, with four older brothers and a father who had never expected his daughter to amount to much. But she was tough. Or at least she had been. It had been years since Bloom had seen Karene, so her call the previous evening had come as a bit of a surprise.

'Where is he, Augusta?' Karene said as fresh tears fell across her cheeks. 'Why wasn't he taken to Derriford Hospital like everyone else?'

'You said he wasn't badly injured. Maybe he did discharge himself?'

'But Derriford has no record of admitting him. I've tried to get the police and the military to help, but they're obsessed with the bomber. Harry isn't a priority apparently.' The bitterness in Karene's tone matched her look of disgust.

'How about the paramedics?' asked Bloom. 'Have you managed to speak to them?'

Karene shook her head.

Bloom made a note to track them down. 'It was a terrorist attack. A suicide bomber. Is that what they're thinking?'

Karene nodded.

'Have you spoken to Harry's colleagues in the Navy?'

'Yes. I called Harry's boss as soon as I realized what had happened. But no one's heard from Harry at work. It's been two days, Augusta. I've just got this horrible feeling . . .'

'That he's in the morgue somewhere?'

Karene blinked a few times.

'Or . . .' said Bloom.

'Or what? What else could it be?' Karene was clearly desperate for answers.

Bloom paused for a moment. The ambulance crew would have been obliged to deliver their patient to a hospital. But no hospital had received him. 'I think the answer's with the paramedics. If that's what they were.'

'What do you mean?' said Karene.

'I'm just wondering what it would take to get hold of a couple of jackets and a stretcher?' she said, thinking out loud.

Karene's eyes widened. 'You think those people weren't medical?'

'I know from working with the police that incidents like this are carefully managed by the emergency services. There would have been a commander in charge making sure that the injured were taken to the nearest possible trauma centre. This feels like an unlikely mistake. Which leaves us with conspiracy. He's missing for a reason.'

'What reason? What possible reason?' Karene looked scared now.

Bloom shook her head slowly. She had no idea.

5

Bloom was back at her desk on Tuesday morning in her rented office, located in the basement beneath a glossy PR firm in Russell Square. The office was small: just two desks, a white board and a couple of extra chairs for clients. Not that they had many visitors. The advantage of the underground space was anonymity; Bloom didn't want some of the characters she dealt with knowing where she spent her time.

Jameson arrived, carrying a bottle of water. He normally had a take-out coffee. He had let his dark hair grow so that the thick curls framed his face and brushed his shirt collar. He strolled to his desk casually, as though nothing had happened in the past few months, as though he'd been here every day. But his eyes, normally alert, looked dull and tired. And he wasn't smiling.

'All right?' he said, taking his seat and unpacking his laptop. There was no jovial accent: no 'G'day Bruce' or 'What's occurring?'

She'd been desperate for him to return ever since the events of the spring, but had doubted it would ever happen. He'd been so angry. And it hadn't eased, not at all. But now, here he was. And after just one phone call. All she'd needed to do was find the right problem. It was obvious. She was irritated that she hadn't worked it out sooner.

'Welcome back,' she said.

'There are ground rules.' He swivelled in his seat to face her. 'I don't want to hear any apologies. What's done is done. My working on this case is to repay you, nothing more, nothing less. It doesn't mean I'm back,' he continued, 'and I do not want to hear her name mentioned.'

Bloom knew he was referring to Seraphine. He'd liked her, maybe even loved her, and she'd hurt him pretty badly. She'd tricked him, and Jameson didn't like being tricked. What he failed to understand was the superior skill a psychopath like Seraphine had when it came to manipulation. It was akin to a superpower. In order to fit in, Seraphine had learned to mimic normality. She'd had years of practice honing a mask of deception. But behind her beautiful face lurked a cold, calculating mind that felt nothing but disdain for the very people she copied. A disdain that made her very dangerous indeed.

'How is Jane?' Bloom asked, moving the subject into safer territory. Jane was the teenage girl whose mother had gone missing earlier in the year, the favour that Jameson had asked of her. And then Jane herself had disappeared, been taken by her mother at the behest of Seraphine. They had managed to secure Jane's return, but her mother, Lana, still remained missing.

'She's fine.'

'Is she seeing much of her father?'

'Every other weekend.'

'It must be nice for her to have stepbrothers.'

Jameson ignored her. 'Where are we starting with this Peterson thing? Because I've made a few enquiries and managed to sort a meeting with his boss this afternoon. Patrick Grey. Northwood Headquarters. We can take the Metropolitan Line. It's only forty-five minutes.'

'Yes, I read your email. Thank you for organizing that. Did you speak to him on the phone?'

'Only briefly. He said it was out of character. That Peterson's the conscientious, reliable type.'

'Interesting. So he's unlikely to have gone AWOL unless he had no choice.'

'Or he's dead.'

Bloom raised her eyebrows. 'So we go to Northwood this afternoon? Good. And we're interviewing Karene this morning. She's coming in at ten.'

'Haven't you spoken to her already?' He was frosty, dismissive. He was here, but it wasn't like before, not at all.

Bloom took a deep breath. 'I thought we should hear it together, properly, from the start: that's what we usually do.'

'Did.'

Bloom frowned.

'What we usually *did*,' he explained.

'So why upset a good system?'

He held her gaze for a moment then looked back at his computer screen.

Karene brought a pad full of notes that detailed her experience of the bombing and its aftermath, and the information she'd gathered from those she'd spoken to over the last two days.

She looked better, stronger. She was wearing loose

trousers with a vibrant green blouse fastened at the front by a large silk bow. Her burnt-orange flats perfectly matched her ginger hair, which was plaited neatly to one side. Karene had always worked in academia and had never felt the need to dress conventionally.

She sat down straightaway and it was immediately clear that she wanted to get on with things.

'Go on,' she said. 'What do you need to know?'

'How long was there between you arriving and the bomb going off?' Jameson asked. His friendly tone and broad smile revealed that Karene's flair and femininity had been duly acknowledged.

'I arrived at Devonport at quarter to eight and the explosion happened fifteen minutes later, just after dinner was announced.'

'Devonport is the naval base?' said Bloom.

'Yes,' Karene replied. 'In Plymouth.'

'And that's where Harry was based?' asked Jameson.

'No. He was based with Rear Admiral Grey at Northwood. But the Commodore at Plymouth was pursuing Harry about a role and the invite was part of that.'

'Reports say the bomb was detonated in the building's reception as people were making their way out,' said Jameson.

'That's right. The bar was inside but dinner was in a marquee on the lawn.'

'Do you know how many were hurt?' he asked.

'Two officers were killed and another two are still in Derriford Hospital. The Commodore lost a leg and his wife was also hurt. Then there were the events staff, two men and two women, all still hospitalized. And another officer's wife is in a coma; she stayed back to text the babysitter.'

'Plus Harry, that's twelve people,' said Jameson. He frowned. 'That's not a lot.'

'It's enough,' said Karene, flashing him a look of utter contempt.

'How many people were there in total?' Jameson asked.

'Over three hundred.'

'So the explosion happened after most people had already left the building?' Jameson scribbled something on his notepad.

'That's a good thing, isn't it?' said Karene.

Jameson sat back in his chair and looked at Bloom. 'Don't you think it's odd?'

'Your average suicide bomber wants to wreak as much havoc as possible,' Bloom explained. 'So why wait until the majority of people are out of the room?'

'Maybe he didn't realize they'd move so quickly?' said Karene.

'I'd say if he's in the building with a bomb strapped to him and people start leaving, he flicks the switch straightaway,' said Jameson.

'So he arrived too late?' said Bloom.

'Or he didn't want to wreak havoc,' said Jameson. 'That wasn't his intention.'

'How do you mean?' asked Bloom.

'I'm not sure,' said Jameson. 'It's just strange. I'll see what I can dig up on the bomber.'

'And that's why you're here,' said Bloom, smiling.

She knew she couldn't do this without him. She'd managed a few cases in his absence, but this one would be impossible. Jameson's background was shadowy. He was very secretive but he'd spent time with MI6, secret service rather than military, but still under the Ministry of Defence. So this case was right up his street.

She only hoped he'd stick around long enough for her to convince him to stay permanently.

6

On the tube, Bloom found herself thinking of a similar trip they'd taken to Leeds earlier in the year. Marcus had chatted happily then. Now, he avoided eye contact and there was a scowl plastered across his face.

'How are you?' she said.

'I told you. I don't want to talk about it.'

'I'm not asking about *it*. I'm asking how you are here, now, today?'

Jameson glanced at her. 'Fine.'

She didn't think he looked fine – he was pale and his shirt hung too loosely over his shoulders – but this wasn't the time.

Jameson was staring at a spot on the carriage floor. He'd been gazing at it on and off since they sat down. 'What do you make of Karene?' he asked. 'Is she kosher?'

'I wouldn't have called you if she wasn't.'

His lip twitched. 'Yes, but *you* didn't call.'

Bloom ignored the jibe. 'What do you want to know? I trust her. She's one of the most unflappable people I've ever met.'

Jameson huffed a laugh. 'Is that so?'

'Not flat and unemotional like . . . you know . . .' She knew not to use Seraphine's name. 'She's simply very robust. All of her research into mental resilience? That comes from somewhere personal. She knows everything there is to know about it. For her PhD, she interviewed hundreds of people: high achievers, people in high-risk professions, those suffering with chronic illnesses. They're all linked by the same qualities, things that keep them fighting.'

'Such as?' The tube pulled into Baker Street station.

'The right mindset: tenacity, optimism, sense of purpose. So it's odd to see her so . . .' Bloom struggled to find the right word.

'Devastated.'

'She does seem devastated, doesn't she? It's odd.'

'You've never been in love, have you, Augusta?'

'Well . . . I wouldn't say—'

'If you can't see it screaming out of every cell in that woman, then you've certainly never felt it.' There was a coldness to his tone that suggested judgement rather than teasing.

Bloom found her own speck to stare at on the floor.

The taxi dropped them at Northwood. Jameson introduced himself to the security guard and explained that their passes had been requested by Patrick Grey. They showed their passports and received red badges in return.

A guard escorted them to Building 410, where the Joint Forces Command was based. The boxy reception was a large white space furnished with black chairs and military photographs. Jameson introduced himself again at the reception desk and they were asked to take a seat.

'This is where it all happens then?' asked Bloom as she looked around. The windows above them were filled with Army, Navy and RAF flags.

'These guys have been responsible for joint initiatives for decades.'

'Which means?'

'This is where all overseas military operations are planned and controlled. Before the mid-nineties, either the Army, Navy or RAF would be assigned overall command of a given operation, but that led to inconsistencies so it was decided a Joint Forces Command was needed, and this is HQ.'

'So operations are planned here with all military assets in mind?'

'Give or take a few exceptions, like our nuclear deterrent.'

'Have you been here before?'

Jameson shrugged, which meant that he wasn't willing to say.

'Here he is,' said Jameson, standing as a man in a blue jumper with gold epaulettes strode towards them with a younger female officer in a crisp white shirt and black skirt.

'Rear Admiral Grey,' said the man, holding out his hand. 'And this is my Chief of Staff, Captain Tessa Morrisey.' Instead of leading them through the glass security pods, Grey took a seat opposite them and Captain Morrisey stayed standing.

'I'm afraid we'll need to talk here.' He turned to Jameson. 'I appreciate your background but you should know your security clearance expires the minute you leave, and your friend here has none.'

'I am well aware,' Jameson said. He sat up straighter, pulling his shoulders tight.

'You said you were with some of ours in Iraq?' Grey either hadn't noticed or didn't care about the change in Jameson's demeanour. Bloom suspected the latter.

'I was. Navy boats provide a nice enough taxi service.'

'Ships,' said Grey.

'Thank you for seeing us at such short notice,' said Bloom, keen to move the conversation on. 'May I ask how long you've known Henry Peterson?'

'Harry and I go way back,' he said. 'I was his commanding officer when he was a newly promoted lieutenant. We got on well. He stood out.'

'How so?' asked Bloom.

'Perhaps we might clarify your role and remit here first,' said Grey, looking from Bloom to Jameson and then back again.

'Mr Jameson and I are private investigators,' she said. 'We've been hired by Karene Harper, Captain Peterson's partner, to locate him.'

'And to do that we need to know about his current role,' said Jameson.

Grey raised an eyebrow but kept his focus on Bloom. 'I spoke to the regulators after Mr Jameson called. And we have this in hand.'

'Royal Navy Police,' said Jameson to Bloom. 'They're looking for Peterson, are they?'

'Investigations are underway, yes. And, of course, the

civilian police are working on this too. It's in the hands of the professionals. Perhaps you should leave it there.'

Bloom had been doing this job a while: she knew they were being dismissed and chose to ignore it. It was nothing more than a power play. She had experienced the same thing many times in her work with senior police officers. Leaders like Grey liked to be in control. It had nothing to do with organizational sensitivities and everything to do with personal ones. It was not insignificant, for instance, that his second in command remained standing. Here was a junior officer who knew exactly what her boss demanded, and Bloom suspected that was compliance.

'None of the hospitals in or around Plymouth have any record of admitting Captain Peterson,' she said, 'so it's unlikely that he discharged himself. A more plausible hypothesis is that he came to in the ambulance and somehow wandered off in a disorientated state. But if that were the case you'd expect the paramedics to file a report.'

'And they haven't?' said Grey, betraying his lack of research.

'We've not been able to locate them,' Jameson replied. Bloom knew he had made some initial enquiries to the ambulance service after they had spoken to Karene this morning. They had no record of a Harry Peterson but were looking into unidentified casualties matching his description.

'There are protocols for these things,' Captain Morrisey said. Her voice was deeper than Bloom had expected.

'There are processes to follow. We can't ignore the fact that a man has just blown himself up on a military base. The priority at present is finding out his identity and preventing further breaches.'

Bloom kept her eyes on Grey. 'Are you not worried that he's missing? Do you not have a duty of care, as his employer, to help us find him?'

Grey rolled his shoulders backwards, expanding his chest. 'I am assisting and will continue to assist the designated investigators. This is not a civilian matter.'

'But as your colleague rightly says,' said Jameson, 'the investigators are focusing on the terrorist attack, and not on one missing officer.'

'We're good at finding people, Rear Admiral,' said Bloom, hoping the use of his title might play to his need for respect and recognition. 'It's what we do. And we don't want to interfere with the investigation. We always cooperate fully with the police. In fact, we have a meeting with them in the diary.' This wasn't entirely true but she'd asked the question and was confident they'd grant her a meeting. 'But if we want to get to the bottom of this then we need to know more about Captain Peterson.'

'What's the nature of his job?' asked Jameson.

Grey said nothing. He'd been happy to put Jameson in his place earlier, but had avoided eye contact with him since. Yet more evidence that this was a man who did not like to be challenged.

'You're not at liberty to say?' said Bloom.

'Oh, I'm at liberty.' Grey smiled. 'I'm simply choosing not to. Because I can't see why it's relevant.'

'Is it controversial?' said Jameson.

Grey pressed his lips into a thin line.

Bloom could see his reasoning. Why share potentially sensitive information with two outsiders if it had nothing to do with Harry's whereabouts?

'Maybe you could tell me a little about him as a person?' said Bloom.

Grey sat back into his chair. 'How do you mean?'

'How does he conduct himself? And how does he lead people? Is there anything that might make him a target?'

'Harry is the consummate people person. And that is no small thing in our world. Command and control is about inspiring as much as it is instructing. You need to inspire loyalty, inspire effort. It's not enough to tell people what to do; you have to make them want to do it for you.'

Captain Morrisey masked her micro-expressions quickly, but Bloom spotted the slightly widened eyes and raised eyebrows followed by a brief smirk. Bloom deduced from Morrisey's surprise that Grey probably didn't live up to his definition of leadership. Bloom was starting to get a sense of the sort of boss Grey might be; one whose modus operandi was much closer to instructing than inspiring. Did he know this about himself or was it in his blind spot?

'So Harry's popular?' asked Bloom.

'I'm not sure popularity is our aim. He's fair and clear.'

Bloom nodded. 'And have you noticed any changes in his character or behaviour of late?'

'Such as?'

'Has he been under any stress at work or in his personal life?' She wanted to know if there was anything that might make him use this opportunity to escape his life and responsibilities. They couldn't rule out that Harry Peterson had orchestrated his own disappearance.

Grey sighed. He was clearly bored. 'The Navy is a promiscuous mistress,' he said. 'Many a marriage has disintegrated due to her interference. I was sad to hear about Harry and Caroline. They always seemed solid. But it never affected his work. Never.'

Grey looked at Morrisey. She checked her watch and nodded. Grey rose from his seat.

'I think it was clear to everyone that this new lady was making Harry very happy,' said Morrisey. 'He seemed content.'

'So this disappearance is definitely out of character?' asked Bloom. 'You'd have expected to hear from him.'

'Not just expected, Dr Bloom, but demanded,' said Grey. 'We afford our leaders some autonomy but not much.'

Grey turned and walked towards the glass security pod.

'So this is not just out of character, it's potentially career damaging. Does that not suggest to you that Captain Harry Peterson might be in trouble?' Bloom asked, raising her voice despite the silence.

Grey didn't reply. He simply stepped into a pod and the doors closed behind him. He exited on the other side without looking back.

Jameson smiled at Morrisey. 'Well he's a character.'

'You have no idea,' she said in a low voice and then shook both of their hands. 'Goodbye, Mr Jameson, Dr Bloom.' She disappeared into a pod, stepped out the other side and walked down the corridor.

Jameson raised his eyebrows.

'What do you think Harry was working on? Can we find out?'

'Sure,' said Jameson. 'It'll be on the news. Whatever's on there, that's what he's working on.'

'Russia?'

'Or North Korea? Or the ISIS terrorist threat? It could be any of those things.'

'You think this was ISIS? The bomb?'

'They haven't claimed responsibility but it certainly makes a statement, doesn't it? Infiltrating a military base. But then again . . .' Jameson paused when a security guard arrived to escort them back to the main gate. They didn't speak until they were alone again.

'You were saying,' said Bloom, as they waited for a taxi.

'It's been bugging me. Why use a bomb to kill so few people? If this was a statement to the establishment and the military, saying, I don't know, "We can get to you and we can harm you," then why didn't they do just that?'

'You think the bomb was a distraction?'

'Perhaps. Sleight of hand. We're all looking over here so we don't see what's going on over there.'

'So maybe this does have something to do with Harry's work?'

'Why else would he be the only person unaccounted for?'

Bloom nodded. 'So we have a bomb that did far less harm than it could have and a missing naval officer who was working on something unknown. Plus if I'm not wrong, his employers don't appear to be taking his disappearance as seriously as you would have thought.'

7

Eighteen Months Earlier

Karene unpacked her overnight bag and changed into a turquoise wrap dress and wedges. She washed her face in the hotel bathroom and reapplied her make-up. She was expected to circulate at these conferences, which she didn't mind at all, but she wouldn't be speaking until tomorrow and so tonight she'd be walking into a bar full of strangers.

She took the lift down to reception and followed signs to the conference bar. The event had started the afternoon before, so the social dynamic was set already. In the bar people clustered in small groups and, as she walked through the crowd, she was offered very little eye contact and only one friendly smile. Human beings were pack animals and it was never more obvious than at a business conference.

She decided that wine was in order before she looked for a suitable group to approach.

'Good evening,' said the barman. He was wearing a crisp white shirt, a black waistcoat and burgundy bow tie. It was a nice hotel.

'A large glass of dry white, please.'

'Karene Harper?' said the man beside her waiting to

be served. He had neatly cut dark hair and friendly eyes the colour of copper. His smile was broad as he held her gaze and there was something familiar in it, as if they were old friends.

'Sorry,' she said. 'Do we know each other?' She was usually good with faces and she was sure she wouldn't have forgotten his. He wore an open-neck blue shirt that on first look was smart and conservative, but she now noticed the mustard-yellow piping to the cuffs and collar, suggesting a man with a touch of flair in this room of corporate suits.

'Harry Peterson.' He held out his hand and smiled again.

The name sounded familiar but she couldn't place it.

'You don't know me,' he said. 'I saw you speak last year. At Naval Headquarters? I really enjoyed it.'

'Well, you were obviously paying attention, Mr Peterson. Because most people call me Karena or Karen.' She shook his hand. His grip was strong.

'Harry, please.'

'Are you in the Navy then?'

'I am.'

'And what do you do in there?'

'Oh, you know, play with ships mainly.'

Karene smiled. 'I had heard that about you boys. What brings you here?'

The Strategic Business Leadership Conference was aimed at the country's blue-chip heavy-hitters. And she'd been invited to speak on her specialist subject: the nature and necessity of mental resilience.

'I'm speaking tomorrow,' he said.

'Really? I didn't notice a Harry on—' Karene stopped. She had studied the agenda. She always did. It helped to know your competition. And she knew that Harry was derived from Henry. 'Captain Henry Peterson.'

'Like I said, Harry is fine.'

The barman slid Karene's wine towards her. Captain Peterson was known to be something of an enigma in the world of military leadership. He was revered for once ignoring the powers that be to save migrants off the coast of Europe. He had said that no man, woman or child was expendable and that as a nation we had a responsibility to protect lives. Which was quite a statement from a military leader; it was an institution set up primarily to fight and defend.

'I tried to get an interview with you once for my research,' she said feeling very self-conscious, like a saleswoman with a naff pitch.

'I'd be happy to,' he replied. 'How about now? I hate these networking things.'

Karene took a sip, not quite believing that she was going to turn this opportunity down. 'I don't actually have any ongoing research at the moment. I'm too busy presenting on the last lot. But, thank you, really. Any chance we could take a rain check?'

'Sure.'

'Could I take your secretary's number? So I know how to get in touch?' Karene hated doing this but if she didn't it would never happen.

Captain Henry Peterson took out his wallet, removed a business card and then asked the barman for a pen. He wrote a mobile number on the back along with a single word, *Harry*.

The conference organizer walked towards them. He was a short man probably in his sixties with white hair and a thick moustache to match.

'Good evening, Sir,' he said to Harry. 'We're so pleased to have you here. I have arranged for you to join the VIPs for dinner tonight. They're very excited to meet you.' The man glanced in Karene's direction and clearly saw nothing of interest. 'Would you like to come with me now?' he asked.

'Is Ms Harper on the VIP table too?'

The conference organizer frowned and looked at Karene again. 'Oh, hello,' he said. 'Karen, isn't it?'

She nodded half-heartedly. 'Nice to meet you at last,' she said. She went to shake his hand but he'd already turned back to Harry.

'Karen, you'll be on a table with our other speakers. Table six, if I'm not mistaken. It'll be a good opportunity for you to find out how today has gone from those who have already presented.'

'Sounds lovely,' said Karene with her nicest smile.

'I think that would be useful for me too,' said Harry. 'I'm not the most experienced presenter.' But his protests were in vain. The conference organizer insisted that Harry join the VIPs.

'Sorry,' he said as he was led to his special table. A moment later he turned back. 'Save me,' he mouthed.

Karene smiled. She liked him.

*

The presenters on table six were typically extroverted, which made for a night of competing stories and anecdotes. Karene hadn't laughed so hard with a group of strangers for a long time, so she didn't think about Harry again until he joined her at the breakfast buffet table the next morning.

'Thanks for coming to my aid,' said Harry as he filled his bowl with bran flakes.

'I expect you're rarely in need of anyone's help.' She filled her bowl with yogurt then topped it with granola. 'Was it really that bad?'

'I always imagined life would be easier with a bit of power and influence but, you know what, it's just dinner with sycophants and self-centred bores.' They moved along the tables until they reached the drinks section. Harry gestured for Karene to go first and she chose an Americano from the machine then added fresh milk as he selected his own coffee. 'Where are you sitting?'

'Over by the window.' She pointed to the table where she'd hung her suit jacket over the chair.

Harry walked with her. He was wearing his uniform and it was eliciting stares from all corners of the room. He placed his bowl and coffee down on her table.

'Join me, why don't you?' she said.

'Only if you promise not to be a sycophantic bore.'

'I'll try my hardest. I genuinely have no interest in how you became such an impressively brilliant human being.'

Harry smirked and sat down. 'Are you sure? I mean, it's a great story?'

'What are you speaking on today?' she asked, unable to stop smiling at him.

'Why are you asking? You already know the answer.'

'I know the title but not what the point of it is.'

'You can't work out the point from the title? "Ships, sailors and secret missions" isn't giving it away?'

Karene shook her head with a slight laugh. 'That's not your title.'

'Crap, really? Well, that's what I've prepared.'

'I doubt they'll notice.'

'Thanks.'

'No. I mean they'll all have their heads stuck in their emails. Most of them are here to be seen and do business rather than to learn anything.'

'Well, why would they need to learn anything? We VIPs know all there is to know.'

Karene was enjoying herself. It was rare to find a man with such a knack for quick banter. 'So you never married. Was that a career decision?'

Harry held his drink just below his mouth. 'That's a subject change. What makes you think I'm not married?'

Karene blushed. Why had she said that? 'You don't wear a ring and there's no mention of a family in any of your profiles, plus . . .' She stopped, realizing the error of what she was about to say: *you're flirting with me*.

'Plus?'

'Nothing. That's it.'

He studied her for a moment then finished his coffee. 'I need another.'

He left the table and Karene fought the urge to put

her head in her hands. He returned with another Americano for her with just the right amount of milk. The guy was paying attention.

'Caroline and I have been married for eighteen years. We have two kids, Sophie and Jake. I don't mention them because it's not relevant and it's nobody's business.'

Karene hoped the heat on her face wasn't showing. 'Sorry,' she said. 'That was rude of me. Most of the resilient people I've studied have very strong support networks. Their husbands and wives are often critical to their resilience. So I was intrigued as to how you'd achieved all of this without that. But clearly I was mistakenly assuming that social media holds all truths.' She had no idea where this shit was coming from but he seemed to be buying it.

'That's interesting. Caroline is a doctor but she put her career on hold to raise the kids.' He looked thoughtful for a moment, as if something new had just occurred to him. 'I expect your other half is well versed in how to support you, given your specialist insight.'

'Of course. It would be remiss of me not to educate them in the matter.'

'He or she?'

'Excuse me?'

'You said educate them, not he or she, so which is it, a he or a she?'

'How is that relevant?' She didn't want to admit to being single right now.

'Just interested.' He didn't seem at all embarrassed to

be quizzing her on her personal life. 'But it's fine if you don't want to tell me.'

'It's not that I don't want to tell you.' She stopped again because that's exactly what it was.

'It's fine, Karene. I was being nosy.'

'Why?' The question was instinctive and she regretted it instantly.

Harry looked momentarily stunned. His eyes widened and he shook his head.

Karene watched him recover and felt her regret morph into something far more dangerous: hope.

Three weeks later, Karene received her first email from Henry, Captain Peterson, Royal Navy. She stared at the sending address for a few seconds before opening it, thrown by the formality. The subject title was 'Conference Speaking' and she half expected to find a request to attend some event and deliver a talk.

Karene

I hope you don't mind my saying hello. I meant to contact you earlier to say how much I enjoyed meeting you and if you ever do want that interview, I would be happy to oblige.

Yours,
Harry.

Karene read and reread the short paragraph. For some reason she felt a lurch of some emotion deep in her gut. It was ridiculous. She dealt with powerful people all the time. She thought for a minute or two then tapped out a quick reply.

Well hello, Harry,

How lovely to hear from you. I too found our meeting very pleasurable, one of the nicest breakfasts I've ever had

Karene stopped, then deleted the breakfast comment. It sounded a bit too suggestive. She tried again.

Well hello, Harry

How lovely to hear from you. I too found our meeting enjoyable. I had hoped to catch you before you left to tell you how much I enjoyed your presentation on Ships, Sailors and Secret Missions. But sadly you'd already left the building – how very Elvis!
An interview sometime would be great, thank you.

Karene.

She hit send before she had time to rethink the Elvis thing. He had enjoyed her humour in person so there was no reason why he would turn his nose up now. And why the hell did she care so much? Did it really matter if he never replied? If his email was just a polite way of keeping in touch and one of many he had sent to other speakers?

Yes. Yes. It really did. She wanted a reply.

She made a fresh cup of tea, returned to her desk

and checked her inbox. Nothing. She pressed the refresh button. Still nothing. And this was how it went for the rest of the day. She told herself he was in a meeting and then that he'd been called away on some important business. She began to re-analyse her response the following morning. Had it been too informal? Should she have kept it professional? Had she been too keen?

She continued to check her emails incessantly. On day fifteen, she interrogated her sent items and outbox in case some unprecedented glitch had frozen her message. On day twenty-one, she decided that it had been just a polite email and that she needn't have replied at all. The following Saturday she returned home from a party late in the evening and checked her laptop as she reheated a bowl of leftover curry. Her inbox contained one message. From Henry, Captain Peterson, Royal Navy.

She placed her food on the table and opened it.

Karene,

I am so very sorry for the delay. Can you forgive me?
I'm in London next Thursday. Could we meet for the interview then? Maybe early evening? (I would happily buy you dinner too.)
How's life treating you? Are you still basking in the success of your research?

Harry

She wanted to reply immediately but forced herself to finish her food. She needed to sober up.

Dear Harry,

Of course you are forgiven. I understand you're a busy man so there's no need to apologize. I'm afraid next Thursday won't work for me. Perhaps we could look at next month?

She deleted the whole thing. Sod it. What did she have to lose?

Hi Harry,

Thursday sounds great. Name the time and place and I'll be there.

Karene.

She pressed send. A reply pinged back almost immediately.

5.30pm. Bistro Pierre on the Southbank. It will be quiet at that time and it does a great moules marinière.

H

Karene looked at his initial. The informality gave her confidence and she replied.

Having dinner then, are we?

8

'I've found him, Augusta, but you need to come now.'

Bloom checked the clock. It was two a.m. She switched on her bedside lamp. 'Where are you, Karene?'

'Exeter Hospital. Harry's here. But it's wrong, Augusta. It's all wrong. You need to come. Now.' Karene sounded a little hysterical and Bloom feared the worst for Harry.

'I'm on my way,' said Bloom. 'I'll call you from the car.' She hung up and dressed quickly in trousers and a cashmere jumper.

When she was on the motorway, she called Karene again. 'I'll be there in three hours thirty according to the satnav. Is Harry OK?'

'He's in a coma.'

A coma would explain his lack of contact. At least he was alive. 'You said it was all wrong? Why do you say that?'

'What's he doing in Exeter? It makes no sense. Why would they bring him here?'

'It was a chaotic situation,' said Bloom. Before leaving she had checked the location of Exeter Hospital and found it was nearly fifty miles from Devonport Naval Base. 'The hospitals might have been overwhelmed.' It sounded logical enough but she knew the most logical explanation was not always reality.

'But there were only twelve injured.'

'They wouldn't have known that when the ambulances were dispatched,' said Bloom. 'Perhaps they requested some from the surrounding areas? Has he been there the whole time?'

'But there's more,' said Karene, ignoring her question. 'It's his injuries, Augusta. I saw him before the paramedics took him away. I remember thinking how lucky he had been. How lucky I had been. Do you remember? I said to you, didn't I, that he seemed OK?'

Bloom could tell that Karene was on the verge of tears. She softened her voice. 'But the medic did say that it might be worse than it looked?'

'He said there might be internal injuries. Things I couldn't see. Not this . . .' The line went quiet.

Bloom waited.

'Augusta, his face is covered in bruises and they're telling me he has significant head injuries. He had no head injuries. It was just a small scratch on his face. I checked him. I felt his head. There was nothing.' She took a juddering intake of breath. 'He's in a coma. He has a huge wound on the side of his head. He'd have been bleeding. I wouldn't have missed that. They say he may have brain damage.'

Bloom felt a churn of discomfort at her friend's words. What had happened to this man? 'I'm on my way. Don't do anything. I'll be there soon.'

Bloom called Jameson as she pulled up to the hospital. It was early, but she needed to fill him in and she didn't

49

know when she'd next get the chance. She listened to the phone ringing. She still felt a pang of dread whenever she dialled his number, the fear that he might not answer.

'Give a man a chance,' he said.

'Karene's found Harry. He's at Exeter Hospital.'

'Well, great. Then we're done, right? Mystery solved.'

'Not exactly. Karene says his head injuries are more severe than she remembers, far worse than anything he sustained in the explosion.'

Jameson sucked in a short breath. 'How could she know that?'

'She checked his head in the immediate aftermath and found nothing but a small cut on his forehead. She says he has major bruising, and they think he may have a brain injury. I expect the bruising could have come up later, but she says he has a large impact wound to the side of his skull.'

'She'd have been under a lot of pressure. Are you sure she didn't miss it?'

'It's a possibility but she's smart. I think it's unlikely. So we need to consider that something might've happened to him later. Maybe the ambulance was involved in an accident, or they made a mistake, didn't strap him in properly. That would explain why they haven't come forward to report anything.'

'Or . . .'

'Have you found something?'

'Maybe. I checked with the security team at Devonport. They recorded three ambulances arriving at the main gate, two at Albert Road and three at Camels Head.

So eight in total. But when I spoke to the ambulance service, they said they only dispatched seven, four from Plymouth Central and three from South Western.'

'How many came to Exeter?'

'None. All were instructed to go to Derriford. It's closer and specializes in military medicine so they're equipped for these injuries.'

'Could they have made a mistake?'

'Sure. Human error can always play a part.'

'But you're guessing not?'

'I think something odd's going on. Does he have any other injuries?'

'I'll check and let you know.'

'Ask if he has any localized trauma: small burns, digit breakages. You know the kind of thing.'

Bloom was surprised at this leap. 'Torture?'

'If someone went to all this trouble to get Harry alone, I'd say they seriously wanted his attention ... or his compliance.'

Karene was sitting on a row of plastic chairs in the corridor of the Intensive Care Unit. She was hunched forward. Her hair hung loose and covered her face and her left foot was tapping a steady rhythm.

'Hey,' Bloom said, sitting down beside Karene. 'Any news?'

Karene didn't look up; she just shook her head.

'Have you had anything to eat?' Bloom touched her friend's arm. 'Karene, have you eaten anything since you arrived?'

There was no response.

Bloom reached into her bag for the banana she'd thrown in on the way out of the house. She peeled it half-way and handed it to Karene. 'Eat this.'

Karene accepted it without a word and took a bite.

'I spoke to Jameson on the way over. He's exploring a lead linked to the paramedics. Everything's going to be fine; it'll all make sense soon. Did the doctors say he's been here since Saturday night?'

'They said they'd check.'

'They don't know?'

'Shift changes, apparently. His notes say he's been on this ward since Tuesday evening.'

'So he could have been elsewhere in the hospital before that?'

Karene finished the banana and folded the skin into a neat parcel. 'It's unlikely.' She finally looked up. Her eyes were swollen. 'The notes follow the patient.'

'And there's nothing recorded before last night?'

'Nope.'

Both women were silent for a moment. Bloom suspected Jameson might be right about the sleight of hand. She could see how Harry's missing days might be explained by some miscommunication but something didn't add up. It felt wrong and she knew that was an instinct to be interrogated.

'His injuries are worse than they were before, Augusta. Much, much worse. He didn't have a head injury, only a small cut on his forehead. I checked him from head to toe. I'm not imagining this.'

'I believe you,' said Bloom, and she did.

'So what happened to him?'

'I don't know, Karene, but we'll find out. I promise.'

Karene looked hesitant. 'What if it doesn't matter?'

Bloom was pretty sure she knew what was coming next but she asked, 'What do you mean?'

'What if he never comes round, or—'

'Has some permanent brain damage?'

'You know how devastating head injuries can be. He might wake up with a totally different temperament. Instead of quick-witted and fun-loving, he might be aggressive and depressed. He might not be my Harry any more.'

'Well.' Bloom wasn't sure what to say. 'You'll have some tough choices to make if that's the case. But there's no point worrying about that yet. OK?'

Karene's eyes filled with tears and she gritted her teeth in an effort to stay in control.

'And you know as well as I do that personality changes are usually only associated with frontal lobe damage. Do you know if that's what he has?'

'No.' Karene wiped her eyes with the back of her hand. 'You're right. I need to focus on the positives.'

A tall, slender man in a shirt and tie walked over to them. 'Miss Harper?'

Karene stood. 'Yes, that's me.'

'I'm Mr Lyle, Harry's consultant.'

'Can I see him? Is he conscious?'

'He's stable but it may be a while before he regains consciousness and until then it's hard to know what damage he's sustained.'

'If any?' said Bloom.

The consultant looked Bloom's way for the briefest of moments, but it was long enough: long enough to know that when he then said 'Indeed' he didn't mean it at all.

'If you follow me, I can take you through to see him.'

9

France

Timothé Durand parked his van in a small lay-by. He was early for his next delivery so he reckoned he could take ten minutes to smoke and stretch his legs a bit. The schedule these days was ridiculous. What with online shopping and the ever-widening delivery zones, there was barely any downtime for the drivers. It didn't bother him too much. He liked being out in the countryside of his homeland; the farmlands and small towns of Normandy and Brittany were breathtaking.

It had been a perfect summer but now there was a cold wind. He cupped his hand around the end of his cigarette as he lit it, strolling down the lane to his left. The house at the end was a traditional French dwelling, stone-built with a slate roof and white-shuttered windows. He wandered over to get a better look. He'd always wanted a place like that.

The door to the small house stood ajar.

Timothé could hear a dog barking. He smiled. His childhood pup had been the same, always warning off imaginary invaders. He wasn't sure what to do, so he stood awkwardly in the yard, taking in the last few drags of his cigarette.

Suddenly a wiry black and white mongrel ran out to meet him, barking and frantic. It sprinted from one side of the yard to the other then rounded on Timothé.

He almost took a step back but then reconsidered. It wasn't a big dog, maybe ten to fifteen kilos. And Timothé knew dogs. If he stayed calm and still the animal was likely to relax. And that's exactly what happened.

'*Bonjour, mon petit.*' Timothé bent down to stroke the dog and then jumped back in horror. His fur was covered in blood. It coated his every paw and was smeared down the animal's left side. Timothé didn't think it was coming from the dog – there were no obvious injuries – and the fact that his paws were coated suggested he had walked through the blood of another.

Timothé looked at the house with its open front door. The blood on the dog was dark and thick, so probably not fresh. Should he call the police? He figured they'd want more details than just a bloody dog, so he walked towards the house, the dog trotting at his side. It was only when he reached the door that he realized the barking had stopped. He looked down at the dog panting heavily and wondered how long he had been howling for help.

'*C'est bien, petit chien. C'est bien.*' He scratched behind the dog's ears.

The smell in the house was bad, a combination of rotting meat and metal. Timothé had done work experience at the local undertakers as a teenage boy and recognized the scent. Something or someone was certainly dead and had been for a while.

Timothé followed his new companion into the square kitchen. There were maps along the wall – Kent, Dover, Canterbury. He paused at the door to take in the scene. The dog walked over to his owner and sat in the blood that had pooled at his feet. The man was tightly bound to his chair with plastic cable ties around his ankles and wrists. It was hard to judge his age because his body was so bloated from decomposition. But it was clear that he had suffered significantly in his dying moments. Timothé saw that the man's toenails had been pulled out and he was missing a finger on each hand. His head was tilted up to the ceiling and a deep wound ran the width of his neck, his mouth open wide in a silent scream.

10

Jameson was already at his desk when Bloom arrived in the office on Thursday morning. She'd missed seeing him there every day.

'What?' he said, over his shoulder.

'I didn't say anything.' Bloom took her seat and powered up her laptop.

'Why were you staring?'

Bloom smiled. He'd sensed her watching. 'You've had a haircut.'

Jameson ran his hand through the mop of curls. 'It was getting unruly.' He turned to face her. 'Let's review what we've got. Any more details on Harry's injuries?'

Bloom shook her head and opened the OneNote document for Karene's case. Jameson had access to this too. It was where they recorded any insights or evidence of value. It was a process that ensured they both had all of the available information all of the time. 'I checked with the consultant and there were no additional minor injuries, no signs of having been tied up or tortured. It seems he was admitted on Tuesday evening, seventy-two hours after the explosion. An A&E nurse found him unconscious on a gurney in the hallway. They couldn't find the crew who brought him in but it was a busy shift; there'd been a fire at a local factory so there were lots of walking wounded.'

'Clever. Bring him in and dump him when people are too busy to notice. They were probably watching the hospitals, listening to ambulance call-outs. That's what I'd have done. Any CCTV?'

'I spoke to the security manager. He wasn't particularly helpful. He says we need a police request.'

'But they do have it?'

'Yes. I took a walk through. A&E is well covered.'

'Could the hospital determine when and how he'd sustained the head injury?'

'The consultant said it was consistent with trauma sustained in an explosion or impact of some kind. He doesn't seem to think it occurred separately.'

'So maybe Karene's wrong? And, if not, whoever did this knew what they were doing. They posed as paramedics, got him out quickly, and then managed to drop him at A&E without being seen. And whatever they did to him in between, they made it look like it was a legitimate injury from the bomb. This is a professional crew.'

'Military?'

'Or agency.'

'Like MI5?'

'Or just a well-funded group.'

'You mean criminals?'

'Motivated individuals working outside of the law, so yeah. But what could their motivation be?'

'To get information. Something related to Harry's work?'

'Or to shut him up,' said Jameson in his typical matter-of-fact tone.

'But why not just kill him?' said Bloom. 'Two people died in that explosion. If you wanted to keep him quiet, surely that'd be the best way? Unless the bomber messed up?'

'They had a fake ambulance ready to go,' replied Jameson. 'So they didn't want to kill him. They needed him alive.'

'They needed him alive,' echoed Augusta, liking the familiar rhythm of their conversation. 'So we have to find out why.'

Jameson's phone started ringing and he walked out of the room to take the call. He would never have done that before. He'd always been happy to speak to anyone in front of her. The change brought a fresh wave of guilt and then irritation. She was tired of feeling guilty; it was a waste of energy. She needed to stop.

Jameson returned with a coffee for himself, nothing for her. 'The bomber was a young lad from the Plymouth area. A born and bred Brit with a Somali mother.'

'How old?'

'Nineteen.'

Bloom groaned. 'His poor parents.'

'He'd never been out of the country apart from a family holiday when he was a boy, so we know he's not been to any camps. They got to him online.'

'How are parents supposed to protect their kids from that?'

'The parents aren't always innocent, you know. Sometimes they lay the foundations.'

Bloom considered that. 'Any idea who's behind it?'

'ISIS have said it's probably theirs but it sounds like an opportunistic claim to me. It's early days. I'll keep on it.' Jameson took a long sip of coffee. 'We could go back to Peterson? Perhaps there's a link to ISIS somewhere there, something they're keeping under wraps.'

'We shouldn't rule out something personal yet. He's divorced and that can raise some powerful emotions.' Bloom knew the dangers of confirmation bias: focusing all your energy on proving one hypothesis. It had been the source of many a miscarriage of justice. They had to keep an open mind.

'This is a bit slick for a jilted lover or a pissed-off wife, don't you think?'

'Perhaps. But I still think we should look at his ex, Caroline.'

'Is she military?'

'No, she's a doctor. A consultant anaesthetist at Luton and Dunstable Hospital. But I'm wondering who she's with now.'

'You're thinking another military man?'

'I've known stranger motivations than wanting vengeance on behalf of a new love.'

'Didn't you say the wife left Harry?'

Bloom nodded. 'She had an affair, yes. But these things are never in isolation. We need to ask why she had the affair.'

'Fine. Let's speak to the wife.'

'I'll get her number from Karene.'

'Ooh I bet she'll love that,' said Jameson with a small laugh. He returned to his computer screen and took another gulp of his drink. 'I'll keep digging into Harry's career.'

'Have you come across anything useful so far?'

'Nothing yet. He joined the Navy on a scholarship from Liverpool University in '95.'

'What did he study?'

Jameson checked his notes. 'Geography. He joined the aviation fleet and trained as an officer and pilot then moved up the ranks pretty quick. He was promoted to lieutenant in three years and made captain last year at forty-three.'

'Is that young?'

'It's not bad.'

'So he's a bit of a high-flyer. Any idea what he's worked on?'

'He was a helicopter pilot in Iraq in 2003 and again in Afghanistan in 2007 and 2010. He was also deployed on a number of humanitarian exercises including acting as the CO of aviation during the 2015 Migrant Crisis.'

'CO?'

'Commanding Officer. He was attached to HMS *Bulwark*, the search and rescue ship.'

'And did they? Rescue?'

'Oh yeah.' He checked his notes. 'Nearly three thousand migrants travelling from Libya were recovered and delivered to Italy.'

'All those people risking their lives for a better future.'

'Three thousand is a drop in the ocean.'

Bloom grimaced at Jameson's inappropriate pun. 'I'll see if we can visit Harry's ex-wife tomorrow,' she said picking up her phone to call Karene and ask for Caroline Peterson's number.

'Do I need to be there? I could crack on with the background research.'

'I think we should stick to our tried and tested approach, don't you?'

'You managed OK the last few months. You don't need me holding your hand.'

Bloom took a deep breath as she looked at the back of his head. She would not let him continue to make her feel bad and she certainly would not let his anger affect the quality of their work. Whether he liked it or not, Jameson was coming to see Caroline Peterson with her.

11

Eighteen Months Earlier

Karene arrived five minutes early. She had spent the last few days stressing about what to wear. She kept telling herself it was an interview, not a date. But the need to pitch her outfit perfectly was overwhelming. She had settled on a blue day dress; not too smart, not too casual.

Harry was standing at the bar with his back to her. He wore dark grey chinos and a purple shirt. His shoes were smart and polished.

'Why am I not surprised that you're a punctual man?' she said as she joined him. The restaurant was set back from the Thames and nestled under the railway arches. It was stylish and trendy; a long thin building with wooden floors and antique furniture.

'I took the liberty of ordering you a drink,' he said as he slid a tumbler of clear liquid towards her. 'I hope that's OK.'

'Thank you,' she said, and took a sip.

'No need to say cheers,' he said and smiled.

She laughed and held her glass up in front of his. 'How uncouth of me.'

He held her gaze. 'You look beautiful,' he said.

She opened her mouth to speak and then closed it again. *Was this a date?*

'Sorry. I didn't mean to embarrass you,' he said. 'Right. Shall we get a table before we begin?'

Their small square table was topped by a single white candle and positioned in a quiet corner of the restaurant. Karene took out her notebook and pen while Harry scanned the menu.

'I'm just going to have the *moules*.' He placed the menu down and spotted her notebook. 'Oh, right,' he said. 'Straight in then.'

On the left-hand side Karene had written a dozen questions. 'Is that OK?' she said. 'I can wait until after we eat if you're hungry.'

'No. No. Go ahead. It's why we're here after all.' The smile on Harry's lips implied that the statement was tongue-in-cheek.

'Are you making fun of my work, Captain Peterson?'

'Absolutely not. I'm endlessly impressed by your work.'

'You do know that sarcasm is the lowest form of wit.'

Harry took a sip of his gin and tonic. 'That may be true but I'm not being sarcastic so my wit remains high.'

'Your wit remains high. Is that so?' Karene raised her pen in mock anticipation. 'Perhaps we should start the interview with where you got your substantial ego from?'

'Sure,' he said. 'If you like.'

She wrote the word 'ego' in large letters on the top of the right-hand page and then looked up to meet Harry's eyes. His laugh was unexpectedly fresh. It made him seem young and carefree. 'I don't have a huge ego. Let me prove it to you,' he said. 'Why don't you ask me one of your real questions?'

'OK. What would you say is the most satisfying aspect of your work?'

'Getting to boss people around and make them do what I want.'

'You like being in charge?'

'No,' he said and he smiled again. 'I'm joking. I'm not a big command and control type.'

'Good thing you don't work in one of the country's most prominent command and control environments then.'

'I know. Phew.'

'So . . .'

'You actually want me to answer your questions?'

'Yes. Harry. I do. That's why we're here.'

'Is it?' He held her gaze.

Karene felt her cheeks flush.

'Humanitarian work. That's the most satisfying part, as you'd probably expect.'

'I wouldn't expect that actually.'

'You think boys join the Navy to go to war?'

'Or to strut about in that pretty white uniform.'

'You think the uniform is pretty?' He laughed again. 'Well, the Royal Navy has a long history of humanitarian work. It's not just conflict. And if we like to look pretty while we do it, what's so wrong with that?'

'Nothing at all. I read in your bio that you've made

some controversial calls on the migrants crossing from Africa.'

Harry watched the waiter deliver water to the next table. 'I expect future generations will look back and judge us on how we've handled that. Imagine travelling for over a year with no sense of safety or certainty. Taking your whole family on an arduous journey because the alternative is just too desperate. And then discovering that others are comfortable to let you starve or drown.'

Karene's pen hovered above the page.

'But my actions weren't controversial. I had the full support of the Navy.'

'Really?'

'Of course. I wouldn't say that independent thought is really encouraged.'

'Now I know that's not true. At your level you're supposed to be making judgement calls, are you not?'

'It's truer than you'd think.'

Harry talked about his approach to challenging and stressful situations and Karene did her best to keep up, scribbling as much as she could in her notebook. He spoke quickly. She liked his animated style and the way he used his hands to illustrate his point. Often the people she interviewed – the mentally strong – were emotionally controlled but Harry was the opposite. He spoke with genuine emotion about the things he had seen and then, just when she felt tears sting her eyes, he would break the tension with a witty aside that made her laugh out loud.

'Shall we order food? I'm starving after this grilling,'

he said. The waiter passed them for the umpteenth time, clearly frustrated that they were taking up a table and hadn't yet spent much money.

'Can I ask you something personal?' she said, keeping her eyes on the menu.

'Have you not already?'

'Your wife. Would she be OK with us having dinner like this?'

'Caroline and I have separated.'

Karene had not been expecting that. So he wasn't on the hunt for an extra-marital affair. Her relief was a surprise. She hadn't realized she'd been feeling anxious about it.

'She ran off with a man called Robin six months ago.'

'*She* left *you*.' Karene couldn't hide her surprise.

Harry gave a tight nod.

'Well I'm sorry. And . . .'

'And?'

Karene studied the menu again. 'She's an idiot.'

They ate and drank as the restaurant filled with trendy Londoners chatting about their day. Their conversation was easy and fun. And by the time they left the restaurant Karene's cheeks were aching from all the smiling.

'Have you seen our ship on the Thames?' Harry said as he held the door open for her. The evening was chilly and she pulled her jacket tighter around her.

'Our ship?' Karene asked. He placed his hand on the small of her back as they exited on to the street.

'HMS *Belfast*. It's a museum ship now. Not far from

here. Would you like to see it? It might help you to put my world into context.'

Karene had hoped they might find an excuse to extend their 'date' and so happily agreed to the walk along the riverside and towards London Bridge. The drinks had made her tipsy and she bumped into Harry as they walked.

'You OK?' he asked.

'I'm great.' This was the loveliest evening she'd had in the longest time. She smiled at him; this man who she felt she'd known her whole life. What a cliché; the sort of thing that usually made her roll her eyes.

Harry smiled and then he stopped. 'Do you think . . . ?'

Karene turned to look at him. 'Do I th—'

Before she could finish, Harry had taken her face in his hands and was kissing her.

She wondered what everyone must think of two adults kissing like this, there in full view of the world. She'd never been kissed this way before and then suddenly, in the middle of the whole dizzying thing, she had the craziest thought: this man kisses me as if he loves me.

12

Caroline Peterson's home was tidy and clinical. Bloom had grown up with a hospital consultant for a mother so she knew how one environment could infiltrate the other. The house was a large detached property with a spacious hall carpeted in cream and had walls lined with tasteful black and white photographs of the Peterson children. Caroline led them through to her lounge, which was so pristine it belonged in a show home.

'What's your role in this again?' Her dark hair was cropped short and her elfin face covered in freckles that made her look younger than her forty-two years. She hadn't offered them a drink and clearly had no intention of prolonging the visit.

'We're exploring Harry's head injury and investigating the delay that occurred between the explosion and his hospital admission.'

'You and Karene are personal friends?' Caroline said.

'We studied together.' Bloom caught the hint of a smile on Jameson's lips. She had lectured him on the dangers of working for friends when he had asked for her help earlier in the year.

'Don't get me wrong, I like Karene,' said Caroline, 'but I think she's being a little hysterical about this. The system is never perfect. In an ideal world we'd be able to track the patient's entire journey but that's simply not possible.'

Bloom would never have described Karene as hysterical, but she knew such character assassinations were not unusual between an ex and a current lover. It boosts the ego to imagine your competition as a lesser person. 'We're not talking about a lack of background information here,' she said. 'We're looking at seventy-two hours in which no one can account for Harry's whereabouts. That's not just imperfect; it's highly suspicious.'

Caroline held Bloom's gaze and then she acknowledged the point with a crisp nod of her head.

'We think that someone either wanted to question Harry or to silence him,' said Jameson.

'We're wondering if it's to do with his work,' added Bloom. She didn't want Caroline to think she was in any way under suspicion.

'And you need me to fill you in because the Navy won't?' Caroline looked smug.

'Are there any incidents that you think might be related to this?' asked Jameson, ignoring the dig.

Caroline shook her head slowly.

'Do you recall him being upset or angry at any point?' asked Bloom. 'Or being distant and secretive?'

Caroline smiled. 'They're always secretive, whether they've good reason or not.'

'They?' said Bloom.

'The men, the military, the officers. It's all part of the glamour.'

Out of the corner of her eye, Bloom saw Jameson raise his eyebrows.

'Has Harry done any jobs that would make him a target?' asked Bloom.

Caroline paused.

'Just go with your gut,' said Jameson.

Bloom tried again: 'If you had to rank Harry's jobs in terms of controversy or danger, what would be at the top?'

'As far as I'm aware he hasn't done anything particularly controversial or dangerous.'

'He did a tour of Iraq and two of Afghanistan. You don't consider that dangerous?' Jameson asked. 'Did he not tell you what he'd seen out there? What he did as a pilot?'

'I never asked.'

'You never asked?' Jameson failed to hide his disdain.

Bloom stepped in. 'We'll explore that line of enquiry with his colleagues then. How about in your personal life?'

'Excuse me?' Caroline sat up a little straighter. This line of questioning clearly offended her.

'You'd be surprised how often the cases we investigate are linked to a person's private life. It's usually where the emotions are strongest so we have to ask.'

'You don't *have* to ask. You're not the police. You're just two interfering amateurs on that crazy woman's witch hunt.'

Bloom paused in the hope that a brief silence might de-escalate things. Caroline may have left Harry for another man but clearly she felt some significant resentment towards Karene. 'You think Karene is crazy?' asked Bloom, keeping her voice slow and calm.

'I think she's interfering in something that should be left to the proper authorities. A man blew himself up on a military base. It's clearly a terrorist attack.'

'You must have been to a fair few military balls in your time,' Jameson said.

'A couple, yes,' said Caroline. 'But to be honest they're not my cup of tea.'

'But you've been to enough to know that with a bomb strapped to your back, you could cause some pretty major destruction. I mean, how many people typically attend. Two hundred? Three hundred?'

Caroline nodded.

'We're wondering why so few were injured,' said Bloom. 'Less than four per cent of the guests.'

'And why do you think eight ambulances arrived but only seven made it to a hospital?' asked Jameson.

Bloom said, 'You know Harry better than anyone, Ms Peterson. You were married for eighteen years and you have two children. We need your help. Anything you can tell us would be useful.' She held Caroline's gaze. They needed to win her back. 'What sort of man is he?'

'Not one for conspiracy theories, that's for sure.' Caroline sighed. 'Harry's a hard worker, very ambitious. But he's also a great father; the get down on your knees and play type, not that they need that now they're teenagers.'

'And as a husband?'

73

Caroline thought for a moment. 'A little detached. Not so much in the early days. He's an entertainer at his core and in need of an audience. But behind the façade he could be distant and emotionless. He didn't give much away.'

'Is that why you separated?'

'You get to the point in your life where you need more: someone who's really present.'

'And did you find that?'

'I did.'

'Another military man?'

'Robin?' Caroline laughed coldly. 'Oh no, he's a consultant like me. I'm done with the old club.'

'What type of consultant?' she said.

'Orthopaedic.'

'A bone breaker,' said Jameson.

Caroline kept her eyes on Bloom. 'The best of his kind.'

'Isn't she a peach?' said Jameson as they climbed into Bloom's car.

'Typical senior medic. Precise, logical—'

'Cold. How can you not ask about your husband's experience at war? I get that you might not want all the gory details but surely you'd at least want to check in?'

'Every relationship is different.' Bloom pulled away from the kerb and drove out of the exclusive housing estate.

'She's got a bee in her bonnet about Karene.'

'I know.'

'I still think this is more likely to be about Harry's work, but I wouldn't put it past that cold fish and her boyfriend to have a hand in this.'

'Agreed. Let's keep in touch with the ex-Mrs Peterson and maybe we should take a look at the new man too.'

13

'Thank you for seeing us at short notice,' said Bloom as she approached Detective Superintendent Matthew Drummond at the entrance to Plymouth Police Station.

'Grace Briggs at the Met spoke very highly of you,' he replied. Grace had attended one of her first *Psychology of Crime* courses and had kindly put Bloom in touch with Drummond. 'Grace said that if I wanted to know what motivated the bomber, there's no one better to speak to than you. So come on through.'

Bloom and Jameson were led into an office with a small wooden table in the middle and they sat down on stiff chairs upholstered in a coarse blue fabric.

'We wanted to talk to you about an idea we've been exploring. We're wondering if the bomb was a cover for something else,' said Bloom.

'Go on,' said Drummond, clearly intrigued.

'One of the officers injured in the blast was taken away in an ambulance,' said Jameson. 'However, the emergency services have no record of dispatching the ambulance, and it never arrived at Derriford Hospital.'

'No,' he said, shocked. 'That's not possible. Are you sure?'

Jameson answered with a sideways nod.

'An extra ambulance? Where did it go?'

'We don't know. But three days later the officer in question, Captain Henry Peterson, turned up on a gurney at Exeter Hospital's A&E during a particularly busy shift. No one saw him arrive and no one knows how he got there, and that's the first record the hospital has of him.'

Drummond was taking notes. 'So where'd he been?'

'We think someone may have taken him somewhere to question or coerce him,' said Bloom. 'He's in a coma at the moment, so we know very little. What we do know is that the injuries he arrived with were more severe than those he was seen to have immediately after the explosion. The hospital has CCTV but they need a police request to release it.'

'Why am I only just hearing about this?' His tone was admonishing. Bloom knew the police well enough to know that his irritation wasn't directed at them.

'The Navy haven't flagged it?' asked Jameson.

'Do they know about it?'

'We spoke to Captain Peterson's boss three days ago,' said Bloom. 'So if they weren't aware initially, they certainly are now.'

'We've been working closely with the Royal Navy Police. We're scheduled to talk later so it will probably come up then. So what's your connection to Peterson?'

'He's the partner of our client. She came to us when she couldn't find him at any of the hospitals,' said Bloom.

'Why didn't she come to us?'

Bloom and Jameson exchanged a look.

'She did,' said Bloom. 'She reported him missing with

you on Sunday afternoon when she couldn't locate him.' Bloom decided not to mention that they'd failed to take Karene seriously. No need to antagonize Drummond at this early stage.

'I see. I'll look into that.'

'And can you have someone check the hospital CCTV?' asked Bloom.

'Already noted,' he said, tapping his pen on the piece of paper in front of him.

'So whose remit is this investigation? Is it with the Navy Police or with you?' asked Jameson.

Drummond neatened the stack of papers in front of him. 'The RNP are responsible for policing the base and their ships. We are responsible for civilian matters. So, in the case of a civilian bomber on a naval base, we're in this together.'

'And have you identified the bomber?' asked Jameson. Bloom knew this was a test. His contact at MI6 had already given him the details and he was checking if the police had caught up.

'We have. Bashir Forrest. He was a young man from the Plymouth area. British father, Somali mother. He'd actually worked at the base for a time as part of an outside catering company and we think that's how he gained access. He was an ISIS sympathizer as far as we can tell. He'd posted a few things online in support of the attacks in Paris and Manchester, but nothing extreme. Other than that, he was a good kid. Worked hard in school. Never in trouble with us. He was on a watch list but very near the bottom.'

'So any idea why he'd do this now?' said Bloom.

'Finding out is our priority at this stage. We have his phone and computer so we're looking to identify who he's been in touch with.'

'And will you consider the possibility that the bomb was a cover for the kidnapping?' asked Bloom.

'It would explain why there were so few casualties,' said Jameson.

Bloom watched the police officer carefully, gauging his response. He came across as a measured and thoughtful man, but some people were very unwilling to consider alternative theories.

'In my experience, anything's possible, Dr Bloom,' Drummond replied. 'We were relieved but admittedly surprised by the number of casualties. It could be due to an inexperienced bomber, but I'm not one for putting all my eggs in a single basket, so I appreciate your input. We'll look into it.'

'You liked him,' said Jameson when they were back in the car.

'He was open-minded. You know how easy it is to get stuck on one theory and only see the evidence that supports it.'

'I think he liked you too.'

Bloom tutted. She'd forgotten how easily Jameson could flip from serious work mode to frivolous nonsense.

'I mean it. He wasn't wearing a ring. And I'm sure he had a thing for you. You should keep in touch. Look at Karene. Don't you want a bit of that?'

'And go through what she's going through? No, thank you.' Bloom fought a smile. Not because of Drummond. But because of Jameson's tone. He was teasing her, just like he used to. Was it a slip? Or a sign of him loosening up?

14

Eighteen Months Earlier

Karene had no idea where she was. The room was dark and the iron bed frame unfamiliar. She searched for any hints, any memories of the large bay windows and smoked-glass light fittings. Then she felt the warmth of Harry's body by her side and everything flooded back. She lay as still as she could, trying not to wake him as she replayed their evening in her mind.

She had travelled to Portsmouth on the afternoon train to find Harry waiting on the platform. He was wearing tan shorts with a blue checked shirt and deck shoes; the uniform of the off-duty naval officer. It amused Karene that those required to wear uniform for work still adhered to a set way of dressing in their free time. Part of her wanted to encourage some individuality but truthfully she found it endearing.

'Hey, honey,' he had said before pulling her into a long kiss.

'I could have caught a cab,' she said, taking his hand.

'Every second counts.'

His apartment was in a double-fronted white building right by the coast. He had the whole of the second floor. It was furnished in neutral colours and the southern sunshine flooded the living area with a bright yellow glow. Karene deposited her bag in the spare bedroom knowing full well she had no intention of sleeping in there. But the façade seemed appropriate for what was essentially their third date.

Half an hour later they were sitting outside a seafront bar drinking.

'Happy?' said Harry.

'Nah, this is rubbish.' She placed a plump olive in her mouth. 'So, this is your life? Seems pretty tough.'

Harry nodded, his expression grave. 'This is why I need to be so resilient. Do you see that now?'

'It's becoming clearer.' Karene sat back in her chair. 'I never fancied living by the sea. It's so smelly and the buildings always look a bit tragic. Then you have all the tourists crowding the place with their inappropriate clothing and their greasy chips and ice creams.'

'Are you done insulting my home town?'

Karene laughed. 'Sorry,' she said. 'I just meant that I'm surprised by how much I love it here.'

'You love it?'

'Uh-huh.'

'Must be the company.' Harry held her gaze. 'I love it too. It's a shame I can't be here all the time.' He had recently put an offer in on a property near St Albans where his wife and children were now living.

'You can always come back some day,' she said, concerned to see the sadness in his expression. She couldn't believe that this handsome, intelligent, sensitive man could be hers.

'You can never really go back, can you?' He looked out over the sea.

She watched him for a moment intrigued by his words and the deepening sadness in his eyes. 'What have you seen?' she asked.

'Huh? Sorry, I was just admiring the view.'

'But what have you seen? What have you had to . . . see?'

'You don't want to hear those stories.'

'Why not? '

'Because . . . there are some things you shouldn't have to know.' He turned to her. 'I had a friend at university. He went on to be a copper on one of those graduate schemes. He was doing really well but then quit out of the blue, retrained as a web designer. And you know what he said when I asked him about it?' He waited for her to shake her head. 'He said, "You know what, Harry, every day I had to pick up a rock and look at all the bugs living underneath while the rest of the world walked past, oblivious. Nothing I did ever reduced the number of bugs and it got to the point where I just wanted to put the rock down and walk by like everyone else."'

Karene leaned across the table and took Harry's hand. 'I get what you're saying. But I want to know the good and the bad.'

'So let's start with the good, yeah?'

'Have you ever talked about it with anyone?'

Harry hung his head with a laugh then looked her way. 'Yes, Miss Psychologist. I have, thank you. The Navy is fairly good at dealing with these things; we've been doing it a while.'

'I'll have to take your word for that.'

'Look, I saw a lot in Iraq and Afghanistan and it's not nice, but it's war so you can kind of compartmentalize it. The hardest stuff to deal with is what people do to each other outside of a war zone.'

'Which is why your policeman friend found it so hard.'

Harry raised his eyebrows.

'What? You think I don't get this stuff?'

He gazed out at the ocean again. 'The hardest memories to shift are the children struggling to survive because they were born in the wrong place or because they belong to the wrong religion.'

Karene squeezed his hand. 'Tough childhoods can grow tough kids though. I should know.'

Harry looked at her. She couldn't read his expression. Whatever it was, he shook it away and stood up. 'More fizz?'

Karene watched the waves while she waited for Harry to return. Why was she so obsessed with getting inside this man's head? She wanted everything: his views, his experiences, his likes and dislikes and she wanted them instantly. If it was possible to download someone's mind into your own she'd have taken Harry's without hesitation. It was an obsessive attraction that she'd never felt before and no amount of rationalization seemed to calm it.

15

Harry is awake.

The message flashed up on Bloom's phone and they diverted to the hospital, arriving forty minutes later.

Karene was pacing the corridor outside Harry's room.

'Have you seen him yet?' asked Bloom, intercepting her friend's strides.

'They're checking him over. The consultant, Mr Lyle, is in there now.'

'OK. Let's see what he says.' She touched her friend's arm.

'Will you come in with me?'

Bloom nodded. She didn't want to intrude but if Karene needed support, she'd do whatever was required.

'Have you found anything?' Karene looked at Jameson who was hanging back.

'It's looking like one of the ambulances wasn't legitimate,' he said. 'But we'd guessed that. We're trying to work out why.'

'I should have gone over. I knew I should have gone over. If I'd been with him – stayed with him – then this wouldn't have happened. What else? What else do you know?' Karene moved in an agitated manner as she spoke; running one hand up and down her opposite arm at an ever-increasing pace as she rocked her weight from one foot to the other.

'We reckon it's a professional crew,' said Jameson moving a little nearer to the two women. 'So, if it helps, I'm not sure you'd have suspected anything even if you had spoken to them.'

'What sort of professionals?'

The door to Harry's room opened and Mr Lyle exited with a couple of junior doctors in tow.

'How is he?' said Karene.

'He's a little disorientated but that's to be expected. He knows who he is but he can't recall what's happened to him, but that's not unusual at this stage. He's also a little vague on a few facts but I'll examine him again in a few hours. You can go in whenever you're ready.'

'What sort of facts?' asked Bloom and Karene paused at the door.

'The month. The year. That kind of thing. But try not to worry. He's doing well. His motor functions are good. It may just be a touch of swelling. He's been in a coma so it can take a little time for things to settle.'

Bloom nodded and Karene led them into the room.

A nurse was standing at Harry's side checking the monitor and writing notes on his chart.

'I'll wait here,' said Bloom, hovering by the door.

Harry lay staring at the ceiling. Karene approached and took his hand. 'Hey, you,' she said, her voice soft.

His eyes moved slowly towards hers.

'You're OK, Harry,' she said. 'You're going to be OK.' Karene smiled nervously. 'Harry? It's me. It's Karene.'

Harry stared at Karene and then at Bloom. 'Caroline?' he said.

Karene's smile faltered. 'Caroline's not—'

'Where am I?' he asked.

'You're in Exeter Hospital, Mr Peterson,' said the nurse. 'As Mr Lyle explained.'

'*Captain* Peterson,' corrected Karene and the nurse's jaw twitched.

'What happened?' He pulled his hand free of Karene's and she swallowed hard as she slid it off the bed and on to her lap.

'There was an explosion at the ball you attended on Saturday night,' Bloom said when it was clear that Karene wasn't able to answer.

'An explosion?'

'A bomb. A man blew himself up in the reception of the building.'

'How many?' Harry closed his eyes and took a deep breath. Bloom glanced at Karene who was looking similarly queasy.

'We can talk about that later,' Karene said eventually. 'Concentrate on getting better first.'

'Do either of you know where Caroline is, please?'

'He doesn't want to see her.' Karene slumped into a chair in the corridor.

'He asked for her,' said Bloom.

'He just asked if she was here, where she was. Like the consultant said, he's disorientated.'

'Karene?'

'He looked OK, didn't he? He was alert and he was speaking clearly. That has to be a good sign.' Karene's resilience training was kicking in.

'It could certainly have been worse, yes.'

The nurse approached them. 'He's asking for Caroline.'

'Caroline's his ex-wife,' said Karene. 'They're divorced. I'm his current partner.'

'Oh, I see. I'm sorry. Have they been divorced a while?' A troubled expression crossed the nurse's face.

Karene shook her head. 'A year or so, but separated for longer.'

Bloom took her friend's hand. 'If he's disorientated, Karene, it might be wise to simply respond to his requests. Would she come, do you think?'

Karene's expression went blank. 'I'll call her.'

16

Jameson chose a table in the far corner of the cafeteria. He wasn't sure what he'd expected when he'd agreed to work with Bloom again, but he should have predicted that she'd carry on as if none of it had happened. It was classic Augusta. He knew she was the focused professional when it came to work but he couldn't help feeling irritated by her complete lack of remorse. He picked at his ham and cheese panini. He'd told her not to mention Seraphine Walker, but that didn't mean he wanted her to pretend it never happened. He had hoped her behaviour towards him would be conciliatory at the very least.

'Do you ever stop eating?' She sat down in the seat opposite him.

'Do *you* ever stop pretending everything's normal?'

'What does that even mean?'

He took a bite of his sandwich and said nothing. This was typical. She was deflecting his question to avoid accessing her emotions.

'I don't think Harry recognized Karene,' she said.

'What?' Jameson felt for the woman. He remembered what it had felt like when his mother's Alzheimer's had set in and he'd seen blankness in her eyes when he had walked in.

'I know. It's worrying.'

'I thought they were soulmates.'

'He's asked for Caroline.'

'Ouch. How did she take that?'

'Not well. She's calling her now. We just spoke to the consultant again. They think it's some sort of amnesia.'

'You're quite similar, aren't you?'

'Karene and I? Not really. I mean, we're both psychologists—'

'Throwing yourself into work instead of facing up to the truth.'

Bloom sighed. 'Which is?'

Jameson finished his sandwich and sat back. 'You know I'm not back for good, don't you?'

'What were you planning to do instead?'

'I have a few irons in the fire.' This was an outright lie. He'd done nothing to find other work. He had a good pension so he could live without any further income but working with Bloom had been fun. It had kept him alert, staved off the boredom, given him a purpose. But he couldn't work with someone who had shown the cool disregard for his life that she had in that dank room under the dark arches of Leeds only a few months earlier. She was supposed to be different. She was supposed to be better than the men and women he'd worked with in his past life.

'Well, I should make the most of you while I have you then.' Bloom's smile was a little sad. It was the first sign of upset that she'd shown and it made Jameson feel good. 'So,' she said. 'Do you think this was a genuine terrorist attack that someone took advantage of, or was the whole thing about Harry?'

'If I had to put money on it, I'd say it hinges on Bashir Forrest. Either someone got wind of his plans and piggy-backed them or they groomed him to do their bidding.'

'The low number of casualties really strikes you as significant, doesn't it?'

'It makes me think it's a military operation; get in and get out with as little collateral damage as possible. They ensured that Harry was close enough to the explosion to need an ambulance but far enough away to survive. How did they do that?'

Bloom looked out of the window and tried to imagine the scene. 'They put someone in there with him.'

'They must have planned it all: where the bomber needed to be, where Harry needed to be, that their fake ambulance would reach him first. It's impressive.'

'So too orchestrated for the likes of ISIS?'

'Accessing a military base and setting off a bomb would be huge for ISIS. If it *was* them they'd be singing their involvement from the rooftops.'

'But they've only made that one statement.'

'Exactly.

'So who then? If it's military in style, could it *be* military?'

'It could certainly be someone's military, yeah. And given Harry's job in the Navy it makes a certain amount of sense. Maybe some other country is sending our military a message: we can get to you.'

'How do we find out who?'

'We interrogate the hell out of Peterson.'

'I'm not sure it's going to be that simple.'

17

Caroline walked down the hospital corridor with Mr Lyle and all the authority of a woman comfortable in her environment. She was a consultant anaesthetist. Hospitals were her domain. Karene eyed her grey trousers and white blouse, the NHS lanyard hanging around her neck. She remembered the first time she'd met Caroline when she'd accompanied Harry to collect his children. She was hoping to find a plain and dumpy housewife, ideally a little ugly, so was rather annoyed when an attractive woman opened the door.

She watched as Caroline and Mr Lyle discussed Harry's condition, the acronyms flying back and forth between them, too quickly for a layperson to interpret.

Caroline nodded hello to Karene as they reached Harry's door and mouthed, 'How are you?'

'Fine,' Karene mouthed in response, fighting the urge to ask why it had taken her so long to get there. She had called her last night and the woman had chosen to wait until morning to come. Augusta had suggested they go for breakfast but Karene needed to be here, she had to see this, even though she knew it might hurt.

She watched Caroline approach the bed from the doorway and braced herself.

'Thank God you're here.' Harry's face lit up as soon as he saw his ex-wife. 'Honey, where have you been?'

Karene leaned against the door frame for support. He had always called her honey. She knew it was irrational to think he hadn't used the same term of endearment for the woman he'd married and yet she had naively assumed the term was hers and hers alone.

'What have you done now, darling?' Caroline said as she took his hand and kissed his cheek.

Karene gripped the door frame. Caroline must be loving this. She wanted to shout out, '*She cheated on you. You hate her!*' But she swallowed the words. Not only because Mr Lyle had warned them against forcing memories, but because she loved him and couldn't bear to see him receive such painful news.

Mr Lyle had confirmed that Harry's episodic memory from the last four years was missing. He had no recollection of his wife's betrayal and their subsequent divorce, and no recollection of meeting and falling in love with Karene. His mind was anchored sometime in 2013. Lyle had made it clear that the best course of action was to go along with it for now and to allow Harry to recover at his own pace. If he ever did.

'They said there was an explosion at Devonport.' Harry's elation quickly turned to concern. 'What was it? How many were hurt?'

Caroline sat on the chair next to his bed and kept hold of his hand. 'It was terrorism. A suicide bomber. A dozen or so were hurt and a couple died.'

'Three deaths,' Karene said through gritted teeth.

Caroline's conviction irritated her. They didn't know that it was terrorism. Not for sure.

Caroline and Harry looked at her. 'I thought only two had died,' said Caroline.

'One of the bar staff passed away this morning.'

'You were here yesterday,' he said, acknowledging her for the first time. This was a good sign. He was able to form new memories.

'Yes. I was.'

'Karene is a friend,' said Caroline. 'She called me when she found out you were here.'

Harry nodded. It made total sense to him. Why wouldn't it?

'You work here?' he asked.

Karene started to shake her head and then realized that was probably the easiest explanation. He could think she worked for the hospital, that she knew Caroline through work. She couldn't tell him the truth and at least this way she had a reason to be here.

Bloom found Karene leaning against the door of Harry's room with her shoulders rigid and her jaw tightly set. Whatever had happened in there had not been pleasant.

Karene took the vending-machine coffee and yogurt from Bloom and walked to the nearest row of chairs. 'He thinks I work in the hospital. That I'm Caroline's friend.'

'OK.'

'He looked so happy to see her. Oh God.' She passed the food back to Bloom. 'I think I might be sick.' She buried her head in her hands. 'I'm sorry; I'm a mess.'

'It's fine, Karene. You've had a shock. It's normal to be upset.'

'I just never thought that . . .' Karene stared at the door that separated her from Harry. 'You'll think I'm an idiot . . . but I never imagined him loving her.'

'Why would you? By the time you'd met him, he no longer did. Most couples don't get to time travel.'

Bloom opened the yogurt and handed it to Karene.

'I'm nobody to him now,' she said.

'Listen to me.' Bloom waited for Karene to look her way. 'You know very well what you are to him. Lyle's advised you not to tell him what he's missed, but that doesn't mean you can't help him to remember. The brain is still a great mystery. Who knows what might trigger his memories: your voice, your touch, even just your presence.'

'He might never remember.'

'True. But despite what you saw in that room, you know how he felt about his wife's betrayal. That won't have changed. She still did that and he's still going to find out.'

Karene took a deep breath. 'I know.'

'And then he'll need you. He'll need someone on his side. A lot of trauma is coming his way. I mean, how old are his children now?'

'Seventeen and fourteen.'

'So they'd have been thirteen and ten when he last remembers seeing them. That's a big age difference. He'll feel like he's missed so much.'

'But he didn't. He's been amazing with them. He really stepped up when their mum left.'

'They know that and you know that. So he'll need you with him.'

'What am I supposed to say?'

'I don't know. I'm not sure it matters. Talk about the weather. Ask him how he's feeling. Anything. Just be there.'

Karene sat a little straighter. 'OK,' she said. 'I can do that.'

When Caroline had left, Karene went back into Harry's room.

'Is it OK if I keep you company?' she asked, her tone deliberately light.

He shuffled up in the bed, his hospital gown gaping to reveal his tanned torso. Karene felt a pang of longing and averted her eyes.

'Sure,' he said. 'Grab a seat. Caroline said you're a friend of hers?' The colour had returned to his cheeks and an alertness to his eyes.

'I'm not sure I'd call us friends, but I've known her for a year or so.'

Harry's smile creased around his eyes. 'I hear you. She can be a hard person to befriend.'

Karene felt a twinge of hope. Maybe he didn't love Caroline after all. 'She can be a little high maintenance,' Karene said, hoping for confirmation.

'At times, maybe, but she means well. She keeps things together. They're my world, her and the kids.'

Karene knew she was staring too intensely but she couldn't bring herself to look away.

'Are you a doctor too?'

He didn't seem to notice her distress. 'Psychologist.' She wasn't sure she could do this. How could she listen to him talk about his wife in this way? It was too hard. 'Sorry, would you excuse me?' She went to stand but he interrupted.

'Before you go,' he said, placing a hand on her forearm. She looked at his hand, feeling it hot on her skin. 'Will it come back? My memory?'

She met his eyes. She could see the fear and the anticipation. 'I'm not . . .' She faltered, unsure what to say. 'I think it depends.'

'On?'

'Which part of your brain has been damaged. Whether this loss is due to a temporary factor like swelling or a more permanent injury.' She wasn't sure if she should be telling him this. She didn't want to scare him or give him false hope. He stayed quiet, waiting, and so she continued. 'Sometimes memories come back gradually, sometimes spontaneously, and we don't really know how or why the brain is doing that. And sometimes they're permanently gone. I'm afraid we don't really know enough about it.'

'Is there anything I can do to help it along?'

Karene placed her free hand on top of his. 'Rest and try not to worry.'

Harry closed his eyes as he spoke. 'Easy for you to say.'

She wanted to shout, *'No, it isn't. None of this is easy for me,'* but instead she said, 'I suppose.' Her urge to run disappeared. He looked lost. She wanted to climb into the bed beside him and tell him that everything would be OK. But she couldn't. So she sat back down and hoped that just being here might help.

20

Harry had been moved from the Intensive Care Unit on Sunday evening. He was now in the neurology ward of Exeter Hospital and visiting hours were fixed: eight a.m. to eight p.m. It was very nearly eight a.m. on Monday and Karene was heading towards the ward and checking her emails. She planned to spend as much time with him as possible. She stopped abruptly when she saw a new message in her inbox.

From: ANONYMOUS   07:59
Subject: What do you know about the man you love?

There was no text in the body of the email, only the question in the subject line. She clicked on ANONYMOUS. The full address was ANONY0433@gmail.com.

Who would send that to her? And why? She knew Harry. They told each other everything. It was one of the things she loved most about their relationship: their ability to be totally open and honest. She wasn't naive enough to think she knew everything about the man, but she knew the important things. Was someone implying that Harry had been hiding something from her?

She entered the ward and approached the nurse behind

the desk. 'Morning. Can you tell me where I'll find Harry Peterson, please?'

'Is he new?' the nurse said, as she checked the computer screen.

'Yes,' she said. 'He was moved here last night.' She refreshed her inbox, but there were no other emails.

'I'm afraid he's not on this ward.'

Karene looked at the name behind the desk. She'd definitely come to the right place. 'I spoke to the ward sister last night. She said he was here and settling well.'

'Are you sure it was this ward?'

Karene stood to her full height. 'Absolutely. Could you please check again?' She had all the time in the world for those who dedicated their lives to the NHS but she couldn't stand incompetence.

'Nope. He's not here. Give me one moment.' The nurse dialled a number. 'Carla, I have a lady here looking for a Mr Harry Peterson. She said she spoke to Felicity last night and—' She stopped and listened. 'I see. OK. Thanks.' She hung up.

'Mr Peterson was discharged this morning.'

'What?'

'Yes. At six thirty.'

'Who would discharge him? He's in no fit state to be moved!'

'Well, he must have been.'

'Believe me. He was not. He suffered a significant head injury resulting in serious memory loss. You can't just send him home.'

The nurse shrugged. 'Well he's not here any more.'

21

Eighteen Months Earlier

The country pub near Karene's home town of Bakewell was full of walkers sheltering from the rain. Karene and Harry sat in the corner farthest from the bar, away from the noise. They had ordered five starters to share and a bottle of wine.

'Are you looking forward to it?' Karene picked up a piece of whitebait, and dipped it in the tartare sauce. Harry was starting his new job the following Monday, and would be working out of Northwood Headquarters in London.

'It'll be the same old drill. Peacocking until everyone finally calms down and gets on with the work.'

'I take it that's you doing the peacocking?'

'With a full-on turquoise suit. You know me, honey.'

Karene picked up his left hand and kissed the back of it. 'My little show-off. Will the work be interesting?'

'I expect so. It's advisory for the most part, so no rolling up my sleeves and actually doing something.'

'Will you miss being in the thick of it?'

'Not when we have a habit of going to war, no.'

'Bit of an occupational hazard that.' She watched as he topped up their wine glasses. 'Was it awful? War, I mean.'

Harry's laugh was low and sarcastic. 'Yeah.'

'Tell me about it?' She wanted to listen to him talk about it, to make sure he'd processed it in a healthy way. She wanted to take care of him.

'You don't want to hear it.'

'Stop saying that. I wouldn't be asking if I didn't want to know. Were you ever in danger?'

'Of course. We came under fire plenty of times.'

'I really don't get why anyone would do it. I understand that big-picture-wise we need to defend the nation and protect those in danger, but on an individual level I don't get why you'd sign up to put yourself in harm's way.'

Harry shrugged. 'Some like the thrill of it, others want the skills and the discipline and the rest of us probably want to put right the wrongs we've seen.'

'Is that why you signed up?'

'I suppose.'

'What wrongs had you seen?' Karene asked. This was the most he'd ever said to her about his experience in the Navy and his reasons for joining.

'You!' he laughed. 'Always trying to get inside my mind!'

'I'm interested,' she said. 'Aren't I allowed to be interested in the man I love?'

'I guess,' he said. When she didn't say anything else he sighed and gave a small shake of his head. 'Have I told you about my sister?'

'You have a sister? Older or younger?'

'Older. She had a stroke when I was in my teens. She's in a care home now.'

'I'm so sorry. That's awful.' She laced her fingers through his. 'Is she why you joined the Navy?'

'I didn't think about it when I signed up but I can see now that it was a big factor. I suppose I—'

Karene waited.

He pushed a king prawn around his plate. 'She told me.'

'Told you what?'

'That she'd been feeling weird: getting headaches, feeling disorientated. They were probably mini-strokes. But I didn't do anything about it.'

'What could you have done?'

He shrugged.

'How old were you?' she asked.

'Sixteen. And Lucy was twenty. If I'd told Mum or encouraged her to go and see the doctor . . .'

'You couldn't have known. How long after she told you did it happen?'

'A few days. I could have checked on her, made her stay at home instead of going back to her dingy flat. If we'd been there when it happened we could've reacted faster. Reduced the effects.'

Karene squeezed his hand. 'You said she's in a care facility now?'

'She lost the ability to speak, walk, go to the bathroom without help.'

'Oh, Harry, I'm so sorry. How awful for her, for all of you.'

'I've never told anyone this before.'

'That she'd told you she felt ill?'

He took a sip of wine.

'You didn't tell your parents?'

'They'd have hated me.'

'No they wouldn't.'

'Grief's a funny thing. It makes people look for a reason, for something or someone to blame. It would've landed on me; I know it. Mum's convinced the anti-sickness drugs were responsible. She's spent years campaigning against their use but there's no evidence they had anything to do with it. She just needs something.' He took his hand away from hers and used it to pick at the seam of his jeans.

'Anti-sickness drugs?'

'She had persistent morning sickness.'

Karene placed her glass down as she processed this extra level of tragedy. 'Your sister was pregnant?'

Harry looked away from her and out of the window, taking a moment to compose himself before he nodded.

She took his hand back. 'What happened to the baby? Did she lose it?'

'No. Well, not technically. She carried him to full term. Little Max. Mum named him after my dad. They delivered him by Caesarean and we all went to see him, but his scrote of a dad wasn't interested. And mum suffers with rheumatoid arthritis so there was no way her and Dad could cope with a baby and what was happening with Lucy at the same time.'

'He was adopted?'

'If I'd have done something I could've stopped him losing his real family.'

Karene sipped her wine as she watched Harry pick apart the prawn on his plate.

'So did you join the Navy to . . . escape?'

He laughed a low laugh. 'Did I run away to sea, do you mean? I suppose I did. I wanted to do something that mattered, I guess.'

'I'm sure she'd be very proud of you.'

His smile didn't reach his eyes.

22

Bloom was walking across Russell Square when Karene called.

'He's gone, Augusta.'

'Who?'

'Harry.'

'What do you mean, gone?' Bloom stopped and stepped to the side of the path to allow a runner to pass. Was this because Karene had found him? Had he been taken once, and then taken again?

'He was discharged from the hospital.'

'To where? By who?'

'The nurse says that the Navy collected him. He's been discharged into their care. Apparently they have their own rehabilitation centre.'

Bloom stepped on to the grass and away from a woman with two large Alsatians. 'But that's a good thing, surely? The military rehabilitation centre will be cutting-edge.'

'That's not the point. They won't let me see him. It's a closed facility. Military only. I need to see him, Augusta. I need to help him.'

'How convenient.' Of course they wanted him back in their own care; this made perfect sense.

The line was quiet for a moment. 'What do you mean?'

'They're closing ranks,' said Bloom. 'Making sure no

one pokes about in their business. Maybe we shouldn't have spoken to Rear Admiral Grey.' She needed to sound out Jameson.

'That's who returned my call. Harry's boss. He said this was procedure and not a civilian matter.'

'So they've moved all the injured personnel to their own facility?'

'I don't know. That's what he implied. Shall I ring Derriford Hospital?'

'I'll get Jameson on it.' Bloom also suspected that Jameson might be able to get them in to see Harry but she didn't want to raise Karene's hopes. She started walking again.

Karene didn't respond. Bloom wondered if the connection had failed; the signal in hospitals was notoriously patchy. 'Hello?' she said pressing the phone to her ear.

'There's something else,' said Karene.

'Go on?'

'Someone's playing games, Augusta. Someone knows something and they're taunting me.'

'What kind of games?' asked Bloom. She didn't like the sound of this.

'I've had an email. It didn't say much – just asks how well I know Harry – but they're implying he's done something wrong.'

'Is this someone you know?'

'The email was anonymous.'

'Do they know Harry?' asked Bloom.

'If they did, they wouldn't be suggesting what they're suggesting. He's a good man. He's dedicated his whole career to helping others. I'm not having anyone say otherwise.'

'We should try to be open-minded.'

'They're saying that I don't really know him, that I should suspect him of God knows what.'

'Karene?' This was why she never worked with her friends and family. They expected total support without even the hint of a challenge.

'No,' said Karene. 'I'm not having it. With everything he's going through, everything he's got coming. I'm not having some idiot thinking they can attack him when he can't defend himself.'

Bloom thought about that as she crossed the road to her office and an idea began to form. 'Can you come into the city later today?'

'I've got nothing else to do.'

'Karene. You're an expert in resilience. Be resilient.' They said their goodbyes and Bloom walked into the building and down the stairs to her office to brief Jameson and to see if he could find any roads into the rehabilitation centre.

'I've had three more emails from this idiot,' said Karene as she walked into the office and dropped her bag on to the spare chair by the door. 'Where's Marcus?'

'He's working on something for me. What do the new emails say?'

Karene sat down in Jameson's chair and swivelled to face Bloom. 'They're all the same. No text in the body of the email, just a question in the subject line.' She took her phone from her jacket pocket, unlocked the screen and handed it to Bloom.

There were three consecutive emails at the top of Karene's inbox.

From: ANONYMOUS   11:00
Subject: Is he a good man?

From: ANONYMOUS   11:45
Subject: Does he help or does he hinder?

From: ANONYMOUS   12:00
Subject: Can you prove it?

'Have you replied?' asked Bloom.

Karene snatched her phone back. 'Absolutely not. I'm not dignifying this nonsense with a response.'

'What time did the first one arrive?'

'Eight o'clock.'

'And then these came clustered between eleven and twelve.'

'Is that significant?'

'Not necessarily. But patterns are useful. People reveal more than they realize through their habits.'

'Would you reply?'

'Maybe. But let's think it through first.'

Jameson arrived carrying a blue cardboard folder. 'Make yourself comfortable,' he said to Karene.

She stood. 'Sorry.'

'He's just messing, Karene. Sit down,' said Bloom.

'Am I?' He placed the folder face down on Bloom's desk and stood against the wall. 'What's occurring?'

Bloom smiled at his Welsh accent. She hadn't heard that in a while.

Jameson looked uncomfortable. She could see that he was fighting to keep things awkward. This slip back into his jovial style was probably nothing more than habit but it gave her hope that in time things could return to normal.

'Karene's received some odd emails,' said Bloom. 'Someone asking questions about Harry and how well she knows him.'

'Excellent. Let's trace the email. See who's showing off.'

'Do you think it's the people who hurt Harry?' asked Karene.

'It's worth a shot. Sometimes people are too cocky.'

'But it might be from someone else,' said Bloom.

'Who else would be goading her?' asked Jameson.

'You don't even know what the questions are yet,' said Bloom, exasperated with his knee-jerk heroics. He often behaved this way in the company of attractive women.

'I can guess.'

Bloom raised her eyebrows.

'They were asking how well she knows him, yes? So I expect they're implying he's hiding something. What hasn't he told you? And so on. Am I close?'

Karene looked impressed. 'That's pretty much it, yes.'

'No, it isn't,' said Bloom firmly. 'We don't know that they're goading you. Why would they? Other than to indulge some perverse pleasure? Look at the wording, the questions. They're relevant, helpful.'

'Relevant?' snapped Karene. 'Are you kidding me? *How well do you really know the man you love?*'

'Open up that first message. Did it say "really"? How much do you "really" know him?'

'Yes.'

'Can you check?'

Karene did nothing.

'Please,' said Bloom.

Karene sighed and checked her phone.

'OK, you're right. It says, "What do you know about the man you love?" No "really".'

'You're inserting the tone of judgement, Karene. That's why you added "really".'

'It *is* judgemental!'

'Just for a moment try thinking of it another way. What if there's no judgement at all? What if it's just a question?'

'I don't understand what you're saying.'

'That makes two of us,' said Jameson.

'What if someone is asking questions to make you think?'

Karene thought for a moment. '"Can you prove it?" is not without judgement. It's quite pointed. It means, *Is he a good man?*'

'Again, it's your judgement, not necessarily theirs. That's the problem with written communication. What if it's an innocent query? Would you say that Harry is a good man?'

'Yes. Absolutely.'

'And does he do good things?'

'He's done some amazing things; he's dedicated his life to helping others.'

'So you'd say he helps rather than harms?'

'Totally. It's what I love most about him. The choices he's made within an organization trained for warfare.'

'But Harry can no longer remember some of those things.'

Karene acknowledged the point without speaking and her eyes became a little teary.

Bloom leaned forward in her chair. 'So it may well be incumbent on you to speak for him.'

Karene's eyes widened. 'To prove it.'

'Exactly. I wonder if our mystery emailer is a friend rather than a foe.'

Jameson coughed. 'We should check out the alternative too, though. It might also be the bad guys showing off or some sicko playing games.'

'Of course,' said Bloom. 'Glad you've been listening all these years, Marcus.'

Jameson gave a small shake of his head. 'Why are you being so magnanimous anyway? If they're a friend and they want to help, they should do just that. We don't need the cryptic messages. I think you're reaching with this.'

Bloom wasn't sure if she should air her theory yet. There were too many angles she still needed to consider, but Jameson and Karene were looking at her expectantly. They both knew her well enough to know that she had a hypothesis brewing.

'Marcus and I think that whoever took Harry needs him alive. If that wasn't the case, he'd have died during the explosion or shortly afterwards. It would have been easy to make it look like he was another unfortunate victim.'

'But they haven't yet got everything they want from him,' said Karene.

'Possibly. But something struck me earlier when you said that Harry wouldn't be able to defend himself due to his memory loss, Karene. If they needed information but wanted him alive they could have opted to harm him in a safer way. Why not break his bones?'

'Presumably they needed him unconscious when they left him in A&E,' said Jameson.

'So drug him. A head injury is really risky. The brain is so unpredictable. If we're right and they need him alive – to do something or help them in some way – wouldn't they need him to be competent too?'

'Well, they failed there then, didn't they? The guy's lost four years of his life,' said Jameson.

'Exactly.' Bloom looked from Jameson to Karene. 'What if they needed him to forget?'

'Surely you're not saying—' began Karene.

'What if all of this is about Harry's memory? If we set the bomb aside, Harry disappeared for seventy-two hours then reappeared with no recollection of the past four years.'

'You're thinking something happened in the last four years that someone wants him to forget?' said Jameson.

'Maybe he did something. Or witnessed something.'

'Or they got him to do something in the time he was missing,' said Jameson. 'And they needed him to forget that.'

'This is ridiculous,' said Karene. 'You can't decide which memories someone is going to lose from a head injury. It doesn't work like that. You know that as well as I do!'

'You say that.' Bloom opened her notes on memory loss from the research she'd done that morning. 'But there are case studies of retrograde amnesia limited to one or two years where there is specific damage to the CA1 field of the hippocampus.'

'But head injuries affect different people in different ways. You can't predict it,' said Karene.

'We know which parts of the brain are involved in episodic memory and which control procedural memory. We know that certain regions lead to anterograde amnesia and others retrograde.'

'Wait,' said Jameson. 'You've lost me.'

'Sorry,' said Bloom. 'We have two main types of memory, procedural – which is how we learn skills and the performance of tasks – and declarative – which covers our recollection of events and facts about our lives, like the names and faces of family and friends.'

'And they are managed by different areas of the brain?' he said.

'Yes. Harry has lost his episodic memory. He can't remember what he's experienced or learned over the past four years but he will still recall how to drive, for example. So only his declarative memory is affected. And we know that the hippocampus in the brain is heavily involved in that specific function. For instance, there was one unfortunate chap who underwent brain surgery to reduce his epilepsy and, because little was known about what different brain regions did at that time, his hippocampus was removed which resulted in severe retrograde amnesia.'

'H.M. The most studied patient in neurology,' said Karene.

'And retrograde?' asked Jameson.

'Memories of the past,' said Karene. 'As opposed to anterograde amnesia, which is our ability to form new memories.'

'So he has a very specific type of memory loss, controlled by a very specific part of the brain?' said Jameson.

'Exactly,' said Bloom.

He looked at her. 'And you're saying that if you wanted someone to lose the last few years of their memory, you could cause localized damage to the hippocampus.'

A deep frown creased Karene's brow. 'But that would require surgery not a head trauma.'

'A head trauma doesn't require seventy-two hours,' said Jameson. 'They could have done that in the ambulance. Interrogated him, beat him up a bit and dropped him at the hospital to arrive with the other bomb victims.'

Bloom nodded. 'So why did it take so long?'

'Because he wouldn't talk?' said Karene.

Jameson narrowed his eyes. 'Maybe. Or they needed the seventy-two hours to do something more intricate.'

'We need to find out what Harry has forgotten,' said Bloom.

Jameson smiled. He looked at Karene. 'What do you know about the man you love? What has he done, good and bad? Tell us everything.'

23

'Do you think she'll come up with anything useful?' asked Jameson.

Karene had returned to her accommodation to spend the evening gathering together everything Harry had told her about his life and work in the past four years. She'd said she would also check in with his closest friends about the couple of years before she had met him.

'Hard to say,' replied Bloom. 'But we have to try. If there are gaps, we can investigate with Harry's colleagues and the rest of his family.'

'Yeah, let's hope the others are a bit more engaged than his ex-wife.'

'Any insights on her new boyfriend?'

'He seems clean. Nothing controversial. He's been a doctor in the same hospital since he qualified; never in trouble, no military training or weird hobbies. I'll keep digging but it's not looking promising. He and Caroline were on holiday with the kids the week of the ball.'

'I've had a call from one of Detective Superintendent Drummond's team and the CCTV at the hospital drew a blank too. The hours in question had been erased or recorded over.'

'How convenient. Cock-up or conspiracy?'

Bloom shrugged. 'We'll never know.'

'No, but I'd say it's one more thing that suggests some-one sophisticated might be behind this.'

'Not just a lone bomber or a bungling ambulance crew covering their tracks,' said Bloom, acknowledging the point. 'Can we get in to see Harry, do you think? We need to get some more information, and fast. We've got so many theories and hardly any facts.'

'He's not on a military base: it's a medical facility.'

'And have all the military personnel from the explo-sion been transferred there?'

Jameson shook his head. 'Just Harry, as far as I know. But I expect the Commodore who lost a leg will end up there too.'

'Grey told Karene it was procedure for all military staff to be moved there.'

'Really? It's a specialist trauma centre: limb loss, head injuries, spinal injuries. So I can't see why other casual-ties would be transferred there.'

'And he said she wouldn't be allowed on site.'

'That could be for a couple of reasons. He's been moved to Stanford Hall in the Midlands. It's not offi-cially open yet. They're in the process of transferring activities there from Headley Court in Surrey.'

'So it might not be set up for visitors?'

'Possibly not. There's still a lot of construction going on.'

'And what else?' asked Bloom. 'You've got something else.'

Jameson collected the blue folder from the desk and opened it. He placed two printed images on her desk.

A man was tied to a chair, his corpse bloated and disfigured and surrounded by a large pool of blood.

'This is Harry Peterson's cousin, Julian. He was found on Wednesday by a delivery driver.'

'Where?'

'In the kitchen of his house in a small village in Normandy. He'd been tortured pretty brutally. Not a professional job, but toenails pulled out, fingers chopped off. I'd say whoever did it enjoys their work a little too much.'

'I take it you're thinking a psychopath?'

'Ha . . . although, actually, yeah. One of your criminal ones.'

'How long had he been dead when he was found?'

'The autopsy will tell us more but from the bloating and discolouration I'd say probably somewhere between one and two weeks.'

Bloom looked up. 'Marcus, that could mean he was murdered just days before Harry's kidnap.'

Her partner nodded slowly. 'I'm thinking whatever it is that Harry's just forgotten, this guy knew too.'

24

'Have you seen this?' The next morning Bloom thrust an open newspaper on to Jameson's desk. He looked down. There was a picture of Devonport Naval Base surrounded by police vehicles and a small photograph of Harry Peterson. The headline read:

Hero's Memory Tragically Wiped by a Terrorist Bomb

The article described Captain Harry Peterson's tours in Iraq and Afghanistan and included a quote from a colleague that said he was an exemplary pilot and universally liked by his colleagues. It said that he had lost four years of his life and that doctors at the Defence and National Rehabilitation Centre expected that the damage sustained would be permanent. There was a profile of the suspected bomber, a short description of the bomb and details of those killed and injured.

'Is that right?' said Jameson, finishing the article. 'About his memory loss being permanent?'

'It's early days. Although they could have done an MRI or a CT scan, I suppose.'

'They haven't named the doctors. It's probably some hack wanting to make the story as dramatic as possible.'

'I agree. But it's going to upset Karene and no doubt his children too. It's irresponsible journalism.'

'You say that as if journalism is usually responsible and not all about selling papers.'

'They should be investigators and purveyors of the truth.'

Jameson laughed. It was a sound she hadn't heard in a long time. 'For such an intelligent person, Augusta, you can't half be naive.'

Bloom took the paper back. 'I need to go and see Karene and tell her about Harry's cousin before we head out there. Are you coming?' Jameson had booked them both on a flight out to Normandy that afternoon and arranged for them to meet with police at Julian's residence.

They walked the short distance from Russell Square to Cartwright Gardens where Karene had rented a studio apartment. The room was small but well-equipped with a bed, kitchenette, table and two chairs. The blind on the window matched the throw on the bed and above the headboard hung a large picture of Audrey Hepburn looking back over one shoulder with a cigarette holder to her lips.

There were notes spread across the small table.

Karene ushered them inside. Her red hair was wet from the shower and the drips of water had created dark patches on the straps of her pink sundress. Her feet were bare and her toenails painted deep purple.

'I've had another email,' she said as Jameson sat in the spare chair and Bloom perched on the edge of the bed.

'It arrived just before you.' She unlocked her phone and handed it to Bloom.

From: ANONYMOUS   11:00
Subject: Is Harry safe?

'They're just trying to spook me,' said Karene. 'I should block them.'

Bloom showed the message to Jameson who raised his eyebrows in response.

'Perhaps we should check in?' Bloom said.

'Got it.' Jameson went out of the apartment and into the hallway.

'What are you doing?' asked Karene. 'Where's he going?'

'Sit down for me, Karene.'

Her expression flashed panic but she did as instructed.

'Did Harry ever mention a cousin in France?'

'Julian?'

Bloom nodded. 'I'm afraid I've some bad news. Julian was found dead on Wednesday morning.'

'Oh my God. How? What happened?'

'He was murdered in his kitchen.'

Karene opened and closed her mouth but said nothing.

'Murdered how?' she said eventually, her voice low.

'He had his throat cut. But he'd been tortured too.'

Karene placed her hands over her mouth. Her eyes were wide and Bloom could see that her friend had joined the dots.

'The pathologist estimates that he was murdered ten to twelve days before the body was found. So around the weekend before the ball,' said Bloom.

Jameson came back into the room and nodded to Bloom.

'Harry's safe?' she asked.

'Yep. I spoke to the Head of Security and he's going to keep an eye on things.'

'Why did they torture him? What did they want?'

'We think it might be linked to Harry,' said Jameson. 'That they might both have known the same secret.'

'Have you come up with anything that involves Julian too?' asked Bloom.

'Does Caroline know?' asked Karene. 'I think the kids visited Julian regularly when they were little. He has a stepdaughter who lives over here with her mum. They used to take her with them to see him.'

'Probably not,' said Jameson. 'It's all being kept very low-key at the moment but we can tell her if you like.'

Karene nodded then picked up the papers on the desk and began to sift through them. 'Julian ran his own business. He wasn't military and he retired ages ago and moved to France. I don't know what they'd have in common other than their family.' She stopped sifting and looked back at Bloom. 'Is this a personal thing? Is someone coming for him again? Why is my emailer asking if he's safe?'

25

Bloom and Jameson disembarked their flight, collected their hire car and started the hour-long drive to Julian Peterson's home in a rural village near the town of Avranches in Normandy. While Jameson drove, Bloom read through Karene's notes.

'Obviously she has a lot more detail from the time they've been together. But she's pieced together plenty from before that. She starts with the routine of his life over the past twelve months. He works pretty much nine to five, has had no deployments or lengthy trips away, only the odd overnight. His children stay with him two weeks out of every four. He's bought a house in St Albans near their mother so that he can be as involved as possible. He's a keen cyclist like you. She says he trains three or four times a week, often cycling to and from work which is about twenty miles. He does half a dozen or so races a year. She's listed his most recent ones. They have a small group of couples they socialize with and she's included their names and contact details. And once a month he travels to the Cotswolds to visit his sister Lucy who's in a care home there.'

'What's wrong with the sister?'

Bloom skipped a few pages to the notes on family. 'She had a stroke in 1989 when she was just twenty.'

Jameson sucked air in through his teeth. 'Tragic.' He took the exit signposted Rennes and Le Mont-Saint-Michel.

'She's also given us some details on his current role. He develops scenarios for how the Fleet Air Arm should respond to potential conflicts or humanitarian disasters. Is that the Navy's aircraft division?'

Jameson nodded. 'So he's not working on a specific threat. That reduces the chances of him becoming a target. Strategic scenarios are just that: scenarios that may or may not come to pass. We need to check that with Rear Admiral Grey. Harry may have been working on something that he couldn't talk to Karene about.'

'She's listed his deployments: where he went and for how long. I'll let you take a look at those in case anything jumps out.' Bloom turned to the last few pages. 'Good for you, Karene. She's gathered all the information to answer the emailer's questions. "What do you know about the man you love?" Age, birthplace, career, places he's lived, family members including Caroline and their two children, a list of likes and dislikes. He likes entertaining and dislikes injustice.'

'Sounds like your average Miss World.'

'He just wants world peace and happiness for all.'

Jameson chuckled.

'Then, she's written a paragraph on how she views him. She says he has a fun-loving and light-hearted exterior but underneath is a competent professional who genuinely cares about his work and the people it affects. Apparently, he has an uncanny visual memory and can often recall the smallest of details about somewhere they've been or someone they've met.' Bloom lifted her eyes to look out through the windscreen. 'That's interesting, isn't it?'

'So has he witnessed something? You said different types of memories are stored in different areas of the brain. What about his visual memory? Can we find out if he's noticed something about his kidnappers?'

'I don't know but it's worth a shot. Can you get us in to see him?'

'I can keep trying.'

They met a French police officer at the house, and were shown through to the crime scene. Bloom had a basic grasp of French, but thankfully Jameson was fluent. She left them talking and slowly walked around the kitchen to where Julian had been found. The body and its restraints had been removed but the chair remained on the stone floor, which still bore a dark stain where the blood had been. The rest of the room was neat and tidy. A single plate, wine glass and chopping board sat on the drainer next to the deep porcelain sink. Had he been interrupted while washing up? She put on a latex glove and opened the fridge. She was hit by a strong aroma of cheese. The vegetables in the salad tray had turned brown and were dissolving into mush. On the middle shelf sat a half-eaten Camembert next to an open packet of sausages. She closed the door.

'Apparently they think he was tortured with his own kitchen equipment. The scissors and three knives are with forensics,' said Jameson.

'Does that mean they didn't intend to hurt him? If they didn't bring their own tools?'

'There's always something you can use. And it's safer not to be carrying anything that can incriminate you.'

'Are you still thinking amateurs?'

'Probably highly experienced amateurs.' He held up a document written in French. 'Autopsy report. They found nothing to indicate any hesitation in the injuries inflicted. The attacker was confident and competent.'

'How did you get that?' she said.

'A little bit of charm, a little bit of coercion.'

'Anything else of interest in it?'

'I'll take a closer look.'

Bloom continued circling the kitchen, searching for anything that might suggest who was here or why. She had no idea what she was looking for and everything appeared to be normal. It was only when she closed the kitchen door in order to see the dresser better behind it that she spotted the noticeboard. 'Marcus?'

He came over to look at the cork board hung on the back of the door. It had a few business cards for electricians and plumbers, a take-out menu, a photograph of a woman in her fifties wearing a sunhat and large shades, and a postcard. Bloom pointed to the latter. It showed forty or so people crammed into a small fishing boat and she read aloud the words printed beneath: 'To help or to hinder. Your choice.'

'Migrants?' said Jameson. 'What's on the back?'

Bloom removed the pin and turned the postcard over. The back was blank apart from the name of the print company in the bottom left corner. 'Quickcards. Aren't they British?'

'Yes. As was Julian.'

She turned the postcard around and re-pinned it. Then she photographed it on her phone. 'What are the chances he'd have that question pinned here? It's very similar to Karene's email.'

'What did that say?' asked Jameson.

'Does he help or does he hinder?'

'I told you we should chase them up,' said Jameson.

'Let's get in touch with Superintendent Drummond. Maybe he can get something out of Quickcards.'

'What will they tell us?'

'Perhaps who sent it. Or if Julian ordered it himself. Maybe he ordered more than one and sent them to other addresses.'

Bloom placed her phone back in her pocket and removed her gloves.

'Also,' she said to Jameson, pointing at the photograph of the woman, 'we need to find out who that is.'

26

The flight back to Southend took less than an hour. Jameson sat beside her reading a book on cycling while Bloom used the time to update her case notes.

They hadn't spoken to anyone who had suggested that Harry might be mixed up in something dangerous. And yet, here was his cousin, tortured and murdered in the most brutal way. Harry and Rear Admiral Grey had both signed the Official Secrets Act – so perhaps there was something there that no one knew about. But Julian Peterson had no other military connections. So was it a personal matter? In which case, why attack a military base? Why not grab Harry on the street or in his home when he was alone and vulnerable?

Somebody wanted to make a scene.

Was it a show of strength? A warning shot?

She took out her phone and sent the picture of the postcard to her iPad. She linked the image to her case notes and enlarged it.

The bright blue boat tilted ominously to one side in the water and was packed with people clinging on, sitting on the roof and jammed into every space on the small deck. She could see children and only a handful of orange life vests. The picture quality wasn't good enough to make out faces or expressions, but she could imagine the desperation.

To help or to hinder. Your choice.

Harry had assisted the migrant relief effort. She recalled Jameson saying that some people felt that not saving drowning migrants would deter others. Could Harry have made that call? He would certainly have been senior enough to stand down air support. But would he? Karene would think it impossible.

Rear Admiral Grey described Harry as reliable, a safe pair of hands, a man who could be trusted not to let others down, someone who inspired loyalty and knew how to get what he wanted. His ex-wife had expanded on that, saying that if Harry wanted something he could turn the full force of his personality on the recipient. She had called him an entertainer. Which matched Karene's description. Bloom imagined a gregarious, engaging man who could turn on the charm. But Caroline had also said he could be distant and secretive, especially towards the end of their marriage.

Bloom checked her notes to confirm when the Peterson marriage had ended. She raised her eyebrows. It was sometime in late 2015: the same year that Harry had been deployed on the search and rescue mission. Was that significant? She made a note to speak to Caroline again and check it out. Finally, Karene had told them that Harry's light-hearted exterior masked a conscientious professional who disliked injustice and had chosen to spend his life helping others. She had also mentioned his uncanny visual memory.

Bloom turned to his career history. He was a decorated naval officer and an experienced pilot, so clearly dedicated and intelligent. He had been to war three times and had experienced things others couldn't imagine. Karene's expertise suggested that this either rendered people realistic and resilient, or very much damaged. Karene felt that Harry was the former, but people were good at masking their true selves, especially when it came to their mental health. Caroline had described her ex-husband as emotionless. Was he in denial or repressing his trauma?

Bloom recalled a press article that Karene had sent her when they were first looking for Harry. It had seemed irrelevant at the time, simply a way of demonstrating what a great guy she had fallen for. But in light of the postcard Bloom opened it and re-read the editorial. It described the decision taken by the newly promoted Captain Peterson to airlift migrants from a stricken vessel off the coast of Italy even though no one had agreed to take them in. He was quoted as saying, 'No man, woman or child is expendable, not one single one, no matter who they are or where they are from. As a nation, we have a responsibility to save any and every life.'

The plane began its descent. Bloom saved her files, sat back and closed her eyes.

To help or to hinder?

Your choice.

She sat up. Jameson looked over and raised an eyebrow, asking if everything was OK. Bloom nodded and sat back in her seat again, but her mind raced as she connected the pieces together and firmed up her theory, or rather, her fear.

27

The window opposite Harry's bed looked out on to a partially landscaped garden. He could see raised beds, some with hardy perennials, the others still bare. There was a lawn with a circular seating area surrounded by a neatly cut privet hedge. The path leading towards it was bordered by pairs of box-cut trees. Beyond that, there was another building still under construction and heavily scaffolded.

One of the porters, a skinny, balding chap called Freddie, carried a box of supplies into the room.

'Afternoon, Sir,' he said.

'Afternoon,' said Harry. He had encouraged Freddie to call him Harry but the porter was having none of it. Harry was one of the first patients here, but many more would be transferred from the military rehabilitation centre in Surrey in the coming months and Freddie had said he was expected to treat all of them with the respect they deserved. It was no good starting bad habits now. 'Busy day?'

Freddie placed a box of latex gloves in the cabinet and carried a few toilet rolls into the en-suite. 'I'm all done, Sir. Shift change in ten. This is my last job of the day, then two days off.'

'Very nice. I wish I could escape for a few days.'

'You'll be out of here soon enough.'

And then what? thought Harry. Caroline had been refusing to bring the kids to see him. She had said all in good time, but he could tell she was hesitant. She'd only been in once – before he was transferred – and even then she'd spent most of the time talking to medical staff. He sensed something was off. She'd never been the most attentive wife, but this was unusual. He'd struggled to read her expressions, had noted the lack of physical contact. He'd forgotten something important, he just knew it. Christ, he'd forgotten four years of his life, of his children's lives, he was missing *everything* important. He couldn't imagine Sophie at seventeen, Jake at fourteen. He'd asked to see photographs but Caroline had said, not yet, to wait until he was stronger. He'd tried to bring it all back, lying there for hours on end willing the memories to return. But the blank space was dense and dark.

'You take care now,' said Freddie as he left the room.

'Have a good weekend.' Harry had no idea if it was the weekend or midweek. He had no access to a television, computer or even a newspaper. Maybe they were shielding him from all the changes, the ways the world had moved on, or maybe those luxuries were yet to be installed. He'd been told he was here to be treated by a leading team of neurologists, but he suspected some other motivation too. The location was remote and the facility unfinished. Was he being hidden? And, if so, why?

He must have drifted off because when he awoke it was dusk and his room felt dull and cool. The man standing at the foot of his bed was unfamiliar. Harry thought he'd met all the porters. Maybe this one was new. His uniform was too big. It hung loose around his shoulders revealing a large tattoo that covered the lower part of his neck. It looked like some sort of bird. The man pushed a wheelchair to the side of the bed.

'Get in . . .' he said. 'Please.' The man had a thick accent, possibly North African.

Harry sat a little higher in the bed. It would be good to get out of this room. Other than an MRI scan on arrival, he'd spent his whole stay looking at these four walls.

'Where are we going?' He manoeuvred his legs from under the covers and sat in the wheelchair. As he did he noticed that behind the new porter, standing in the doorway, was Freddie. Harry was confused. Freddie had said he was leaving and that he wouldn't be back for a couple of days. What was he still doing here?

Before he'd had time to form the question, Freddie's colleague pulled out a gun.

28

The knock on the front door came just as her phone began to ring. Bloom placed her pen down on the pad and answered her phone as she walked into the hallway.

'Hello?' she said.

'Augusta,' said Karene.

Bloom opened the door. Jameson was standing on her doorstep looking just as anxious as Karene sounded. 'What's happened?'

'I've had another email,' said Karene in her ear. 'It says, "I told you he wasn't safe."'

'It's Harry. Can I come in?' said Jameson.

'Is that Marcus?' said Karene. 'What did he just say about Harry? What's happened to Harry?'

'Karene's on the phone,' she said to Jameson. 'She's had an email saying, "I told you he wasn't safe." What's happened?'

Jameson walked down the hallway and into her kitchen. He'd never been here before, never been invited. He perched on a bar stool at the kitchen island. 'Put her on speaker,' he said.

Bloom did and placed the phone on top of the counter. She turned over her notepad. She wasn't ready for Jameson to see her latest theory just yet.

'Karene, it's Marcus. I've just had a call from the Head

of Security at the rehab centre. There's been a shooting.'

'Oh God,' said Karene.

'Two fatalities.'

'Harry?' asked Bloom.

'They wouldn't reveal details on the phone. I'm going up there now.'

'*We're* going up there,' said Bloom.

Jameson nodded.

'Pick me up,' said Karene.

'You don't have to come. We can check—' started Jameson.

'Pick me up,' she said again.

29

Alina sat at the kitchen table in her new flat in a city she was still getting to know. She was on her laptop, searching online. She knew she shouldn't, but she always deleted the history afterwards so she figured she was fine. This time the name 'Peterson' brought up two news articles. She read the newest one first; it was written in her native French.

Dammit. Julian had been a nice man, kind to her. The article didn't say how he'd died but it was clear that someone had hurt him. The same someone who had tried to hurt Harry. Were they coming for her too?

She knew that Julian hadn't revealed her secret. For the simple reason that he never knew it.

She went back to the older article and re-read it. She'd done this so many times in the last few days and it always brought about the same gut-wrenching panic.

Hero's Memory Tragically Wiped by a Terrorist Bomb

Harry had lost the last four years of his memory, it said, permanently. Which meant *she* was permanently gone. How would she cope alone? He had always told her she was stronger than anyone else he knew, but that was when she had him to guide and protect her. The men who had come to check on her since could never replace him. She could see in their eyes that she was just the latest job. They had said that her new identity was part of a witness protection scheme. She was finally safe, finally anonymous.

Which meant that Harry would never be able to find her again.

30

'How do you cope without a television?' Jameson said as they drove to collect Karene from the rented London apartment she had remained in so she could be close to Bloom.

Bloom said, 'You don't know that I don't. You only went into my kitchen.'

'I walked past the lounge door and saw in the mirror on the back wall that there wasn't one. Only a small sofa that looks unused and a comfy chair angled away from the window because the house is south-facing, which was confirmed by the faded pattern on the armrest nearest the window. The cushions on the chair are indented because that is where you sit to read and probably always in the same position.'

'You noticed all that?' Bloom sounded shocked.

Jameson enjoyed showing her she was not always the most observant in their partnership. 'I also noticed the floral tea set on your kitchen dresser that is not your style at all, so I assume you've taken it from your parents' house as a keepsake which tells me you've either sold the family home or are in the process of doing so. You have three separate locks on your front door, the only door into the property, two locks on each window and a high-spec intruder alarm which tells me that you don't feel safe in your own home.'

'Or that I want to feel as safe as I can.'

Jameson's mouth twitched. 'Same difference. There were some unexpected things too. Like the large painting of those little sheep in snow and Banksy's *Girl with Balloon* print in the kitchen. I wouldn't have thought those were your style.'

He chose not to mention the other picture of a girl: the photograph carefully placed beside the reading chair in the lounge. Something told him he shouldn't. He also didn't let on that he'd seen her turn her notebook over when she thought he wasn't looking.

'All right, Mr Spy. That's all very impressive but you can stop now,' said Bloom.

The two-and-a-half-hour drive from London to Loughborough was tense with long periods of silence. Karene sat in the back staring out of the window.

'They never said he was in danger. They only asked if he was safe.' It wasn't the first time Karene had pointed this out. 'How were we supposed to know?'

Jameson overtook an elderly woman driving at fifty miles an hour in the middle lane of the motorway. He had warned the Head of Security at Stanford Hall Rehabilitation Centre. They couldn't have done anything more. He'd explained this. But Karene wasn't hearing him.

He moved back to the inside lane. 'Let's focus on who's sending the emails. We thought someone was trying to tip us off, which now seems to be on the money, so why aren't we discussing that?'

'Do you have a theory?' asked Bloom.

'It's clearly some sicko who's getting a kick out of pushing my buttons,' said Karene.

Jameson continued, 'The Head of Security is a friend of a friend. That's how I heard about this so fast.' Bloom caught his eye and he shrugged. 'The world of warfare is small. I'd tipped him off to a possible threat; he returned the favour.'

'But you're wondering how our emailer knew?' said Bloom.

'They must be an insider.'

'Or even better connected than you are.'

'Have we looked at where the emails are coming from?' asked Jameson.

'Do you mean have *I* looked at where the emails are coming from?'

'All right,' said Jameson. 'Have *you* looked? Or do you need me to do it?'

'No, no, I'm perfectly capable, thank you. I've asked Lucas to check it out, but all he found was the Gmail account and the IP address of a London hotel and other public wifi spots around the city.'

Jameson had heard all about their new technical wizard Lucas George. He was a freelance cyber-crime consultant recommended to Bloom by a police constable they had worked with earlier in the year. And by all accounts, he was impressive.

'So, whoever it is, they're in London.'

'And smart. Lucas said it could literally be anyone with a laptop,' said Bloom.

Great. Another dead end. This case was going nowhere.

Jameson parked outside the entrance and called his contact. A few minutes later a security guard drove out to meet them and they moved into his vehicle to be driven on-site. When they reached the gated military area they produced their passports and were handed red lanyards with the word ESCORTED written on both the pass and the fabric. The Head of Security, Greg Taylor, met them just outside the redbrick building. He was a short man with thick grey hair and a muscular frame, probably in his fifties.

Jameson had said to let him lead the conversation so Bloom and Karene stood silently as the men exchanged hellos and briefly discussed their friend in common. Finally, Jameson said, 'So what happened here?'

'It looks like they posed as porters. Came in on this afternoon's shift change.'

'Armed?' said Jameson.

Taylor nodded.

'How the hell did that happen?'

'We're still in preparation.'

'You're still a military facility.'

'What about Harry?' said Karene. 'I need to know,' she said in response to Jameson's glare. 'Is he alive?'

'He is,' said Taylor.

'He is?' said Jameson. 'I thought you said there'd been an attack on Peterson?'

142

'I did. But the deceased men are the two porters.'

'One of your guys intervened?' Jameson figured this might redeem them a touch. How can a military facility allow armed intruders through the gate?

Taylor shook his head. 'They shot each other.'

'*They.*' Jameson's laugh was one of disbelief rather than humour. 'You're not serious?'

31

It took all of her willpower not to run and wrap him in her arms. Harry was sitting in a long open space with tiled floor and minimal décor, staring out of the window. The full head bandage he'd been wearing in hospital had been replaced with a small square patch that seemed to have been stapled to his scalp. The bruising on his forehead had darkened to deep purple.

'Hey,' she said, softly. 'How are you?'

He turned to the sound of her voice. A smile formed and then faltered. 'What are you doing here?'

Harry looked from Karene to Bloom to Jameson.

'We need to speak to you, Harry,' said Karene.

'You're Caroline's friend? And who are you two?'

Karene pulled up a chair and sat beside him.

'I'm not Caroline's friend, Harry, I'm—' She swallowed and met his gaze. 'Harry, I'm yours.'

'Mine?'

She nodded.

'My what?' His voice was solid, unmoved.

She took his hand and squeezed it gently. 'Just yours. I know we're not supposed to tell you ... things ... things you've forgotten but you're going to need me. We have no idea who these people are and why—'

'Mine as in ...' Harry looked at Bloom and Jameson

again. 'Is that why Caroline hates me? Oh, no.' He removed his hand from Karene's and stood up. 'I never would, never could. No. That's why she won't let me see the kids. They hate me.' He ran his hands down his face. 'I thought today couldn't get any worse.' He looked at Karene. 'I'm sorry,' he said. 'You're not mine. Whatever this is or was . . . it's not any more.'

He walked away and she was left staring after him.

32

Karene sunk down into the seat that Harry Peterson had vacated and Bloom rushed after Harry. Jameson guessed that Karene might want some time alone so he went to find Greg Taylor in the reception, where a construction manager in a shirt and tie with a high-vis jacket and hard hat was surveying the space.

'Can I take a look at the scene?' he asked.

'You know I can't let you in,' replied Greg.

'Just a view from the doorway?'

Greg paused. 'OK,' he said. 'Follow me.'

The small ward had four beds but only one had sheets and those were now strewn across the floor and soaked in blood. The dead men had been removed but Jameson could guess from the pools of blood where each had fallen: one just in front of where he was standing and the other on the far side of the bed.

'How the hell did they both end up dead while Harry walked out unscathed?'

'Incompetent idiots, I expect.'

Jameson looked around the walls then crouched low and examined the floor. 'The weapons?'

'Bagged for evidence.'

'Any idea what they were firing?'

'Handguns. A Sig Sauer and a Glock.'

Jameson nodded. A popular choice for your average tooled-up criminal. 'And you have no idea who the deceased were?'

'We thought they were agency staff with a full set of references. We're looking into it now. One had been here since Monday but the other only started this afternoon because one of our regulars failed to turn up.'

'So they got one of their guys in to scope the place as soon as Harry Peterson was moved here. And then they sent in reinforcements. I'd check on that regular staff member if I were you.'

'You think he's part of it?'

'Or someone forced him to take a day off. Hopefully not permanently.'

How had Harry survived this? What had he done? Bloom had said that skills can remain despite memory loss because they're stored differently in the brain. So perhaps Harry had defended himself. But, whatever had happened, it was clear someone wanted him dead. Which blew their previous theory out of the water.

33

'She won't tell you,' said Bloom. 'And it's because she couldn't stand to see the look on your face when you hear it.' Harry turned to look at her. 'But I'd want someone to tell me the truth if I were in your shoes.'

They were in a small side room with comfy chairs and a television. Bloom studied Harry: she wondered if there was something breakable there or just a very resilient soul. When he lifted his chin a touch, she continued. 'Caroline left you. It wasn't because you met someone else, but because *she* did.'

Bloom was pleased that Karene wasn't there to see the pain move across Harry's face. He took a deep breath and looked towards the corner of the room. 'And who exactly are you?'

'I'm Augusta ... Bloom. An old friend of Karene's from university. Marcus Jameson and I investigate unusual crimes.'

'Private detectives?'

'Of a kind.'

'And what have you detected?' There was an edge to his voice.

'Mr Peterson ... Harry ... I believe someone may have made you forget something on purpose.'

'*Made* me? With the bomb?'

'More likely during the time you were missing.'

Harry frowned, narrowing his eyes. He opened his mouth then shook his head. 'Missing?'

'Have you been told about this? No. OK. Of course you haven't. Shall we take a seat? I'll explain it all.'

Harry didn't move. 'I met your friend Karene *after* Caroline left me?'

'Yes. That's my understanding.'

'And she's hired you?'

'Correct.'

They stood for a moment in silence before Harry said, 'Then she should tell me everything. If it's as you say and she's the person who cares the most.'

Bloom smiled. She could see the effort it was taking for him to suppress his shock.

'She really does,' said Bloom.

34

Karene hadn't moved. Her eyes were swollen and a little red. Bloom felt terribly sad for her friend.

'He'd like to hear it from you,' she said.

Karene straightened her back and squared her shoulders. Harry led them to three armchairs set in front of a large window that overlooked a neatly trimmed lawn and Karene explained how she and Harry had met and fallen in love.

'And after the bomb?' he said, looking uncomfortable with the details so far.

Karene explained his injuries as they'd been immediately after the explosion and then how she'd searched all the hospitals desperately trying to find him.

'You turned up in Exeter Hospital about seventy-two hours later with head injuries that weren't there on the night. Those cuts and bruises weren't there. I know I couldn't have seen a skull fracture but the wound on your head is severe and would have been bleeding heavily. There was just a small graze.'

'None of the other injured people went to Exeter,' said Bloom. 'They were all admitted to Derriford Hospital on the night of the ball.'

'So, what are your theories?' Harry asked.

Jameson joined them and perched on the armrest of Bloom's chair.

'We're fairly sure someone took you away in an ambulance but after that we're unclear,' said Bloom. 'But during this period you sustained your head injury and possibly the memory loss too.'

'*Possibly* the memory loss?'

'It's impossible to say whether your memory was affected by the initial impact of the bomb, or by whatever caused that head injury, or by something else entirely,' said Bloom.

'Augusta thinks the later injury may have been used to mask a surgical procedure,' said Karene.

'We wouldn't know that for sure without an MRI scan,' said Bloom.

'They did one here. The day I arrived.'

Bloom looked at Jameson.

'Leave that one with me,' he said.

'What are you expecting to see?' asked Harry.

'Well, if someone intentionally damaged the memory centre of your brain we might see evidence of that. The track of a drill, for instance.'

'A drill?'

'You'd have been unconscious,' said Bloom.

'I wouldn't remember if I wasn't.'

Bloom and Karene fell quiet as they both considered the truth of his statement.

'Why would someone do that to me?' he asked.

Bloom sat forward and clasped her hands together.

'As far as I can see there are three possibilities. You've seen something someone wants you to forget, done something someone wants you to forget, or someone wants you to forget what you've told them.'

'But seen or done what?'

'That's the million-dollar question, my man,' said Jameson.

Bloom continued, 'It could be something in your past or—'

'Something that happened in those missing hours,' finished Harry.

'They may have needed your skills or particular insights for something.'

'But . . . that's a needle in a haystack. How do we ever find out if I don't remember what I've seen, what I've done or who I've met?'

'There are some clues,' said Jameson.

'Such as?'

'I'll get to that, but would you run me through this afternoon first? While it's still fresh.'

'I've already told the police everything.'

'It's important we know everything too,' said Jameson. 'If we're going to help.'

Harry surveyed the room, gathering his thoughts.

'When I woke there were two porters in my room. I'd never seen the guy at the end of my bed before, but the one in the doorway was called Freddie. He'd been here since I'd arrived.' He was factual, reporting the details in an efficient, matter-of-fact way.

'Working as a porter?' said Jameson.

Harry nodded. 'Freddie had said earlier that he was nearly done for the day and was taking a few days off so I wondered what might have kept him. This place is pretty much deserted other than the construction workers and new trainees. The new guy pushed a wheelchair up against the bed and told me to get in. He had a heavy accent – North African, maybe – and looked more suited to life as a nightclub bouncer. I did as I was asked. I didn't think much more of it. I was grateful for a change of scenery. I shifted across and had my back to the two of them and I heard the new guy say something in French. I think it was "Who is this?" or "What is this?" And Freddie replied, "It's not your concern."'

'Also in French?' said Jameson.

Harry frowned. 'No,' he said. 'Freddie replied in English.'

'Go on,' said Jameson.

'After that it all happened very fast. The new guy moved to my side and reached for a gun from the back of his trousers and I just hit the floor and rolled under the bed. I'm not sure where I thought I was going, what it would achieve; it was just instinct. The guy walked around the bed, grabbed me by my top and hauled me out all the while waving his gun and cursing, still in French. Once he had me on my feet, I saw Freddie in the door. His arm was up and his gun was aimed right at my head. The guy holding me went nuts hissing something I couldn't make out. All I heard him saying was, "*Vivant! Vivant!*" and then he pushed me forward on to the bed and I heard the shots.'

'They shot each other intentionally?' said Jameson.

'I'm pretty sure that's what happened.'

'And the guy holding you pushed you out of the way?'

'He saved my life.'

Jameson met Bloom's eye. '*Vivant.* It means alive. They need him alive.'

Bloom considered that. 'Did Freddie get carried away? Start threatening to kill Harry?'

'Maybe he's the torturing psycho,' said Jameson.

'Torturing psycho?' said Harry.

'Sensitively done, Marcus,' said Karene. 'Perhaps you two might take a walk and I can fill Harry in on other developments?'

'That was unfortunate,' said Bloom as she and Jameson walked outside. He was looking suitably ashamed. That hadn't been the best way to tell Harry about his cousin.

'So, what do you reckon?' he asked. 'Who are these jokers? They insert Freddie as a porter, make him invisible and then – what? – he loses it? Or changes the game mid-play?'

'Or they're too disorganized to fully brief their team. What if they'd received separate instructions?' said Bloom. 'Not every group is a cold, calculating team of practised professionals.'

Jameson stopped. 'What's with the back-handed digs? I thought I was the one who was pissed off?'

'And why is that, Marcus? What exactly do you have to be pissed off about?'

'You know very well.'

'Do I?' Bloom folded her arms across her chest. He was referring to how she'd kept him in the dark about Seraphine's identity. 'I made a judgement call, in the heat of the moment and perhaps it was the wrong call, but I did not intentionally put you in harm's way.'

'That's not what I'm angry about.'

'Isn't it?'

'God no. You did what you had to do. I'd probably have done the same.'

Bloom raised her hands in a show of exasperation. 'So what are you angry about then?'

He bit his lip hard as he looked up into the sky. When he looked back at her his face was a picture of disgust. 'That you never thought it wise to tell me what you are.'

Bloom took a sharp intake of breath.

'What you really are,' he said and then walked away.

She watched him go in disbelief. He still believed Seraphine's assessment of her: that Bloom was also a psychopath.

35

Harry and Karene sat in silence. She wanted to reach over and take his hand, to feel him pull her close and hold her tight. She missed how he used to look at her. It broke her heart that all she saw in his eyes was confusion and a total lack of recognition. She couldn't even detect any hint of attraction, which made her doubt that the last two years had really happened.

'Who was tortured?' he said eventually.

'Is there any way of getting a drink in this place?'

Harry shook his head. 'There's a kitchen that probably has tea and coffee. Who was tortured, someone from the ball? Who's the psycho?'

'No, Harry. Marcus shouldn't have said that. I'm sorry.'

Harry studied her. 'Tell me.'

'A week or so before the ball, Julian was attacked in his home. I'm sorry, Harry. He was murdered.'

'Julian?' He looked momentarily confused and then his eyes widened. 'My Julian? My cousin?'

Karene closed her eyes and pressed her lips together.

'Why would . . . how? What has Julian got to do with anything? He's a retired engineer.'

'We were hoping you might be able to tell us that.'

Harry's laugh was bitter. 'You figured a man with no

memory could give you answers. I'm starting to worry about the quality of your investigators.'

Karene had heard this hard tone before. When he used to talk about Caroline and her new partner Robin. 'It's the biggest clue we have. He was killed a few days before the bomb attack. That has to be related given—' She stopped because she didn't want to say this.

Harry's eyes watched her. 'Given what they did to him?'

'I don't think you need to hear that now. You're recovering and you've had a shock.'

'It is not your job to protect me.'

Yes. Yes it is. 'Marcus can explain it. I don't really know the details.'

'You can tell me the gist, though. He was tortured how?'

Karene studied the floor. The tiles had a thin coating of dust from the construction work. 'They removed his toenails and cut off two fingers.'

'Jesus.'

'They wanted him to tell them something.'

'That's usually how torture works, yeah.'

She used to love Harry's sarcasm but his words had no humour, only judgement.

'How did he die?'

She met his gaze. 'They cut his throat.'

Harry stood and paced the floor with his hands on his hips. The bandage on his head looked stark white against his dark hair. He was dressed in grey cotton trousers and a grey T-shirt and he had shaved. She'd heard that a major philosophy for the rehabilitation of service personnel was to maintain their routine for smart dress. Let your stand-ards drop and it weakens the mind.

'Harry?' she said.

He continued pacing.

She wanted to say, '*I'm here for you, lean on me, I love you*', but she remembered Augusta's advice: don't tell him you care, just care. 'We'd assumed given the attack on the military base that this was all to do with your job, maybe something you were working on or had worked on in the past. But the attack on Julian suggests it may be more personal.'

'As in?'

Karene shrugged. 'Augusta says most crimes are motiv-ated by either need or emotion, and that emotions are usually stronger in our private lives. That's why most mur-der victims know their killer. Apparently over 60 per cent are married to them.' She let that sink in for a moment. 'What can you tell me about Julian?'

Harry stopped pacing and stared out across the garden. 'He's a good man . . . *was* a good man. Like me, he came from nothing. His mother is my dad's sister. He's fourteen years older than me. He learned a trade and built a busi-ness while I progressed in the Navy. He retired early to France and since then we've seen each other once a year at most. Caroline and I would sometimes visit with the kids in the summer. Occasionally he came home to see his stepdaughter, Clara, but they'd drifted apart recently.'

'When did he move to France?'

'Er . . . four years or so ago. He sold his business and moved out there for a change of pace.'

'So . . . would that be eight years ago?'

Harry bowed his head. 'I suppose it would.'

Karene went to stand alongside him and briefly laid the palm of her hand on his upper arm. 'I'll do whatever I can to help and Augusta is the most tenacious and insightful person I know. We'll find out what's going on. I promise.'

'Why would anyone hurt Julian like that? What the hell have I done?'

36

Bloom and Karene arrived at Stanford Hall just after nine a.m. having spent the night in a local hotel. Jameson had left them to dine without him the night before. After yesterday's altercation, that was fine with Bloom. She was both furious and disgusted by his accusation.

He had managed to negotiate a meeting with the Head of Neurosurgery for Bloom and Karene that morning. And Bloom in turn had spoken to Detective Superintendent Drummond and persuaded him to allow Jameson to visit Loughborough police station and view the physical evidence gathered from the shooting. They would compare notes later.

Greg Taylor escorted them through to a room filled with computer screens and introduced them to Mr Avery, the Head of Neurosurgery and an Idris Elba lookalike.

'You wanted to discuss Captain Peterson's MRI.' He had a soft, Midlands accent. He tapped the computer keyboard and the screens on the wall filled with black and white images of cross-sections of Harry's brain. 'How can I help?'

'I'll leave you to it,' said Taylor. 'Give me a shout when you want me to escort them back, Mike.'

Avery nodded to Taylor.

'Dr Bloom and I are psychologists,' said Karene. 'So we have some insight into memory loss, but we have a theory we'd like to check out that requires an MRI.'

'Fire away.'

'Are you aware that Captain Peterson may have sustained his injuries following the explosion? In the seventy-two-hour period afterwards?' asked Bloom.

This was clearly news to Avery.

'I thought that might be the case,' said Bloom.

'What did the Navy say when he arrived?' asked Karene.

'That as we specialize in rehabilitation he was here to recover from his injuries. And apart from the memory loss he's doing remarkably well.'

'Did you notice anything unusual about the MRI?' Bloom was studying the screens. It had been a while since she'd seen a brain scan.

'He has a fracture. There was a little swelling but no bleeding. He's healing well. What is it you're looking for?'

'Is it possible to cause the type of memory loss Captain Peterson has sustained surgically?' she asked.

Avery frowned. 'You'd really have to know what you're doing.'

'How would you do it? Damage the CA1 area of the hippocampus?'

The surgeon smiled. 'Someone's been doing a little research.'

'Just testing a hypothesis,' she said. 'His memory loss feels too convenient.'

'You could certainly trigger amnesia with lesions to the hippocampus but I'm not sure how precise you could be about the type of memory lost.' He walked to the screen on the far left and pointed at one of the images. 'These are the temporal lobes. They sit just behind your ears and are mirrored on either side of the brain. Within those sits the hippocampus. It's fairly central so getting to it would require something pretty invasive.'

'But it can be done?' said Bloom. 'Can you cause a lesion on the brain intentionally? Does that technology exist?'

'It's certainly possible to target specific areas. We do it to biopsy tumours that are deep within the brain. We use navigation computers to guide a needle either to obtain a sample or to deliberately cauterize an area with electricity that heats the needle and destroys the tissue at the tip. But we always screw a frame to the skull to keep it completely still and it leaves four small scars on the head, two on the forehead.' He placed his index fingers on his own head just above his temples. 'Here and here.'

Bloom felt a jolt of adrenaline. 'Exactly where Harry has bruised and damaged skin.'

Karene was biting her lip as she studied the images.

'Don't you think that's a coincidence?' asked Bloom.

The surgeon frowned then moved back to his computer. 'You'd have to drill a hole in the skull for the needle to pass through. It's usually the size of a five-pence piece but it could be smaller, maybe five millimetres in diameter? It could be masked by his head injury.' He pressed a few buttons and the scans changed. He walked over to examine them.

'But the hole would be visible on the MRI?' said Bloom.

'These are the CT scans sent from Exeter Hospital. It

would be easier to spot it on these.' He returned to his computer, flicked through numerous pictures and selected four to display. 'This is the area of the head trauma. We have cracks to the skull here and here, nothing too drastic but . . .' He beckoned for Bloom and Karene to join him. 'Look at this,' he said, pointing to a gap in the thick white line. 'That could be a hole. It's thicker than the other fractures and completely dissects the skull bone. Do you see?'

'So, he did have surgery?' said Bloom.

'Possibly,' said Avery.

'Why has no one spotted this before?' said Karene.

Avery folded his arms and concentrated on the screen. 'If this is a hole, it was cleverly masked by his injuries. It's not unusual for victims of an explosion to have cracks and holes in their skull. You wouldn't find it unless you were looking for it.' He went back to the computer and selected the MRI scans again. 'If he did have surgery to affect his memory, I would expect bilateral lesions on his hippocampus.' His voice was urgent, excited almost.

'Damage done to both the right and left sides?' asked Bloom.

'Indeed.' He enhanced the scan until the section he was looking at filled the middle screen on the wall, then he put his glasses on and walked over to study it. 'Well, well,' he said.

'You can see lesions?' said Bloom.

'But why are they there? This is a perfectly healthy brain.'

'To make him forget.'

The surgeon looked her way. 'The brain is not a filing

cabinet. You can't pick out a section of tissue labelled memories of this or memories of that.'

'Which is why he's lost four whole years,' said Bloom.

Avery considered her for a beat and then said, 'I suppose it's possible . . . No.' He shook his head.

'What are you thinking?'

'We don't use them, but have you heard of functional MRI scanners? They show what areas of the brain are activated by certain thoughts or activities. I suppose it could be used during surgery.'

'If Harry was awake and talking about his memories, then they'd be able to see which parts of the brain were involved,' said Bloom.

The surgeon nodded and removed his glasses. 'Then you could kill that tissue.'

'Like pressing delete.'

'Delete?' mumbled Karene. 'What does that mean?' Bloom hadn't noticed that Karene had been uncharacteristically quiet. She was standing by the door looking pale and exhausted.

Avery said, 'It means they're gone for good.'

37

Karene insisted they find a nearby cafe before driving back to London. Bloom knew she was stalling, hoping for another chance to see Harry. They had asked but were told that Captain Tessa Morrisey was with him, the woman they had met with Rear Admiral Grey in Northwood. Jameson arrived at the cafe shortly after them, having already visited the police station.

'What do you think of Harry, then?' he asked while Karene was at the counter. 'Do you think he's done something sticky?'

'I don't know. But I think it's very sad for them.'

'She's so loved up she'd believe anything he told her. It's pretty easy to be fooled by someone you care about. Particularly when they don't want you to see the truth.'

Bloom knew this was a reference to Seraphine and how easily the woman had fooled him. And yesterday he had the nerve to suggest Bloom was equally as manipulative. She still hadn't forgiven him, wouldn't forgive him. 'Thinking of someone in particular?'

Jameson's lip curled into a snarl. 'So what do you think of Harry? Answer my question.'

Bloom watched Karene chatting to the barista as she waited for their coffees. 'I haven't seen any reason to disbelieve her description of him. Clearly his job has some confidential elements. But fortunately you're well-versed in getting us around that.'

'If I can get in to see him again.'

'Why wouldn't you?'

'If Grey has sent his gopher to see Harry, I expect they're looking to move him.'

'Again? I thought this place provided the best neurological care?'

'But that's not the priority any more, is it? Now it's about security and that means a safe house.'

'You think? She's going to be gutted.' Bloom watched her friend transfer their drinks to a tray.

'They're right to, though. He's at risk here. There'll be more of them.'

'Did you get anything from the evidence?'

'Both porters were wearing bulletproof body armour under their uniforms. Which is why they went for head shots. But their kit was different.'

'How do you mean?'

'Freddie had a well-worn vest, fairly standard quality. Whereas the other guy had brand-new, top-of-the-range gear and a pretty impressive handgun.'

'Is that unusual to have different kit? What does it mean?'

Jameson pulled a face. 'Probably just guns for hire, which would also explain the argument and lack of co-ordination. But well done for dodging my question,' Jameson said to Bloom as Karene sat down. She began handing out the drinks.

'What question is she dodging?' Karene said.

'What she thinks of your lover boy.'

Karene blinked a couple of times and then said to Bloom, 'Avery wouldn't have spotted the surgery without your help, would he?'

'We see what we expect to see. You need to know to look for it.'

'And you did. Thank you, Augusta.'

'It doesn't tell us anything unfortunately. We still don't know who did this or why.'

'Which is why we need to keep interrogating the man,' said Jameson. 'And why I *still* want to know what you think of him.'

'Don't mind me.' Karene hugged her drink to her body, shrinking away defensively.

'Fine,' Bloom said. 'He comes across as an articulate and intelligent individual who clearly wants to know what's happened to him.'

'Is that it? I think you're losing your touch.' Jameson took a gulp of his vanilla latte.

Bloom sighed and looked at Karene. 'You said he was worried that he'd contributed to Julian's murder, that he regularly visits his sister in the care home and that he played an active role in helping his children to cope with the divorce which tells me he has warmth and empathy. Caroline too said that he was a good father. But she also said he was reserved and distant, emotionless and secretive. But he's always been open and loving and fun with you. So Caroline's perspective might reflect their marriage rather than his character.' Karene took a breath and held it in. Bloom continued. 'And his boss describes him as a professional, well-admired naval officer, one who is willing to stand up for what's right.'

Jameson glanced at Karene mischievously. 'But what do *you* think of him?'

'I think he's a typical, decent human being.'

'I thought you said "typical" wasn't a thing?' Jameson was enjoying this.

'You know what I mean,' Bloom said. 'And just because there aren't alarm bells going off doesn't mean he's incapable of doing something wrong or making a mistake. We need to keep exploring his work. There's something we're missing, something we're not allowed to know.'

'But? What else? You're thinking something,' said Karene.

'I'm surprised he has no other symptoms. He's lucid and articulate and if you had no idea he'd lost the last few years of his memory I don't think you'd guess it.'

'Oh, man, you think he's faking.' Jameson's childish grin irritated her.

'I didn't say that.'

Karene sat silently now.

'I'm simply observing that if someone did this, as they appear to have done, it is a very, very accomplished piece of surgery. And that doesn't fit with your useless guns for hire theory, does it?'

Jameson's eyes widened a touch and then he smiled and pointed her way. 'And that's why we pay her the big bucks.'

Ten minutes later they were in the car heading south. Karene had not protested. She knew as well as them that their time with Harry was done for this visit at least.

'What the hell?' said Karene after the buzz of her phone. She held out the open email application for Bloom to see.

From: ANONYMOUS   11:00
Subject: In the land of the blind, the one-eyed man is king

From: ANONYMOUS   11:01
Subject: Tick tock tick tock

Bloom read the messages aloud to Jameson then gave the phone back to Karene.

'And this is a helpful person, is it?' Karene said.

'What does that even mean?' said Jameson.

Bloom thought about it. She wasn't sure. It was cryptic and, no doubt, intentionally so. Was the reference to blindness related to Harry's memory loss or to their inability to uncover what was actually going on? And who was the one-eyed man: them or whoever was behind the emails?

38

Augusta sat at her kitchen island and scrolled through her case notes. She started with Harry's history. If his memory had been wiped on purpose, what had he done in the past four years that could be relevant?

His early career was based out of Yeovilton Air Station forty miles away from his wife and children in Salisbury. In 2013 he was the Commanding Officer of 814 Naval Air Squadron based at Royal Naval Air Station Culdrose in Cornwall, 150 miles further away from his family home. That would put a strain on any marriage. They had separated in late 2015, not long after Harry's promotion to captain. Harry then moved to work at Northwood on the outskirts of London. He had been working for Rear Admiral Grey since summer 2016, which was around the time that Caroline took up her position as a consultant anaesthetist at Luton and Dunstable Hospital and moved with their children to St Albans. According to Karene, Harry had purchased a house nearby so that he could see the children as often as possible. St Albans was a mere thirteen miles from Northwood. Bloom wondered if Harry regretted the strain his job had put on his marriage and his relationship with his children. Perhaps that was why he'd made sure to be as close as possible over the past year.

He had been dating Karene for nearly eighteen months. The honeymoon period had passed so Karene should have a fairly accurate idea of Harry's character, especially considering her profession. Jameson was right that love can make you susceptible to lies, but those rose-tinted glasses tended to clear, certainly within a year or so.

Harry's life had changed significantly over the past four years. He was now a divorced man living apart from his children and in a new relationship with Karene. He had left his life as a pilot and moved into a more strategic role, desk-based and no doubt dominated by meetings and negotiations as opposed to the thrill of active operations. Had he grown bored or frustrated and looked for excitement in the wrong place, with the wrong people?

When was he last deployed? Operation Weald. The international search and rescue mission Jameson had told her about. She reviewed her notes on the operation. It had been an eighty-day mission from mid-April 2015 until early July, off the coast of Italy, searching for migrants crossing from Libya. Three Merlin helicopters had helped to recover over 2,900 migrants from the sea. She brought up the picture of the postcard on Julian Peterson's noticeboard.

To help or to hinder. Your choice.

Karene's mystery emailer had sent a similar question about Harry: does he help or hinder? Bloom knew there was something here. It was a clue. But what did it mean?

Over the course of her career, Bloom had kept the numbers of every police officer, barrister, prosecutor and client she had ever worked with. She scrolled through them now, looking for the one person she knew could help them. When she found the number she was looking for, she typed out a short message but she didn't send it. She placed her phone on the table and closed her eyes.

In the land of the blind, the one-eyed man is king.

She picked up her phone, re-read her message and pressed send.

39

Antony Bello's name certainly fitted. Whether he was dictating orders to a lowly soldier or speaking in confidence to a trusted associate like Abdul, there was always volume. Today was different, though. Because Bello was off-the-charts angry. As Abdul knocked and opened the office door, a glass hit the opposite wall and smashed.

'Bad news, I take it?' said Abdul, closing the door behind him.

The whites of Bello's wide eyes were in stark contrast to his dark skin and his blue cotton shirt was soaked with sweat. 'Why do they fail me? Do they want to spend eternity burning?'

Abdul did not believe in God. Not that he'd ever admit that to the second in command of God's Liberation Army. Bello was devout to the point of radicalized. He was also the nephew of GLA's founder and tipped for the top job when his uncle's battle with pancreatic cancer met its inevitable end. So not a man to disagree with.

Abdul stood in the corner of the room, his hands clasped behind his back, waiting as Bello raged against those who had failed him. It was not that he was scared of Bello. Abdul had never been scared of anyone his whole life and he had met some truly despicable men. No, he stood there because he enjoyed watching Bello's rage. He loved seeing the knee-jerk decisions and impulsive actions of such men, most of which weren't thought through well enough to have the desired impact. There were exceptions to this, of course. Men who'd made it right to the top. But they were rare indeed.

'I should have sent you, Abdul. You would never have been so weak and stupid.' Bello was calming now. He stood behind his desk with his hands flat on its surface. His face glistened with sweat but his eyes were no longer so wide. Abdul dipped his head once in acknowledgement of the compliment. 'Get my commanders together. We will strategize.'

Abdul left to do as he was asked. He didn't give an opinion. If pressed, he would admit that Bello's desire to dominate the women in his life was the source of his weakness. At current count the man had no fewer than eight wives and yet he continued to obsess about the one who had outwitted him. It would be his downfall.

Abdul summoned Bello's four commanders, instructing them to join their leader immediately. He then made his way to the end of the garden where he couldn't be overheard and made a short call. Abdul may well have behaved as if Bello was his boss, but this was far from the truth. His allegiance lay firmly elsewhere; with the person who had placed him in this job for a reason and who expected regular updates on Bello's activities. On his way back into the building to join Bello, Abdul reflected on the irony. Men like Bello spent so much time with their faces to the sky searching for answers that they missed what was happening right under their noses.

40

Bloom finished her morning run in record time. Her mind had been racing with all the questions still unanswered. She took a few moments to catch her breath before fetching a pint of water from the kitchen and taking it outside to drink as she stretched her muscles.

She hadn't received a reply to her text last night. She checked her phone again, but still nothing. Perhaps they'd changed their number. She resisted the urge to call; it was better to wait. Instead she dialled the number for Caroline Peterson. She expected to get the consultant's voicemail but Caroline picked up on the second ring.

She began with the normal pleasantries but Caroline encouraged her to get to the point.

'As far as you're aware,' said Bloom, 'did Julian Peterson have any involvement in the migrant crisis?'

'I wouldn't have thought so.' Caroline's tone was clipped, as though Bloom was intentionally wasting her time.

'Did he have any strong views about the migrant situation, either for or against?'

'As an ex-pat, I'm not sure he'd be in any position to object to migrants.'

'Was he in support of countries taking them in, then?'

'I wouldn't know.'

'I saw a postcard on the noticeboard in his kitchen

with a picture of migrants packed into a fishing boat. Any idea why he would have this?'

'You went to his house? You really are poking your little nose into our business, aren't you?'

'We're only trying to help Harry, as we've been asked to do.'

'By his bit of fluff.'

'Might Harry have sent it?' Bloom ignored the dig.

'Why would Harry have sent it?'

'Because of his search and rescue work in 2015.'

Caroline was quiet for a moment. 'I don't know.'

'Do you recall Harry talking about that operation?'

'A little. He said there was a lot of resistance to taking in the migrants.'

'Did the experience affect Harry in any way?'

'Not that I recall.'

'You separated later that same year.'

'Did we?'

It was clear she was getting no insight from Caroline. 'OK, thank you,' said Bloom. 'One last thing. There was a picture of a blonde woman in her fifties on Julian's noticeboard. Do you know who this could be?'

'That'll be Isobel. She's married but she and Julian have had a thing for years now. It's all very French.'

Bloom thanked Caroline for her time and hung up. Julian Peterson was having an affair with another man's wife. It was unlikely that a cuckolded husband would resort to such levels of torture, but she knew not to ignore an alternative hypothesis. In her experience, people never failed to surprise you.

41

Jameson ate a banana as Bloom talked him through her suspicions. She wanted him to investigate Operation Weald a bit further. 'It's well within the timescale of Harry's memory loss and I can't help thinking that migrants postcard is a clue.'

'Where's the controversy?' Jameson discarded the banana skin into the waste basket. 'It was a humanitarian mission and a successful one at that.'

'To help or to hinder. Perhaps Harry hindered someone's activity: one of the people traffickers, for instance. I expect they're not all opportunistic individuals; some will be organized businesses. The kind of people who don't appreciate you hindering their lucrative operation.'

'Of course. But why wait two years to shut Harry up?'

Bloom pondered this as she opened Julian Peterson's Facebook page on her screen and began searching for a woman called Isobel. There were no female friends by that name. But that made sense if she and Julian were having an affair. She inserted a link to Julian's Facebook page into an email and sent it to Lucas George. Maybe he could find some online contact between them. 'Julian Peterson was having an affair with a married woman,' she said when Jameson looked over to see what she was doing.

'The plot thickens,' said Jameson.

'Doesn't it always?' She turned back to face him. 'Can we speak to someone who worked with Harry on Operation Weald?'

'I'll see who I can find, but I think it's unlikely.'

'You're right,' she said and Jameson raised an eyebrow. 'That it doesn't make sense. If Harry stood in someone's way, or witnessed something they'd done, waiting two years to shut him up would be risky, as would wiping his memory but keeping him alive. They couldn't be absolutely sure that he wouldn't remember something.'

'Discrediting him might be enough.'

'Placing doubt on his recollections?'

Jameson nodded.

'But, still, why wait two years? Harry has been living his life in full view of the world. He would have been easy to find.'

'So why now?'

'And why keep him alive originally and then try to kill him?' Bloom noted the questions on her iPad. 'And it isn't just hindering, is it? To help or to hinder. Maybe he helped someone?'

Jameson tapped his pen against the side of his head and pursed his lips.

'What if he helped a trafficker but then stopped for some reason?' she said.

'They'd just move on and find someone else to use, or kill him and find someone else to use. They wouldn't perform brain surgery.'

'Have you any ideas then?'

He continued to tap for a few moments then stopped.

'If they need him alive, they still need him to do something. And if they've wiped his memory it's because they want him to forget something. Something he's seen or done.'

'But they've also tried to kill him.' Bloom's brain made the connections at hyper-speed. 'That's why they came for him again. Not to kill him. *Vivant. Vivant.* They performed the surgery as quickly as they could, then returned him to the NHS, hoping that in all the confusion no one would notice his absence. They needed him to recover.'

'OK . . .'

'And if Karene hadn't seen him beforehand, just after the bomb detonated, then we wouldn't know that something additional had happened. We'd still be assuming an administrative error, that he was just the unfortunate victim of a terrorist attack. And then when he's well again—'

'They can use him again. And that's why Freddie was inserted as a porter at Stanford Hall.' Jameson shook his head, his expression serious. 'These people are a step ahead all the time.'

42

Nine Months Earlier

Karene woke to the sound of shouting. Her left arm was pinned to the bed. Harry had wrapped his fingers around her forearm and was squeezing tighter and tighter.

'Harry!'

She tried to push his hand away and prise his fingers apart but his grip was vice-like and immovable. 'Harry!' She grabbed his shoulder with her free hand and shook him hard. He continued to call out, words she couldn't understand, as his body rocked from side to side. She pinched the skin on his bare upper arm as hard as she could, digging her nails in, and cried out in pain as he increased the pressure on her arm.

She looked around in panic. Her phone was across the room charging and Harry's was nowhere to be seen. The walls to his flat were thick and the windows closed. She could shout as loud as she liked, but no one was likely to hear; no one was coming to help.

Pain shot up her arm and she cried out again. He would sleep through crushing her and there was nothing she could do. And then she saw the glass of water half drunk on his bedside table. She rolled across his writhing body, grabbed it and threw it in his face.

Their meeting the following Monday morning at Northwood Headquarters didn't take place this time in the middle of the reception area. Lieutenant Commander Adams had arranged for them to speak in one of the side meeting rooms. Bloom and Jameson still weren't allowed past the glass security pods. The area beyond was restricted to those with the necessary clearance.

Adams had been the Medical Advisor on HMS *Bulwark* during Operation Weald and had been in regular contact with Harry Peterson over the course of their mission. He was a tall, skinny man with a prominent red birthmark on his left cheek. 'I was responsible for all the medical staff and supplies on the ship used to assist the migrants we pulled from the sea.'

'Did you know Harry Peterson well?' said Bloom.

'Well enough. He was the commanding officer for the naval air squadron and a good few ranks above me, but Peterson's the sort who ignores all that pomp and deals with you as a human. I've a lot of time for the Captain. How's he doing?'

'He's recuperating, but struggling to remember a few years before the explosion,' said Bloom.

'So I heard. He's lost ten, someone said. Imagine that, thinking you're ten years younger than you are.

That'd be a bit of a shock when you look in the mirror.'

'He hasn't lost that much time, just the last four or so.' Bloom was always amazed by how a story changed as it was retold.

'Captain Morrisey said you needed my help with something specific?'

Jameson had spoken to Tessa Morrisey the day before and explained their working theory: that Harry's kidnap and subsequent memory loss might be related in some way to Operation Weald. She had agreed to arrange access to Lieutenant Commander Adams. She did, however, ask for discretion about Harry's condition and the attacks against him. 'We need some background on the operation. That's all. And Tessa said you'd be the best person to speak to.'

'Ask away.'

Bloom asked for some general information on how the operation had been run and the condition of the migrants picked out of the sea. And Adams explained how the Air Fleet supported the operation by searching the ocean for boats and by airlifting those who needed to be extracted due to their medical condition or because they were in particular danger.

'Where were the migrants coming from in the main?' said Bloom.

'Sub-Saharan Africa. Places like Nigeria, Gambia, South Sudan. We picked up thousands of them but the Italian government struggled to take them in at first. It took a lot of negotiating but eventually we were allowed to drop them in Sicily.'

'Sicily?' Jameson raised his eyebrows. 'Mafia territory.'

'And did Harry Peterson do anything in that time that stood out to you?' said Bloom.

'Like what?'

'Did he go out of his way to save someone? Or did you think he did something wrong or misjudged a situation at all?'

Adams pressed his lips into a thin white line. Bloom expected a challenge about what they were really investigating and why. But after a pause, Adams said, 'I recall one discussion over dinner. It was not long after we'd started and everyone felt a touch overwhelmed by the scale of it, the number of people trying to cross. One of the officers, a Commander like Peterson, said to Harry that they should be blowing up the launch sites along the Libyan coast to stop the blighters from getting into the sea. I remember Peterson's response to that. He wasn't happy. He said something like, "Really? That's who we are? That's who you think we should be?" I liked that. I liked that he cared not only about those desperate people but about the Royal Navy and what it should stand for.'

'So he's not one to step out of line?' said Jameson.

'Absolutely not. He became a bit of a poster boy after the operation. The Navy used him for PR which is not surprising; he's a good-looking chap and a bit of a charmer. I'll find you the articles.' Adams searched through the computer and then printed a couple of pages for them. One was the editorial in *The Times* that Karene had shown them and Bloom pointed out Harry's quote about no man, woman or child being expendable.

'Did anything upset him at all during that time?' said Jameson.

'He's not the sort to get upset. He's the guy you want around when everyone else is flapping. He stays calm and keeps his sense of humour. Everyone will have been upset by what we saw to some degree, because it's an awful situation and people were dying. But if you're asking whether Harry was traumatized? I wouldn't expect so. It was nothing compared to what you see in war.'

'Never even asked why we were asking. You've gotta love the military,' said Jameson as they waited for Patrick Grey, who apparently wanted to speak to them before they left.

'Not everyone is as inquisitive as us,' said Bloom.

'Nah, it's not that. A senior officer told him to answer our questions and so he did. Command and control at its best.'

Rear Admiral Grey greeted them in the reception bang on time at the agreed eleven hundred hours.

'I'd have expected you to move Harry to a safe house,' said Jameson.

'It's not wise to keep him at Stanford Hall, I agree. But this isn't MI6, Mr Jameson. We don't have safe houses scattered around the country at the ready.'

'MI6 is international. It's MI5 who hold the domestic safe houses. But I can call in a favour if you need the help?'

Bloom jumped in before the ego battle really got going. 'We wanted to keep you informed of some progress we've made.'

'Tessa has briefed me on what you found in the MRI scan. You believe this backs up your suspicions around foul play?'

'The second attack sort of backs us up too.'

'Well, we have no definitive evidence that those men were there for Captain Peterson. I doubt he'd have walked out of there unscathed if they had been.'

'You think the bomb and the porter attack are a coincidence?' said Bloom.

'I'm not ruling it out.'

'Which is the real reason you haven't moved Peterson. Why spend the budget when there's no provable business case?' said Jameson.

'The problem is we need Captain Peterson to receive the care he needs as well as ensuring his continued safety. These things take time, Mr Jameson.'

'I know somewhere he can stay. There's a house in Southampton. It's entirely secure.'

'A government safe house?' said Grey.

'No.' Jameson glanced at Bloom. 'It's privately owned, bought for cash. The owner listed is a shell company, and the bills are paid through that. It's nearly invisible.'

'Privately owned by whom?' said Bloom.

Jameson smiled. 'The point is that no one knows. That's what makes it safe.' He focused on Grey again. 'I'm willing to stay there. Keep an eye on him.'

Bloom stared at Jameson with wide eyes.

He shook his head at her. 'Think about it,' he said to Grey. 'It's in no way linked to the Navy and I'm perfectly capable of ensuring Peterson's safety. And Dr Bloom is able to assist with his memory problems and the man's ex-wife is a consultant anaesthetist. We couldn't put a better team around him if we tried. Plus, it's free.'

Ten minutes later Bloom climbed in Jameson's car, shut the car door and faced him. 'What the hell are you thinking, Marcus?'

'It's the best solution. They get to hide Harry. We get to interrogate him.'

'Do you have a death wish? These people coming for him have no qualms about you becoming collateral damage. Look at the people killed and maimed by the bomb.'

'Yes, but they're also so damn incompetent they shoot each other in the head.' He smiled as he started the engine.

'This is not a joke.'

'I'm not laughing. Look. I have an old friend I can call on for help. Someone who'll watch the house for me. And I've no doubt Grey will make sure his lot are watching us too.'

'What is wrong with you? You can't do this.'

'Grey seemed cool with it.'

'Marcus, you could come to serious harm. I can't let that happen.'

'Gosh, you're almost showing some genuine affection there, Augusta. Steady on now!'

'Stop the car. Marcus, pull in there.' She pointed at a lay-by.

Jameson did as she asked, switched off the ignition and swivelled in his seat to face her. His expression was one of amusement.

'Let's get this straight, then,' she said. 'I am not a psychopath. I do not have psychopathic tendencies. I simply understand a good deal about their kind.'

'Or you believe your own propaganda,' said Jameson.

'And you think taking that woman's word is a good call, do you? You think she has a balanced idea of what makes people tick? Grow up, Marcus. I'm a good person, a caring person and you know that. We have a case to solve and a business to run so you either need to let this go or . . . go.'

He locked his jaw and narrowed his eyes. Then he restarted the car and pulled back out into the traffic. 'Fine,' he said. 'I will.'

Bloom didn't dare ask which option he'd chosen.

44

At midday on Tuesday, a blacked-out Range Rover pulled up outside Jameson's safe house in Southampton. Rear Admiral Grey had agreed that Harry could stay for a couple of days while they sourced something more suitable. Jameson thought Grey should have been more grateful: Harry Peterson was vulnerable in Stanford Hall. It made sense to move him as quickly as possible.

Jameson opened the back door of the car to find the seats on the opposite side had been removed and a bed secured to the floor. Harry Peterson was not on it. He had instead chosen to sit in a reclined position in the remaining cream leather seat. He sat up, pulling the hood of his sweatshirt over his head to cover the bandage and nodded hello to Jameson before quickly following him into the house.

Once the two naval officers who had accompanied Harry had checked the house and asked a range of questions about security – Was there an alarm? Was the front door the only access? Were the windows lockable and locked? – they left. They would be staying close by, they said, and checking in regularly.

Jameson showed Harry to the larger of the two bedrooms. 'The bathroom's just down the hall. I'll put the kettle on.' Jameson left him to get settled and when he returned a few minutes later with a mug of tea, Peterson was asleep on the bed. He put the tea down, stood for a moment to check Harry's breathing sounded good, then quietly closed the door and left the man to rest.

45

Bloom and Karene arrived at the safe house around four p.m. They had caught the train to Portsmouth and then taken a taxi to the Fareham Community Hospital, walking the last quarter of a mile to the address Jameson had given them as instructed. The house itself was on a residential street, but it didn't look like a residence. It was a small, single-storey white box of a building with business-style venetian blinds covering the floor to ceiling windows and a large black front door. It sat in a patch of parched, overgrown grass behind a six-foot metal gate. It looked like an industrial unit, the office of some local business that had closed down long ago. Bloom was impressed.

'It looks deserted,' she said to Jameson as he walked to the gate to let them in.

'That's the idea.'

Inside, the place was furnished with a modern white kitchen and open-plan living area. The lighting had been cleverly designed so that it felt airy despite the closed blinds.

'No one followed you then?' Jameson said. He was smiling as though it was a joke, but Bloom knew he was concerned.

'We did everything you said. Paid cash. Travelled

separately to Waterloo. Kept our eye on anyone who was making the same journey as us.'

'Where's Harry?' asked Karene.

'Sleeping. The bedrooms are in the back.'

Karene walked on through.

'How is he?' asked Bloom. 'He shouldn't really be moving around this much with a head injury.'

'I think the journey wiped him out. He's been asleep since he arrived. I've checked on him. He's breathing fine.'

Caroline Peterson arrived at the house at six thirty p.m. in a taxi that dropped her at the end of the street. Harry was still asleep. His body was healing and he'd had a traumatic few days; it was hardly surprising.

'This is a questionable situation, don't you think,' she said on arrival. 'Harry should be in hospital, not shacked up in some godforsaken bachelor pad. What is this place anyway?'

'Invisible. And you need to keep it that way.' Jameson offered Caroline a seat on the couch but she remained standing. 'It's only for a few days.'

'Is this your doing?' she said to Karene. 'Because I think it's incredibly selfish.'

Bloom stepped in before Karene had a chance to bite. 'As I said on the phone, there was an incident at the rehabilitation centre and he wasn't safe there any more.'

'A medical incident?'

'A firearms incident,' said Jameson.

Caroline looked at each of them in turn. 'Are you going to tell me what's going on here?'

'We're making sure Harry is as safe as possible,' said Bloom, 'and that involves keeping a medical eye on his recovery. We want to involve as few people as possible at this stage for security reasons which is why I asked you here to check on him.'

'I'm not a neurosurgeon.'

'No, but as a consultant anaesthetist you know more than us.'

'You said this was for just a few days. Then where are you taking him?' she said to Jameson.

'That's up to the Navy.'

'Another hospital?'

'Possibly.'

Caroline's expression darkened. She was not happy about this and Bloom could understand her reticence. It was nowhere near to ideal.

'He's been sleeping since midday so we left him to rest, but perhaps you could wake him and check that everything is OK,' Bloom said.

'And you should know that he's aware of your separation and divorce,' said Karene.

'Well, if he's remembering things then that's a good sign.'

Karene's eyes diverted towards the floor.

Caroline stepped towards Bloom and Karene. 'You told him?'

'I'm afraid we needed him to know who Karene was so that he would trust us to help him,' said Bloom.

'So you destroyed the trust he had in me without a second thought.' Caroline squared her shoulders and hardened her tone. Bloom guessed that this was the version of Ms Peterson her staff saw.

'I think you did that yourself when you jumped into bed with Robin.' Karene's tone sounded light-hearted but the words were intended to sting and, from the look of fury in Caroline Peterson's eyes, they did.

46

Abdul was summoned to Antony Bello's private quarters just after midnight. He passed through the apartment as discreetly as possible, ignoring the two semi-clad women he could see asleep on the bed through the open bedroom door, and found Bello drinking whisky on his balcony.

'How can I be of service, Sir?' he said as he stepped into the warm night air. It was too hot to be outdoors for any length of time during the day, but the evenings were the perfect temperature.

Bello waved his hand towards one of the free chairs and said, 'How can he disappear without trace?'

Abdul knew that Bello was referring to the British naval officer. Word had passed swiftly through the group that their surveillance had drawn a blank. 'They know he's the target. It is only wise to assume his people would protect him.'

'Are you calling me unwise?'

'I am simply saying that if we think like them, we can defeat them. It is nothing more than a game of chess.'

'He has children. We will use the children.'

'We could, although I believe they will be protected now too.'

'Their protection is no match for me.'

'I think they have proven otherwise.' It always amused Abdul when Bello spoke as if he was the one out there doing the grunt work and risking his life. The truth was this man rarely left his gilded cage.

Bello gripped his glass and took a long swig of alcohol. He didn't like hearing home truths from Abdul, but he was not a stupid man.

'So, if not the children, then how? How do I get to this man?'

'A better question is, how do we get this man to come to you?'

'Yes! Yes. Make him come to me.' Bello stood. The meeting was over. 'Make him come to me,' he said, one more time. And this time it was an order.

47

Harry emerged from the bedroom a few minutes after Caroline had left. His hair was dishevelled but there was now a large white bandage taped rather than stapled to the side of his head. His T-shirt was creased and he was barefoot.

'Hey honey,' Karene said, without thinking.

Harry gave her the sort of smile you'd give to an over-familiar stranger. He sat on the end of the sofa nearest to them and leaned back. They had all heard the conversation in the bedroom; the questions, the accusations and the heated rebukes. It probably wasn't the best way to recuperate from brain surgery.

'I'll get you some water,' Karene said. She needed to do something.

'Can I get a coffee?' he asked.

Karene paused for a moment. Was caffeine advisable? She pushed the worry aside. Harry was having another very bad day in this terrible week; he could have what he wanted. She set about refreshing the cafetière and rinsing the cups as Bloom pulled her seat forward to face Harry.

'Caroline says you're doing as well as can be expected. But how are you feeling?' Bloom asked.

Harry closed his eyes. 'Furious but fine.'

'Furious about Caroline?'

Karene watched from the sink. He had shielded her well from his marital breakdown when they first got together. She had never seen him broken-hearted or angry about it. Did she want to see that?

Harry lifted his head. 'That. And this. Who the hell would do this to me? What have I done to deserve it?'

'Are you feeling up to a few questions?'

'I guess so. Fire away.'

'Marcus and I have been looking into your activities over the past four years with the help of Karene and your boss.' When Harry looked confused, she said, 'Rear Admiral Grey. You've worked in his team at Northwood for the past year. What's the last job you recall doing?'

'I'm Commanding Officer of 814 Air Squadron at Culdrose. I mean, I was. That's what I remember.'

'Well, you've made a few career moves since then, including a promotion to captain in the past few years.'

'Yes. Tessa Morrisey told me.'

'Rear Admiral Grey does not believe your current work at Northwood is controversial enough to warrant an attack on you so we've been looking further back. Do you have any recollection of a search and rescue operation off the Italian coast?'

Harry shook his head.

'You were the Commanding Officer for the Air Fleet in support of HMS *Bulwark* which had been deployed to save thousands of migrants crossing from Libya to Europe. Does that ring a bell?'

Harry shook his head again.

'Operation Weald,' said Jameson.

'OK,' said Bloom when it was clear that Harry had no idea what they were talking about. 'We are wondering if this is significant because this postcard was pinned to your cousin Julian's noticeboard.' She handed Harry her iPad.

He studied the image for a moment. '"To help or to hinder. Your choice",' he read. 'Did I send this?'

'We have no idea. It was blank on the back so we think Julian, or someone he knew, may have ordered it from Quickcards, which is a company that produces cards using pictures you upload.' Contact with the company had drawn a blank. They couldn't identify who had created the postcard without a client account or order number.

'So it hadn't been posted to him?'

'It doesn't look like it. There was no address on it.'

'You think he was planning to send it to me then?'

'We have no idea.'

'Right.'

Karene placed Harry's coffee in front of him. She thought it unwise to join him on the sofa. She didn't want to make him uncomfortable so she perched on the far end of the coffee table.

'Thank you,' he said, attempting a smile.

She knew she made him feel awkward and that broke her heart. They had been so close, the closest she'd ever experienced with a partner, and he'd said it was the same for him. How could that all have gone? She realized that things might have been easier for her if Harry had been killed by the bomb. At least then her memories would be unblemished. The thought made her sick with guilt. She was aware of Augusta watching her and turned her body away.

'I'm sorry I don't remember anything,' Harry said to her when Bloom and Jameson had left them alone.

'There's no need to apologize,' she said. 'We're asking the impossible.'

'Not really. They're my memories. I should know my own life.'

'But if they're gone, what we're actually asking you to do is gaze into your future and guess what you might have done.'

He was quiet for a moment. 'You think they're gone for ever?'

Karene tried to smile but she knew it looked weak.

'And you're absolutely sure someone did this to me on purpose?'

'The MRI scan showed lesions in the region of your brain that controls memories. The surgeon also found evidence that a hole had been drilled in your skull to insert the type of needle typically used to treat brain tumours.'

'And they used it to fry my memories?'

'Yes and no. Memories are not all stored in one place, but the hippocampus is where our memories seem to start. Damage to it can either affect our ability to make new memories or recall past memories. But you still remember everything before 2013 and you haven't forgotten the skills you'd learned in training.'

'So older memories are somewhere else?'

'I'm not one hundred per cent sure. I'm not certain anyone is. We only really know what we know from brain injury case studies. The men who survived being shot in the head in the Second World War taught us more than anyone about the brain. The bullets at that time were fired fast enough to penetrate the skull but were small enough to only cause localized damage. So neurologists could look at the track of the bullet and compare this to the functions that had been lost – sight, movement, memory, etc. – and determine which areas of the brain did what.'

Harry was smiling.

'What?'

'You're quite bright, aren't you?'

She gave an embarrassed laugh. 'I don't know about that,' she said. 'We can all sound intelligent when we're talking about our own field.'

Harry's eyes closed momentarily.

'You know you haven't lost everything,' she said. 'You still have the most important bits, like your personality and memories of your family, your children.'

'Just not you.' Their eyes met and it felt to Karene as it always had. She wanted to take his hand, kiss him, hold him. 'That must be hard for you.'

'A little.'

'How long had we been together?'

'Eighteen months. But I'm not supposed to tell you too much.'

'No, go on. I want to know.'

Karene hesitated then remembered Bloom's advice about helping him to remember. 'We met at a conference where we were both speaking. You'd heard me speak before so introduced yourself and we just hit it off. There was a lot of teasing.'

'What were you speaking on?'

'Mental resilience. It's my specialism. What it takes to remain resilient in the face of stress and pressure.'

'The perfect person to have on my team, then.'

'That wouldn't be the first time you've said that.'

'Really?'

'Yeah. You're pretty helpless and needy.'

Harry laughed for the first time since the ball. The sound filled Karene with joy and she couldn't help grinning.

'Thank you for making me laugh.'

'That's my job.'

'Yeah?'

'Taking care of you, making you laugh, making you think, and I know you don't know me any more but I'm not sure I can stop doing those things.'

Harry leaned back and closed his eyes. 'I'd better get to know you then.'

48

Harry lay on the sofa with his head resting on the padded armrest. Bloom had told him to make himself as comfortable as possible before they started. He had never tried hypnosis before. Truth be told, he always thought it was something for needy neurotics who didn't know their own minds. But Bloom said it was more of a relaxation process, something that enabled people to access subconscious regions of the brain. It had to be worth a shot.

'Close your eyes and take a few deep breaths for me,' said Bloom. She sat on the opposite sofa.

He did as he was told and followed her instructions to find a serene place inside his head. He chose the beach he'd taken Sophie and Jake to when they were little. They'd always laughed there so it seemed as good as any.

'Once you feel completely relaxed and ready, just raise your finger for me,' said Bloom. Her voice sounded a little further away. 'Thank you,' she said when he did as she asked. 'I'm going to ask you a series of questions to reflect on. Then when we're done, you can share any insights you believe may be helpful to your current situation. It is likely that you know something, have seen something or done something that someone wants you to forget. And, as our behaviour is largely habitual, we can often predict future actions by examining those in our past. So I'm going to ask you to think of genuine examples of past life experiences that may be helpful. Are you ready?'

Harry lifted the index finger of his left hand a touch.

'Can you think of a time in your life when you have been given access to someone's secret?' She waited a moment to give him time to think, then said, 'Did you keep that secret? If not, why not and who did you share it with?'

The memory that came to mind was Caroline's second pregnancy with Jake. They had experienced two pretty distressing miscarriages after Sophie and so Caroline was adamant that no one should know about this baby until they had confirmation that all was well at the twelve-week scan. This had been a huge challenge for him, because twelve weeks felt like a very long time to say nothing. There had been a couple of occasions where he'd nearly slipped up and one moment where he had consciously considered confiding in his best friend. But, in the end, he'd done as instructed.

'Have you done something you regret and, if so, how did you respond?'

This was an easy experience to identify. He really only had one regret in life and that was to do with his sister, Lucy. He'd never told anyone how she had confided in him about her headaches and moments of disorientation. If he had alerted someone at the time, she might not have had the stroke and ended up losing her baby and her quality of life. His regret was such that he hadn't visited her in over ten years. He wasn't even sure that Sophie and Jake were aware of her existence.

What did this say about him? That's what Dr Bloom wanted to know. What can you tell us about who you are and what you might have done based on who you were?

It was something else he had hidden. A secret he'd carried his whole adult life.

The realization brought a fog of despair. If he had done something he really didn't want anyone to know about, he was more than capable of hiding it. Maybe he would never know the reason for this attack on him.

'Let me know when you're ready to carry on,' said Bloom's far-off voice. When he raised his finger she said, 'Have you ever witnessed a crime or someone doing something you disapprove of? And if so, what did you do?'

Inside his head, Harry laughed. It was a naive question. Anyone who works in the military is exposed to all sorts of crimes, attitudes and actions they disapprove of and not just in the enemy. The trick was to find your own moral code. This was obviously harder in the junior ranks when you are expected to act without question, but thankfully he'd been led by some impressive men and women. Later, however, he became more conscious of how liberal and accepting his outlook was. He had always fought for the underdog; that was part of his make-up.

Bloom's final questions, 'Do you take risks?' and 'How have you responded to feelings of disillusionment or boredom in your life?', were fairly transparent. She wanted to know if he was the sort of person who might do something rash and stupid. He expected there were people he'd met over the years who would think this possible. He was often told he was a larger than life personality. It irritated Caroline that he would strike up conversations with anybody and everybody he met. But those who observed him for longer eventually saw through the bravado and found a calm professional within. Truth be told, Harry was a chess player, always thinking a few steps ahead; anticipating reactions, influencing opinions and motivating actions. Caroline's father had called him manipulative which wrongly implied that his motivations were selfish.

When they were finished Harry sat up and rubbed his face with both hands.

'What did you conclude?' said Bloom.

'About who I am?'

'Tell me three things you know about the kind of person you are, that you think may be relevant or could help us.'

Harry thought about it. 'I'm pretty good at getting what I want. I tend to fight for the underdog.'

'And?'

He smiled at the psychologist. 'I'm sorry to tell you that I'm good at keeping secrets.'

49

Bloom dropped her overnight bag in the office then crossed the road into Russell Square park. She ordered a green tea from the cafe and took it outside to sit in the sunshine at the table nearest the park perimeter. The text message she had received yesterday had simply read, *Meet me tomorrow. Usual place. 10 a.m.*

She had left Jameson and Karene in Southampton earlier that morning. They had agreed it was wise for her to return to London and carry on investigating Harry's past and links to Julian away from the safe house. She re-read an email she'd received that morning from Lucas. He had found a picture of the blonde woman from Julian's noticeboard posted on Julian's Facebook feed just under a month ago. It was one of those 'share your memories' posts. The picture was taken two years earlier at a social gathering in a garden, possibly the one in front of Julian's house. Bloom opened the attached image and looked at it for a second time. The woman in question was in the foreground with a large glass of red wine raised to the camera. Her smile creased her eyes and she seemed genuinely happy. In the background others stood chatting. Bloom couldn't see Julian. He must have been behind the camera. The other men and three women were untagged so there were no names. Lucas was going to look into it.

He had confirmed, however, that the woman at the front was Isobel Roux, the wife of a businessman who lived in nearby Rennes.

Bloom thought about it. A week before Julian was murdered he had posted this picture on his Facebook feed. If Isobel had seen the picture and liked it, perhaps her husband had finally uncovered the truth or discovered she had gone back on a promise to end things with her lover. That could mean that Julian's death was nothing to do with the bomb at the ball. But Bloom couldn't dismiss the migrants postcard.

And she had a fairly good idea who had put it there.

50

Harry woke at ten thirty. His head ached and his shoulders felt stiff and sore when he sat up. He wasn't sure if that was down to tension or the way he had slept. He took the towel from the radiator and went for a shower. He then found the small, wheeled suitcase Karene had brought him and got dressed. He headed to the kitchen and found Marcus Jameson working on his laptop at the table.

'Morning,' said Harry.

'Afternoon,' said Jameson. 'There's coffee in the pot, tea in the cupboard.'

Harry poured himself a coffee despite his headache and placed a slice of bread in the toaster. 'Is this your place then?'

Jameson continued to type. 'Yes and no.'

'Who do you hide from here?'

Jameson looked up and his expression was amused. 'No one any more.'

'You were MI5?'

'Six.'

'When did you leave?'

'Five years ago.'

'Why?'

Jameson returned to his work. 'The usual reason. To get a life.'

Harry could relate to that. He'd spent more time away from his children than with them when they were young. At the time he'd thought it necessary for his job and career. Only now did he wonder if he had justified it to suit his own selfish ambition. 'I want to see my kids.'

'I'm sure you do.'

'I'm not sharing. I'm requesting.'

Jameson closed the laptop and faced Harry. 'You know why you're here in this house?'

'I need to see them. If someone has come for me twice now, they'll keep coming. You know that and I know that. Whatever I've done or whatever I know, these people want to shut me up. I'm not hiding here until that happens without telling my kids I love them.'

'But if you meet them, you make them a target.'

'They're already a target. The fact I have two children is no secret. I want to see them as soon as possible.' Harry ate his toast then rinsed his plate in the sink and placed it on the drainer. He walked to the lounge where a whole wall was now taken up with photographs linked by red string and held in place with drawing pins. 'What's this?' he called.

'It's the thirty-seven minutes before the bomb went off at the ball.'

Harry followed the string from its starting point. 'Tell me about it.'

'Is that a good idea?'

'Why not? You want to know if I remember anything but I need something to work from.'

'Isn't there a danger of creating false memories?'

'Karene and Augusta seem pretty sure my memories aren't coming back, so why not tell me what you know, see if anything jumps out.'

Jameson took a second to decide and then joined him. 'The first sighting I have of you is thirty-seven minutes before detonation when you are captured in the background of this selfie.'

'That's a photo from someone's phone.' Harry looked around the others again. 'Most of these are. How did you get them?'

'That's not the point. The point is these pictures are all time stamped so I can plot out where you were right before the bomb went off here.' Jameson placed his finger on an impressive picture of the windows blowing and plumes of grey smoke escaping towards the camera. 'According to Karene, you were standing at this window at that point,' he said, indicating a previous image where the windows were intact.

'So I'm first captured at 19:25 and then ...' Harry scanned the pictures. 'I'm caught in the back of this photograph on the steps at 19:32 and then photographed here with Chris Waite at what time is that, 19:42 or 45?'

'19:42. Do you remember being in there with him?'

'No. I lived at Devonport for a year earlier in my career. I know it well and I've known Chris since initial training.'

'Well he's the Commodore there now. He lost a leg in the blast and his wife's only just been discharged.'

'Karene told me. I should call him soon.' Harry tracked the red string. 'I'm not photographed again. So why all these pictures?'

Jameson pointed to the image of a stocky, grey-haired man in the background of a photograph of two couples posing on the lawn. 'This guy appears in a few photos at 19:30, 19:36, 19:45 and 19:52. He's not in dress uniform and not with anyone else. Now, Karene said you were with a man in a white shirt when the bomb detonated.'

'And he's in a white shirt.' The man wore his day uniform of black trousers, shirt with epaulettes and a white cap.

'The only one I can find.'

'OK, so what?'

'So what's he looking at . . . here?' Jameson pointed at the photo showing the man on the lawn. 'And here?' He pointed to the guy standing on the concourse immediately outside the building, staring off to the left of the camera. 'If I look at the other photographs, I can work out that in the first one he's looking in the direction of where people enter and then at 19:36 he's looking towards the wardroom steps, where you were captured just four minutes earlier.'

'You think he's part of it?'

'I think he's watching. He's waiting.'

'For the bomber?'

'Or for you. If someone wanted to kidnap you, they'd need to make sure you were near enough to the blast to require an ambulance, but far enough away to survive. The room you were in had thick walls that would protect you from the explosion and place you behind the main blast area and also the most seriously wounded who would be looked after first. If Karene hadn't sought you out . . .' Jameson moved his hand to the floor plan of the building. 'Look at the stairway to the kitchen. This takes you out to an exit. And it's pretty much opposite the room where you were.' Jameson pointed to the last photo of the grey-haired man at 19.52. 'Ten minutes before the bomb goes off, he's heading up the stairs to the building. Eight minutes later the call for dinner will be made and everyone apart from the twelve of you caught in the blast will leave this building. And I'd bet my money that does not include him. I think he's coming in to see you, possibly to engage you in conversation and keep you where they need you to be.'

'That's a stretch, isn't it?'

'Is it? Look here at the CCTV footage showing all the ambulances congregating along the side of the building, all except this one.' Jameson pointed to the image of a sole ambulance caught on a different CCTV camera.

'It's going around to the back.'

Jameson pointed at the building map again. 'To this rear exit.'

'Was this guy one of the twelve injured?'

'He wasn't with you in the immediate aftermath according to Karene, so he must have been capable of moving away and the Detective Superintendent in charge is certain that all those in attendance are accounted for.'

'Except for this guy?'

'No. He says all those with tickets to attend are accounted for.'

Harry thought about it. 'So he wasn't officially there?'

'If they wanted you injured but alive, his job may have been to ensure that.'

'You think he was in league with the bomber?'

'And the dummy ambulance crew.'

Something flickered in Harry's memory, too fleeting to understand.

'What?' said Jameson.

Harry shook his head.

'You look like you remembered something.'

'Nothing tangible.' Harry tried to bring the memory back but it was gone. 'Why do you think this is happening to me? Any insights from your background?'

'Well . . . there's a few things that don't add up. A terrorist bomb is a sophisticated cover for kidnap but then there's the botched attack at Stanford Hall. On top of that, the brutality of how they tortured your cousin doesn't fit with the surgical precision needed to wipe your memory. And the taunting emails Karene's getting—'

'Taunting emails?' Harry felt suddenly protective of Karene. To him, she was one of the investigators but to the outside world she was more than that. She was his partner and therefore also a target.

'Someone's been sending her questions for the past week. Is Harry a good man? Does he help or hinder? Is he safe? I expect whoever's after you is showing off but Augusta seems to think someone may be trying to help us.'

'If you want to help, don't you just help? You don't send cryptic messages.'

'My thoughts exactly.'

51

'How sweet that you remember where I like to sit.'

Bloom looked up from her table and saw Seraphine Walker in the flesh for the first time in three months. She wore a tailored white dress, simple but expensive, with navy-blue heels. Everything about the woman – from her favourite table in the cafe to her twisted mind games – was permanently etched in Bloom's memory.

'I was intrigued to receive your message,' said Seraphine. 'What exactly is it you think I'm up to now?'

'In the land of the blind, the one-eyed man is king.'

'You've lost me.'

'I doubt that, Seraphine. You believe that you and your kind see things more clearly than the rest of us.'

Seraphine thanked the waitress for her flat white and crossed one long, tanned leg over the other before taking a small sip. 'How's my Marcus?'

Bloom felt her jaw tighten. 'He's not your Marcus.'

'Is he still angry with you?'

'I'm not talking about this, Seraphine.'

'Oh, he's not angry. He's disappointed. Yes. That's much worse for you.'

'Why are you sending Karene Harper emails?'

'Is Marcus seeing anyone?'

'What's your involvement in this?'

'Or is he struggling to get over me?'

'He is more than over you. You were nothing but a lesson learned. Now, are you going to answer my questions or is your coming here just another game?' She was not having this woman messing with Jameson's mind again. She had presented herself as the ideal girlfriend in order to get close to Bloom. He'd been broken by not only the heartbreak but by the deceit too. And what concerned her most was that his continued hurt suggested that his feelings for the woman might still run worryingly deep.

Seraphine smiled.

'What do you know about Harry Peterson and the people who are after him?'

'I know that he's a good-looking fella. And presumably he can't remember his lady love any more so that would pretty much make him single.'

'So you *have* been watching him and Karene. I suspected as much from your little hints and tips. As soon as I saw the phrase *your choice* on that postcard I suspected your involvement.' A year earlier Seraphine had used Bloom's advice about choices to justify playing games with people's lives.

'I've no interest in Harry Peterson and his pretty woman.'

Bloom watched Seraphine. She was undeniably stunning, with long blonde hair and blue eyes. If you passed her on the street, you'd assume she was a model or the trophy wife of some billionaire, rather than a snake-eyed psychopath.

'This is all about Marcus, isn't it?' said Bloom. 'Do you have any insights at all?' Was this a ruse? Nothing more than a way to mess with her and Jameson's lives all over again?

Seraphine waited, watching.

The one thing Bloom knew was that Seraphine Walker never did anything without good reason. The trick was to uncover what that reason was. 'What do you know about Harry's memory loss and Julian's murder? Is this you and your meddlers?'

'No, I'm just an interested audience member.'

'But you planted the postcard?'

'I know you love a mystery and I couldn't help giving you a little clue.'

'One of yours tortured and killed Julian to give us a clue?'

'Oh, that would be far too primitive for us.'

'You expect me to believe you placed the postcard after his death?'

'Indeed.'

'And the picture of Isobel?'

Seraphine shrugged.

'OK then. How did you know he was dead?'

'Because I pay attention, Augusta. Now if you want me to answer your questions, you'll need to do something for me.'

52

Seraphine watched Bloom walk away as she finished her coffee. The woman was more than a match for her in terms of intelligence, but she lacked the imagination to really take advantage of what the world had to offer for people like them. It was a tragedy in Seraphine's eyes. What an asset a mind like Bloom's could be to her little club. Just a few months earlier Bloom had put a stop to Seraphine's elegant recruitment drive: the game she had invented to test the purity and talent of the psychopaths who hide within society. Bloom had not halted it permanently, of course, but her skilful game playing had to be admired.

The cafe was busy today. She liked it that way. Summer had been good and Londoners had taken outdoor living to their hearts. Hardly anyone sat indoors for their morning coffee, brunch or early lunch. They filled the tables or found spots on the grass to sit cross-legged.

Seraphine strolled along the perimeter path where it was quieter and the shade from the trees limited eavesdroppers.

Her call connected within three rings. 'Good afternoon, Abdul,' she said.

'Ma'am.' Abdul's voice was deep and soft with a richness that suggested a man of calm intelligence.

'How is our little warlord today?'

'Still fixated on your British sailor. I've suggested that instead of sending more soldiers to apprehend Captain Peterson it would be wiser to encourage the Captain to come to him.'

'I bet he liked that idea.'

'He did. Very much.'

Seraphine waited for a businessman to pass her on the path. The man's eyes scanned her from top to bottom without embarrassment. She held his gaze and then smiled as she pushed her loose hair behind one ear. The man smiled back and slowed a little. Seraphine turned her body away and resumed her conversation. 'And how do you plan to make that happen?' The businessman picked up his pace.

Abdul was quiet for a moment. 'If he thinks we have her, he will come.'

'And if he really doesn't remember her?'

There was no reply.

Seraphine said, 'I'll see what I can do.'

'Thank you, Ma'am.' The deference was habit rather than true sentiment, but Seraphine liked it.

'And what of your progress more generally?'

'My observations on Antony Bello are of great interest to his uncle. Jacob Bello wants someone trustworthy, devout and reliable to succeed him and that is not his nephew.'

'Now, Abdul, my dear friend. Who could you be possibly thinking he might choose to succeed him if young Mr Bello proves unworthy?'

53

Jameson left Harry and Karene talking in the kitchen. He walked through to the small bedroom at the back of the house where he had been sleeping, closed the door behind him and knelt by the bed as if to pray. Harry was insisting on meeting his children and that meant leaving their safe house.

He removed a black wooden box with a six-digit combination lock from beneath the bed. He hesitated then spun the numbers to a date forever burned into his memory: the date he first killed. Inside the box was an unused Sig Sauer P226. He had obtained a licence and purchased the gun a month after leaving MI6. The Sig was the same model as his old service weapon. It had lived in his loft, where his young nieces would never accidentally find it.

If Harry wanted to go out, Jameson needed to be armed.

He took the Sig out of the box and felt the weight of it. Then he loaded it and checked the decocking lever, ensuring the gun wouldn't be accidentally fired, and placed it in the drawer of his bedside table. Freddie, the porter, had been firing a Sig Sauer. It had been old and well used. Whereas the other man had a brand-new, top-of-the-range Glock. Jameson thought about that – why would someone hire two assassins of such differing calibre? – then closed the drawer and rejoined Harry and Karene.

Harry sat at Jameson's computer flicking through the photographs of the Devonport ball.

'Is that you in green?' Harry said to Karene.

'Yes. That was just after I'd arrived. I was looking for you.'

Jameson had felt sceptical about Karene and Harry's romance when he first met Karene. He knew this was because of Seraphine, but he couldn't help it. His brief relationship with her had him believing in soulmates and then, *boom*, she turned out to be a psychopath who had faked it all to target Bloom. It had never been about him at all.

But he was starting to feel sorry for these two. From what he'd heard, they really had been a great match. Sometimes it was hard to look at the pain on Karene's face.

Harry continued to look through the photographs as Karene began making lunch. She laid out cheeses and deli meats on a wooden board and began to slice a French stick.

Jameson watched the computer screen as Harry flicked from one photo to another. The ball had been an extravagant event with men in uniform and women in evening gowns. The sun had been shining and occasionally a photograph would show the string quartet playing on the lawn, or the opening to a large marquee where round tables were set for dinner with wine glasses and champagne flutes that were destined to remain unused. Harry looked more and more despondent with each picture. At one point he closed his eyes and rubbed his temples as if willing his brain into action.

Karene placed lunch on the table and laid out plates and tumblers of water for each of them. 'Why not take a break and we'll eat something.'

Harry began to close the laptop and then stopped. He pushed the screen back up again and flicked back through a couple of images until he found the one of the grey-haired man standing on the concourse. He zoomed in on the man's face.

'Do you recognize him?' said Jameson.

'No, I just . . .' He squinted at the screen which now showed just the man's head and shoulders. 'Earlier when we were discussing him I had a flash of something, a flicker of a memory maybe.'

Jameson and Karene glanced at each other and then back at Harry.

'His epaulettes. I can't see clearly enough.'

'You remembered his epaulettes?' said Karene.

'They're the shoulder patches that show rank insignia,' said Jameson. 'Are you trying to check his rank because I already did that. He's a sub-lieutenant.'

Karene said, 'I know what they are, but why would you remember his epaulettes?'

'I don't know if they were his and I can't see clearly enough here.' He opened the internet browser on the laptop and typed 'Royal Navy ranks' into Google. He selected a picture that showed several pairs of insignias decorated with a variety of gold lines and loops. 'See the loop on this,' he said, showing them the set above the words *sub-lieutenant*. 'It should be worn so that the braid starts at the front, loops over itself and points to the back. But if you put them on the wrong shoulders—'

'The loop is reversed, starting at the back and pointing to the front?' said Jameson.

Harry nodded. 'Any self-respecting naval officer would know that. It's not the sort of mistake you make.' He looked back at the image of the grey-haired sub-lieutenant outside Devonport. 'This picture's at the wrong angle. I can't see them.'

'You think the guy who spoke to you at the ball had his epaulettes on back to front?' said Karene.

Harry stared at her for a long moment then raised his hands. 'I don't know. How can I know if it's a memory from this night? It's impossible.'

'I think that's the point.' When the other two looked at Jameson, he said, 'That's why they fucked up your memory. So you wouldn't remember anything that happened at all.'

54

Isobel Roux replied within minutes to Bloom's request to speak about Julian, saying that she was devastated and desperate to find out who could do such an atrocious thing to such a lovely man. Bloom headed straight to the airport and within hours they were sitting in a cafe on the main square in the town of Rennes.

Isobel was talking about how she had met Julian five years earlier in this very cafe, one afternoon when her husband was away with work. Victor Roux ran a successful import business specializing in artwork and antiques. Bloom guessed Isobel led something of a charmed existence and this sense of privilege was one of the reasons she had taken Julian as her lover. Her husband was aware, she said, and had been for a number of years now.

'So you have no concern that your husband may have had a hand in what happened to Julian?'

Isobel swore in French. 'No! Victor and I have a happy arrangement. He has a lady in Geneva, a French–Spanish interpreter. It is a situation that works well for us.'

Bloom felt no judgement. What people chose to do within their own marriages was their business so long as no one was getting hurt. She placed in front of her a print-out of the photograph Julian had posted on his Facebook page. 'You said on the phone that you could tell me who these people are.'

'*Oui*. These are Julian's neighbours,' she said, pointing to the older couple on the right of the picture, 'Madame and Monsieur Petit. And the man here, talking to the redhead, is Alain Jacques, a friend from the village. He's a builder. He helped Julian with the house when he moved here.'

'And the redhead?'

'She is Alain's wife. I don't recall her name but I believe she works at the local school. And that girl was a family friend of Julian's who stayed with him that summer.'

The dark-skinned girl talking to Alain's wife looked to be in her mid-teens. She wore a shapeless black shirt over black leggings and had her afro hair pulled back in a wide plaited bun. 'This girl was staying with Julian?'

'I think she may be a friend of his stepdaughter.'

'Julian has a stepdaughter?'

'In the UK, yes. They are not so close these days. It was a source of sadness for Julian. Her mother remarried, found the girl a new stepfather, I suppose.'

'How long did this girl stay?' Bloom indicated the picture.

Isobel shook her head. 'A month or so, maybe more.'

'And do you know when she arrived?'

'Not long before this was taken and this was my fiftieth birthday. So July 2015. About then.'

'Can you recall her name?'

Isobel thought for a moment then apologized. 'My memory is not what it was.'

'Why do you think Julian posted this on his Facebook page?'

She shrugged in a very French way, elegant and refined. 'He always posted these memory pictures whenever they came up. He was a sentimental old fool.' Isobel's eyes filled with tears and she drank the remainder of her coffee.

After saying goodbye and promising to update Isobel when they had news, Bloom called Jameson. He answered immediately and she wondered if he was getting bored of his babysitting duties.

'Did you need to go to France?' he said. 'Couldn't you have spoken to her on the phone?'

Bloom smiled to herself. He was definitely bored. 'I wanted to see her expression and I wasn't sure my French would hold up on the phone.'

'I could have done it. I'm literally sat here with nothing to do.'

It had occurred to her to ask Jameson to speak to Isobel. But she didn't want him to know where the contact number for Julian's lover had come from. 'How's Harry doing?' she asked. 'Any luck with the photographs?'

'What do you make of this?' he said. 'When I showed Harry the photograph of the guy in the white shirt, he said he could remember someone wearing their epaulettes the wrong way around. But we don't know when the memory is from. Could he have remembered something from that night, do you think?'

'It's always possible. Karene said Harry had an uncanny visual memory, so there's a chance he might store and recall such details from elsewhere in his brain. The problem is we could never prove it.'

'Unless someone else noticed. Harry said it's not a mistake any genuine naval officer would make.'

'So that would make him an imposter and definitely part of the team who came for Harry.'

'Exactly. So, was your cross-Channel jaunt worth it?'

'I think so. Isobel tells me the young girl in the photograph was a friend of Julian's stepdaughter who was staying for the summer to improve her French. She can't recall the girl's name but confirms the picture was taken in July 2015.'

'The year Harry worked on Operation Weald.'

'And when I pushed Isobel to tell me more about the girl, she said the teenager appeared to be painfully shy and that when one of the male neighbours attempted to greet her with a kiss on the cheek—'

'The girl flinched?'

'Not only that. Isobel said when she thought about it now, the girl's reaction had struck her as odd at the time, as if she was not so much shy as scared.'

'You're thinking she's a migrant?'

'That was my guess. And possibly one who has experienced a degree of trauma.'

'To help or harm. You're thinking Harry and Julian helped this girl.'

'Yes. And if I'm right she's the key. We just need to find her.'

55

Alina bought some groceries on her way home. She spoke briefly to the man behind the counter about the weather then hurried out. She never liked to interact with people for too long. She'd thought her world would expand when she escaped her past, but it had only contracted. It was partly down to her own paranoia, but it made sense to be safe rather than sorry.

She picked up the post from the mat. The water bill was addressed to Lindsay Adeyemi. She placed the letter on the small kitchen table and put the vegetables in the fridge and the tinned soup in the cupboard. It was taking her a while to get used to her new name. In her new job as a receptionist at the local leisure centre she often failed to answer when people called her Lindsay and she'd had to blame it on poor hearing.

Her shift started in half an hour so she had time to listen to the news on the radio. There had been no further reports about Harry Peterson and she hoped that was a good thing. She hoped that he was safe. God forbid he should suffer the same fate as Julian. She couldn't abide having both men on her conscience.

Alina closed her eyes. The first day she saw Harry was the last day she saw her mother. Their boat had capsized and they had clung to each other in the cold water, her mother singing songs in her ear. By the time they were lifted from the sea, the singing had stopped and Alina had been desperately fighting to keep her mother's head above the waves. In the helicopter a man and a woman fought to bring her mother back as Alina begged and pleaded. When they landed on the ship her mother was rushed inside and that's when Harry came to stand beside her. He held his helmet in one hand. That's how she knew he'd been flying the helicopter. He asked if she was hurt or feeling unwell and then, when the man who had been helping her mother stepped out on to the ship's deck, Harry moved into her eyeline. 'I'm sorry,' he had said.

Alina opened her eyes. The rest of the memory was a blur. She knew the doctor had spoken to her but had no recollection of what he had said. Only later did she discover her mother had perished as a result of a heart attack, probably brought on by the effort of trying to keep afloat and warm in the water.

She didn't blame the doctors, nor did she feel any ill-will towards the men who had taken her mother's money and promised to give them safe passage on an inadequate boat. They were only providing a service desperately wanted by people like her. Mother had said the journey was dangerous but not as dangerous as staying.

Alina Maree blamed only one person: the man who had stripped Naomi Maree of every dignity, the man who had beaten and raped her, the man who had eventually turned his attention to Alina. Antony Bello.

56

Late on Friday morning, Jameson sat on the table adjacent to Harry in the coffee shop by Portsmouth and Southsea station. Karene was there too, as were Harry's teenage children. They'd been talking for nearly an hour and Jameson had noticed nothing amiss. No one appeared to be watching them or lingering nearby. The traffic in and out of the cafe was fairly constant. The only other people sitting inside were a group of teenage girls and an elderly man with a large suitcase who was reading *The Times*. An old friend of Jameson's sat in the small car park outside, also watching and ready to react.

Jameson could only hear snippets of the conversation. It sounded like Harry's children were filling him in on all their achievements over the past few years. He watched the group of girls leave a large pile of plastic frappé cups, napkins, cake wrappers and straws behind them as they walked out chatting and giggling. When he looked back at Harry's table, Harry's daughter, Sophie, was leaning in to Karene for a hug and then she moved around the table to put her arms round her dad's neck. Harry stroked his daughter's back and spoke softly to her. A moment later Harry's son said something that made the whole group laugh.

Ten minutes later, Harry, Karene and the children

stood up and began to say their goodbyes. Karene had brought Sophie and Jake down from London on the train and was going to escort them home. Jameson wasn't entirely sure of the rationale, but he guessed that Caroline had refused to come.

Once they had left, Jameson joined Harry at his table. 'All OK?'

Harry watched his family cross the car park and waved at them as they entered the station. 'Sure,' he replied.

In the car park, Jameson saw his friend Vic get out of the car with a laptop bag and follow Karene. His instructions were to follow them the whole way and to ensure that the group made it safely back to Caroline's house.

57

Antony Bello waved away the youngest of his wives as his phone began to ring beside his bed. The girl skittered away quickly. She looked younger than fourteen. He liked that.

'His children just met him in a cafe,' said George when Bello answered.

He sat up, dropped his legs over the side of the bed and slipped his feet into his flip-flops. 'Where?'

'Portsmouth. On the south coast of England.'

Bello walked to his desk and typed 'Portsmouth England' into the search engine on his laptop. 'Who else is there?'

'The children arrived with a woman and there are at least two bodyguards: one in the cafe with them, one out in the car park.'

'Soldiers?'

'Probably Special Forces.'

'Have they seen you?'

'No, I'm in a vacant office space across the street. What do you want me to do?'

Bello thought about it. Abdul was planning to bring Peterson here, but after all the errors to date, he liked the idea of insurance. He had instructed George Selaissie to locate and track Peterson's children. Selaissie had orchestrated the Plymouth bomb. He knew the UK very well. He was the one who'd said they couldn't just take this Captain Peterson, that they'd be noticed immediately, they had to create chaos. He'd identified the ball as the perfect place for a pretend terror attack and also found their willing bomber. So Bello knew he was a man of talent. He also knew Selaissie was keen to make up for the way things had gone since the bomb. But Bello didn't want to undermine Abdul. His uncle thought highly of the man. And while Abdul came over as calm and measured, Bello knew a snake when he saw one. 'You stay with Harry, but send someone with the children. I want the children.'

'And the woman?'

'Who is she? The mother?'

'No. Peterson's girlfriend.'

'Take her too.'

58

A little later, Bloom met up with Jameson in the same cafe and ordered drinks at the counter. She bought a bottle of water for Harry, a large cappuccino for Jameson, a cup of tea for herself and a flat white too.

'Karene's not coming back,' said Jameson when she placed the flat white in front of the empty seat. 'She's taking the kids home.'

'That was tough,' said Harry. 'They're so grown up, almost adults, it's . . .' He stared out of the window at the station entrance.

'It was always going to be hard,' said Bloom. 'Seeing them again. They're the one thing that makes this real.' Bloom took her notebook out of her bag and removed a printed copy of the picture from Julian's Facebook post. 'It's not as tough for them though. They haven't lost all that time with you.'

'Sophie's struggling with it.' Harry looked down at the picture. 'What's this?'

'Karene will help her. You couldn't ask for a better person to support them through this. It's a picture Julian posted on his Facebook page a week before his murder. It was a memory post, a photograph taken two years earlier at a fiftieth birthday celebration that Julian had hosted for this lady.' Bloom placed her finger on the picture.

'That's his lady friend. What's her name? Isobel, I think.'

Bloom nodded. 'And do you recognize any of the others in the picture?'

'Was I there?' Harry picked up the printout and looked closely.

'No.'

He put it down again. 'Sorry. I don't.'

'You have no idea who this girl might be?' Bloom placed her finger on the dark-skinned girl dressed in black.

'Should I?'

'Isobel said she was a friend of Julian's stepdaughter Clara and was staying that summer to improve her French. But I spoke to Clara this morning and she's never heard of or seen this girl.'

'So who is she?'

'This picture was taken in early July 2015, not long after you'd been lifting migrants out of the sea off the coast of Italy. And we wondered if this girl might have been one of them?'

'Why would she be with Julian?'

'Maybe you needed to hide her,' said Jameson.

Harry picked up the paper again. 'She looks young.'

'Isobel estimated about sixteen or seventeen but I think she could be even younger.'

'And whoever I was hiding her from, you think they're the people who've done this to me?'

'Yes and no,' said Jameson. Bloom looked surprised and he moved closer to the table and turned the photograph over to write on the back. 'Somebody skilled and organized kidnapped you from the ball under the cover of a terrorist attack. They performed intricate surgery to remove your memories and placed you back in hospital to recover.' He drew a series of circles for each event linked with a line. 'Then, while you recovered, they sent people for you again, but this time the men end up shooting each other. One of the men wanted to keep you alive, the other wanted to kill you.' He wrote the words 'Dead' and 'Alive'. 'The thing that's been bugging me is not only did these last two guys have such different motivations,' he pointed at the words 'Dead' and 'Alive' again, 'but they also had such different kit. One of them had the latest top-of-the-range gun and body armour, while the other, Freddie, had well-used gear and a Sig Sauer P226, the same firearm issued to me in MI6. Which means—' He felt someone brush past him to sit in the spare seat at the table.

'You have two separate groups coming after Harry,' said the new arrival.

Jameson knew who it was without looking. He recognized her perfume. The smell of it caused bile to swill into his mouth. He looked to his right. Seraphine was wearing her hair in a neat bun and her fair skin had tanned in the sun. He was unable to look away.

'Hi, Marcus.' She took a sip of the flat white Bloom had placed on the table.

Bloom was expecting her.

Bloom had invited her.

The realization broke through his shock. He took his jacket off the back of the chair and walked out. He heard

Bloom calling his name but he kept going. Once more, she had failed to warn him. After all the apologies of the last few weeks, she had chosen again not to trust him when it came to Seraphine. He was done. He knew he shouldn't have come back. You can't fix a relationship, any relationship, when the trust is gone. Bloom clearly had no regard for his feelings, or respect for his opinion, or she would have told him she'd been in contact with Seraphine. She insisted she wasn't the closet psychopath Seraphine had accused her of being, but then why did she do this, why did she insist on keeping in touch with that woman? The woman who'd not only played with his feelings for her own entertainment, but had him genuinely fearing for his life.

He took the keys to the hire car out of his jacket pocket. Bloom could make her own way back with Harry. It was no longer his responsibility. He was out. The keys felt bulky and he looked down at them realizing he wasn't holding the single car key on an Avis fob but a bunch of keys on a red bicycle keyring. He lifted the jacket from over his arm. It was Harry's. He must have left his over the chair of his original table. 'Shit,' he said under his breath. He would have to go back in. He had no choice.

He checked the back pocket of his jeans and found his wallet. He could get a cab and text Bloom to retrieve his jacket and use the hire car. That was a better plan; anything to avoid spending time with that woman.

He changed course and headed for the taxi rank. Two cabs sat waiting for passengers, and he climbed in the back of one, examining the keys in his hand as he waited for the driver to finish his conversation with a colleague. On the keyring were a car key, three house keys and a small golden key. Jameson studied the last one. Its head was shaped like the clubs symbol from a deck of cards and its barrel was flat with small square chunks cut out in seemingly random places. Jameson opened the taxi door again and climbed out. He was sick of people hiding shit.

59

The journey back to London was very subdued. Karene tried to keep the atmosphere light, talking about how well Harry was coping, but Sophie and Jake were clearly shaken by the reality of their dad's memory loss.

'He doesn't even remember who you are,' said Sophie as they pulled in to Havant station and watched a young family board the train and spread toys, colouring books and a picnic across the table opposite.

'Forgetting me is not the worst thing that could have happened and I'm still part of his life, just in a different way.' She was surprised how unemotional her words sounded.

'He was so happy with you though.' Sophie picked at the skin around her thumbnail. It was red and swollen.

Karene looked down the carriage as a woman carrying a large rucksack apologized to the man sitting a few tables away. The man told her not to worry, he wasn't hurt, and the woman carried on walking holding the rucksack behind her back with one arm so it wouldn't hit anyone else. The man at the table glanced at Karene then went back to his book. Something about how quickly he averted his eyes struck her as curious. She felt a tingle of adrenaline. Marcus had said they were fine if they stuck to public transport. He had given her a route. They were to change trains at East Croydon and take the Bedford train to St Albans, then catch a bus across town to where Caroline lived. He'd even found the right bus stop for her. 'Hide in plain sight,' he'd said. 'As long as you're with other people, you're safe.'

60

Harry watched the interaction between Bloom and the blonde woman with fascination. The dynamic was weird, off somehow. It sounded like Bloom had hired the woman as an investigator but the blonde was dismissive to the point of disparaging. How did she run a business speaking to her clients as though they were beneath her? She kept glancing at Harry, holding eye contact for longer and longer with each look. A less vigilant man might think she was attracted to him, but Harry figured she might be flirting on purpose. But why?

'You wanted to know who kidnapped our lovely Harry,' said the blonde. 'Hi, I'm Seraphine.' She held an elegant hand out to Harry.

'You said that two groups were after him,' said Bloom.

Seraphine smiled. 'I may have exaggerated. There is definitely one group after him.'

'So why did you say there were two?' said Bloom.

Seraphine shrugged and the look on her face suggested she really did have no idea.

'Stop wasting our time, Seraphine. You said you had valuable information for Harry and Karene. That's the only reason I agreed to your coming here. What do you know? Who's after Harry? I take it they have something to do with this girl.' Augusta pointed to the photograph of their suspected migrant.

'Ah, Alina Maree,' said Seraphine.

Before Harry or Bloom had a chance to ask about Alina Maree, Jameson was looming over them. 'What the hell is this?' His expression was dark and his eyes wild with anger. He held a bunch of keys in Harry's face, too close for Harry to focus.

Harry leaned back a touch. 'They're my keys. Did you take my jacket?'

'I know they're your keys, sailor boy, and that's why I'm asking what the hell this is and what the fuck you're hiding?'

'I love it when Marcus is so ... you know ... passionate.' Seraphine tilted her head towards Bloom as she spoke. Everyone ignored her.

'It's a key. I don't know what for. I don't know what any of them are for. They were with me in the hospital along with my wallet and my phone.'

Jameson leaned further over the table. He held the smallest key between his thumb and index finger. 'This is a very specific type of key. The sort normal people don't have alongside their house keys. It's for the kind of place you hide something. So what are you hiding?'

'A safety deposit box?' said Bloom.

'Lots of normal people have those these days, Marcus,' said Seraphine.

When Jameson looked at Seraphine his expression was one of disgust. 'How would you know what normal people do? And for that matter what exactly are you doing here?' He turned to Bloom. 'And why the fuck didn't you tell me what you were up to? Worried I might disapprove of you colluding with the devil?'

'Calm down, Marcus.' Bloom placed her hands flat on the table. 'I had no intention of colluding with Seraphine. She's simply here to tell us what she knows and then she'll be on her way.'

'Back to hell,' said Jameson. 'Well at least that's something for us all to look forward to.'

Harry watched the whole interaction play out, trying to work out the connections between these people.

'Maybe I should make myself scarce,' said Seraphine.

'Be our guest,' said Jameson pointing to the door with an outstretched arm.

'Stay where you are. I haven't finished with you yet,' Bloom said.

'I guarantee she doesn't know a damn thing, Augusta. She's playing you,' said Jameson.

'How do we find out what box that's for?' Harry pointed to the key. Why did he have a safety deposit key? He'd never had cause to use one in his life, so what had he needed to hide in the last few years? Could it be something to do with his divorce? Had he moved money or hidden investments? It seemed unlikely. They were hardly a cash-rich family. Most of his and Caroline's earnings had been ploughed into their home or their annual holidays. He couldn't think of anything he had to hide. He looked down at the picture of this Alina Maree. Did this box hold her secrets?

'We ask you,' said Jameson.

'Well, I don't know,' said Harry. 'It must be a recent thing.'

'Recent being anytime in the last four goddamn years?'

'Marcus. Enough,' said Bloom.

'But what if he's faking? You said yourself it was highly unlikely he'd have no other symptoms from his surgery. It's pretty bloody convenient that he's lost only his memories.'

'Only my memories?' Harry could feel his own rage building. Karene had said these people were friends, but they were looking at him as a suspect.

'Harry, I'm sorry. This is nothing to do with you. This is because of things that have happened in our collective past, things you don't need to be inconvenienced by.' Bloom gestured for Jameson to sit but he stood tall with his back straight.

'Do you two need a minute?' said Seraphine.

'I tell you what we do need—' started Jameson.

Bloom stood. 'OK, Marcus. Let's have this out.' She walked past him, away from the table, and he followed. Harry watched them stop just outside the door. Bloom was talking. Jameson had his arms crossed as he stared her down.

'So,' said Seraphine.

Harry met her eyes. They were unusually blue. He wondered if she wore contacts.

'They're great people and they're trying their best, but they're simply not capable of helping you.'

'How do you know about this Alina?'

'I pay attention. It's sort of my thing. Lots of fingers.

Lots of pies.' She brushed a loose strand of her hair behind her ear. Her movements were smooth and precise. He had the sense that everything this woman did she did on purpose. 'I can give you all the answers you need, from what you've forgotten to why you've forgotten it.'

'You know why someone's done this to me?'

'I do.'

'How? Who are you? What's your involvement?'

Seraphine observed Bloom and Jameson. 'Let's just say I'm an interested party. Someone who won't hold anything back or keep any secrets.' She met Harry's gaze again. 'So do you want to know?'

'Of course I do.' Was she suggesting that Bloom and Jameson knew more than they were letting on?

'Good. There's a condition.'

'Why does that not surprise me?'

Seraphine smiled. 'I like you, Harry. You're very direct. But I am going to have to ask you to choose.'

Harry's every instinct told him to beware, but he had to know what was going on. 'Choose what?'

Seraphine tilted her head to the doorway. 'Me or them.'

61

They had time at East Croydon so Sophie visited the Ladies and Jake bought a movie magazine. The train they boarded was busy with commuters so Karene had to stand in the aisle beside where Jake and Sophie sat. She kept her eyes on them the whole way, still a little spooked by the guy on the last train.

'Mum's working late,' said Sophie, reading a message on her phone. 'She says we should get some tea with you.'

'Great.' Karene smiled. She felt irritated by Caroline's assumption that she would look after the children. She took her phone from her bag and checked if their mother had texted her to ask her, but there were no messages.

They disembarked in St Albans and reached the bus stop just as the bus arrived. It was almost empty so they were able to get three seats together at the front. Jake and Sophie talked about a film. Karene checked the text message with the details of the journey. They had eight stops to go. And there was a family pub around the corner from Caroline's so they could eat there.

She was pleased that she'd taken the kids to see Harry. She could tell he'd really enjoyed seeing them. He loved being a father. She'd never wanted children but when she saw Harry with Sophie and Jake part of her wished they were her children too. She imagined she would have enjoyed family life with Harry.

'There's Katy and Poppy,' said Sophie rising a little from her seat and craning to look out of the side window of the bus. Two girls walked along the pavement deep in conversation. They didn't notice Sophie waving.

'Are they friends from school?' Karene said but she didn't hear Sophie's answer. She had twisted in her seat to see Sophie's friends and was now facing the people sitting at the back of the bus.

Which included the man from the train.

Karene fumbled in her bag while trying to look calm. When she found her phone, she dialled Jameson's number. It went to voicemail. She turned her head a little and cupped her hand around her mouth so she couldn't be heard. 'Marcus, it's Karene. Can you call me back as soon as you get this.' He'd asked if she wanted him to arrange for one of his associates to accompany them, but Karene had worried it might spook the kids. Maybe he'd done that anyway.

But what if he hadn't?

They were still six stops away from Caroline's and even then, there would be no one in. She kept checking her phone but it was black and silent. She called Jameson again as the bus stopped next to a large group of people who snaked onboard. Karene listened to Jameson's voicemail for a second time and then a third time. She needed to call the police. But she couldn't risk this guy overhearing. She glanced back again. He stared straight ahead as though he had no idea she was there. He was seven rows back and between them were half a dozen people standing.

'Get off the bus,' she said, placing one hand on Sophie's arm and her other on Jake's back. '*Now*,' she said when they hesitated. 'Get off the bus now.'

Her voice must have sounded urgent because the teenagers did not protest. The driver began to close the doors as they squeezed past those standing. 'Sorry, can we get off,' she said as they reached him. He nodded and opened the doors wide again. Karene pushed Sophie and Jake on to the street. 'Walk with me, quickly.' She scanned the pavement ahead. There was a left turn coming up and she headed for that. The bus passed them before they reached it and Karene saw the man looking out at them through the side window. He had his phone to his ear.

'Run,' she said and their little group darted down the road on the left then took a number of random left and right turns into a large housing estate.

'What's the matter?' said Jake as they slowed on a quiet suburban road.

'I think someone was following us. I'm going to call the police.' She checked the road name and dialled 999. 'We'll be fine now,' she said, touching Jake's arm. 'We're safe.'

She heard the screech of brakes as the call connected. A van stopped next to them with its side door slid open wide. The man inside was young with dark skin, cropped hair and a large machine gun.

'Get inside,' he said.

The three of them took a step back and the man aimed his gun at Sophie.

They did as instructed. What choice did they have? Karene heard the operator's voice on her phone before a strong hand yanked it from her fingers and flung it out of the door as it slid closed. There was just enough time for Karene to see it smash on to the tarmac.

62

Bloom and Jameson were still arguing on the pavement when Seraphine exited the cafe and walked away with a cheery goodbye. Jameson raised his eyebrows and smiled, hoping to convey 'I told you so' to his partner. Bloom pressed her lips into a tight line and went after her.

Jameson joined Harry back at the table. The guy looked pissed off and he couldn't blame him. It must be a bitch not knowing what's going on and who to trust. Jameson was about to suggest leaving when his phone rang in his jacket pocket. It was still hanging over the back of the chair on the adjacent table. He retrieved it and answered the call.

'I lost them,' said the voice on the other end.

Jameson tensed and turned away from Harry. 'How?'

'Something spooked her and they got off the bus as a load of people got on. I doubled back from the next stop but they're nowhere to be seen. Does Peterson know where they might go? Or should I head for the ex-wife's house?'

Jameson could feel Harry watching him. 'It won't do any good to ask him.' Harry had no memory of living near St Albans and he'd certainly freak out if he heard his kids had done a runner. 'Just carry on as planned.' He made his words as ordinary and unemotional as possible. Hopefully Harry would assume it was an unrelated call.

'Won't do any good to ask me what?' Harry said when Jameson hung up.

'Huh?'

'You said it won't do any good to ask him.'

Jameson put his jacket on and checked for his actual car key. 'Different case. Nothing to do with you. Let's go.' He knew Bloom would be trying to bring Seraphine back to share whatever dubious intel she claimed to have, and he had no interest in hearing her lies.

His phone buzzed and he saw he had four missed calls and a voicemail from Karene. He listened to her pleas and checked the call times. She had last called seven minutes before Vic, either just before or just after she got off the bus. He dialled her number. It rang for a while then went to voicemail.

'Everything OK?' said Harry.

'Absolutely.' Until he knew what was going on, he was keeping this quiet. Hopefully Karene had been sensible enough to follow his advice to stay visible and if in doubt to call the police. Until Vic confirmed whether they'd made it back to Caroline's house there was nothing he could do.

63

Bloom caught up with Seraphine on the other side of Portsmouth's Victoria Park. 'We had a deal,' she said.

Seraphine stopped and faced her. 'And what was that deal?'

'That you would tell us everything you know about who is after Harry and I would let you see Jameson.'

'Very clever, Augusta. You know I meant more than simply seeing him.'

'That was our deal. I did not break the terms.'

'You didn't tell him I was coming.'

'You saw how he was. There's no way he'd have been there had he known you were coming.'

Seraphine looked up at the sky. 'You're a clever woman, Augusta, and I can't argue with your logic, but I'm afraid what you did was not in the spirit of the agreement.' She met Bloom's gaze again. 'So, until you find a way to give me what I want, the deal is off.'

'We're perfectly able to solve this ourselves. I cannot and will not sacrifice Marcus.'

Seraphine began walking again. 'Maybe you already have.'

'This is over, Seraphine.'

'If that's your choice.'

*

When Bloom returned to the coffee shop, there was no sign of either Jameson or Harry. She checked the car park and, sure enough, the hire car had left. She took out her phone. No messages. His childish petulance irritated her even though she could see why he was offended. If he'd just kept a lid on his anger long enough for them to draw out the information, it might all have been worth it. Or was Jameson right? Should she have warned him? Would he have been willing to play the part for the right cause?

Bloom contemplated catching a train back to London but knew she had to face the consequences of her actions so she headed for the taxi rank.

It was unclear how much Seraphine really knew about Harry's kidnappers. Clearly she wanted them to think this migrant girl was key, and with the girl's name and photograph Bloom felt sure they could find her. If Lucas couldn't locate her on social media, then Jameson's contacts in MI6 would be able to. But Bloom also knew that Seraphine was not to be trusted; this could all be a ruse. Alina Maree could be nothing but a dead end.

A more tangible lead was the sub-lieutenant Jameson had identified at the ball. Not only did his attendance and subsequent disappearance raise questions, the fact Harry thought he might have been dressed wrongly and therefore might not have been a naval officer at all was worth investigating. Then there was Jameson's point about the shooting. Different motivations. Different weapons. So possibly different groups. One trying to kill him. Another trying to keep him alive.

This was the real key. It was the same with every mysterious death or disappearance, every crime for that matter. If you understand what someone gains, you can work it all out. Over the years she had learned that if you can think like them, no matter how flawed or unusual their thinking might be, you will finally get to the truth of what they did and why.

She paid the taxi driver and walked the last quarter of a mile to the house. The hire car was not in its usual spot on the street. Was he so furious with her that he would continue to put Harry at risk by not bringing him back here? She knocked on the door anyway, hoping he may have dropped Harry here and nipped out for supplies.

On her third knock the door opened and to her surprise Jameson answered. He was on the phone and walked away, leaving her to follow. He continued through the empty living area towards his bedroom. She heard him say, 'Fine, just do what you can,' before the bedroom door clicked shut.

Bloom filled a tumbler with water and sat at the kitchen table. She retrieved her iPad from her bag with the intention of updating her case notes and then spotted a small square of paper underneath an empty glass. The paper had been ripped from a notepad at a jagged angle and something was written on it. She removed the glass and read it.

Bloom opened Jameson's bedroom door without knocking. He stood talking on the phone, his expression worried.

'You've seen this then?' she said holding up the torn piece of paper. 'Were you planning to tell me?'

'One sec,' he said to the person on the phone and covered the microphone with his hand. 'Karene and Harry's kids are missing. They never made it to Caroline's.'

Bloom checked her watch. 'They should have been there an hour ago.'

Jameson nodded once. 'Karene didn't want someone travelling with them, but I sent my guy as a precaution. But he lost them. They've done a runner and no one's seen them since.'

'They're not the only ones.' She turned the paper around in her hand so Jameson could read what Harry had written.

Too many secrets

'And the car's gone,' she said.

'Vic, I'll call you back.' He hung up. 'How long did we leave him with her?'

'Seraphine? Not long at all.'

'Not long is all she needs.'

64

Harry drove the car to the Southampton airport long-stay car park as instructed and found a spot near the shuttle bus stop. He'd told Seraphine that he didn't have his passport but she'd said not to worry, that it wouldn't be a problem. He took the bus to the airport terminal and then followed her directions back past the multi-storey car park and on to Tinker Alley where he found the entrance to Control Post 11. Seraphine greeted him as she handed over a stack of papers to the security officer. The stack seemed to include two British passports which the man checked and then handed back to Seraphine.

'You made the right choice,' she said to him as the security officer led them through the building and out to a private jet.

Harry desperately hoped she was right. For the sake of his children he had to find out who had done this to him and try to stop any further attacks.

Once onboard, Seraphine spoke briefly to the pilot as Harry walked along the length of the cabin. It was a Dassault Falcon 900B. Harry had never flown one but he knew the French-built jet had a range of over 4,000 nautical miles and an impressive flight ceiling of 51,000 feet. The interior was a muted palette of creams, greys and highly polished wood. It had eight large leather seats that looked to swivel on their base and, at the rear, two leather sofas that faced each other. Beyond that was a well-stocked galley area and spacious toilet.

Harry elected to sit on the right-side front seat ahead of the wing so that he had a good view out of the window. Seraphine took the same seat across the aisle. She wore blue trousers, a white vest top and a fitted white jacket.

'How did you get my passport?'

'I broke into your home, riffled through your things and stole it.'

'You——?' Harry was distracted for a moment as he realized that he had no recollection of where his home was, what it looked like or where he kept his passport.

'That was a joke, Harry. I've not been in your home.'

'So how?'

Seraphine shrugged. 'Not your concern.'

'And where we are going, is that my concern?' They both fastened their seatbelt as the plane pushed back and began to taxi along to the runway.

'We're going to see a man about a girl.'

'Alina Maree?'

'Indeed.'

'Who is she?'

Seraphine studied him for a long moment. 'You really have no idea?'

'None whatsoever.'

She leaned back against the headrest and closed her eyes as the plane accelerated. 'Good. That will be helpful.'

65

George Selaisse called his boss. 'Peterson is at the airport. It looks like he's taking a private charter.'

'Good,' said Bello. 'He's coming to me. Let him come.'

'Does he have his memory back?' asked Selaisse.

'I don't know. A friend said they'd make him come and it seems they've done just that.'

Selaisse knew better than to question his boss any further. 'We have his children and the girlfriend. What do you want us to do with them?'

'Keep them for now. I may need them as insurance.'

Selaisse hung up and made a second call as he walked back to the long-stay to retrieve his car. 'How are they?' he said when his associate answered.

'The young girl is upset but the other two are calm. They're refusing to eat or drink.'

Wise, thought Selaisse. He had researched the investigators helping Captain Peterson's girlfriend and could find no information at all about the man. His digital footprint was light to the point of invisible which could only mean one thing: he was in the business. And if that was the case, he would have advised his clients to avoid food or drink in case it had been laced with something. 'I'll be there in twenty minutes,' he said.

As he drove away, Selaisse smiled at the idea of Peterson's investigators and the police desperately searching St Albans. Little did they know their efforts were futile. The trio was long gone and would remain so until Selaisse decided otherwise.

66

'What next?' asked Bloom. 'What do we do?'

Jameson was still trying to ring Karene but Bloom heard the phone go to voicemail for the second time.

'Caroline Peterson's called the police and she and her fella are out looking right now. As is my guy.'

Bloom typed out a text message to Karene asking her to call as soon as possible. 'If someone has them, who are we looking at? The people who want Harry alive or those who want him dead?'

'Either.'

'Who are they?'

'Like we said before, it could be people smugglers involved in the girl's migration. It could be some other group that she or Harry have crossed and are running from. It could be part of the British military trying to protect or silence Harry, a team of guns for hire employed to do the same, or a combination of any of the above. We still haven't found answers to the most important questions!'

'And in your experience, if any of those were to kidnap Karene and the children, what would be their motive?'

'Easy. Insurance. A bargaining tool.'

'Not to protect them?'

'Without informing the mother?'

'Fair point. That's something. They've been taken as a bargaining tool. Presumably to keep him from talking. Where would you take them?'

Jameson raised his arms to the ceiling. 'Somewhere like this.'

'A safe house?'

'A deserted building, a remote farmhouse.'

'And that could be anywhere in the country?'

'Or outside of it. The trick is to get as far from the point of origin as you can.'

'They won't have their passports.'

'We're likely dealing with people smugglers.'

'They could be locked in the back of a van parked on a ferry?'

Jameson thought for a moment. 'There's only one thing we know for sure.'

'And that is?'

'They won't be anywhere near St Albans.' Jameson looked thoughtful as he leaned against the bedroom window. 'You know the porter at Stanford Hall who'd been there the whole time?'

'Freddie?'

'What if he was there to protect Harry?'

'Wasn't he the one Harry said tried to shoot him in the head?'

'While he was being held by the other porter.'

'You think Freddie was aiming at the other porter?'

'Two separate groups. One well funded with all the latest equipment, the other in possession of standard military-issued gear.'

'Wouldn't Rear Admiral Grey have told us if Freddie was protection staff?'

'Not necessarily. Not if he didn't know. The gun was a standard-issue Special Forces firearm.'

Bloom headed back into the kitchen and found her notes from Harry's account of the shooting on her iPad. Jameson followed and she read the notes aloud.

'Harry said that when he sat in the wheelchair he heard the new porter say something in French: "What is this?" or "Who is this?" And Freddie replied in English, "It's not your concern." Harry thought this was one team member clarifying the nature of their task with the other.' She looked up at Jameson.

'But what if the accented guy was asking Freddie the question?' said Jameson. 'Asking him who he was.'

'Because they didn't know each other?'

'That would explain the first guy going for his gun.'

'And when Freddie reaches for his weapon, the first porter used Harry as a shield.'

'But . . . ?' Jameson said in a tone that implied she was missing something.

'The accented porter needed Harry alive.'

'He pushed Harry away because he thought Freddie might shoot them both.'

'That's not a bad hypothesis.' Bloom heard her phone alert. She had a text message. 'And on the upside it means both parties just want control of Harry. Neither of them wants him dead.'

'Yet,' Jameson said with a frown. 'And there's more.'

Bloom held up her hand. The message wasn't from

Karene, but from a blocked number. She read it to Jameson.

Today 21:05

I'm not one to brag, but this is a unique
situation. The blind leading the blind was
never going to work.
Leave it to one who can see.
Harry says Hi.

'I told you,' Jameson said. 'She got to him.'

Bloom replied to the text. The reference to Seraphine's earlier taunt about the blind leading the blind made it clear Jameson was right about who the sender was.

Today 21:07

Harry's children are missing. Is that you?

A couple of minutes later her phone rang. Caroline Peterson sounded livid rather than distressed.

'What are you meddlers doing to find my children? If your friend Karene thinks this is funny, she'll have a shock coming.'

'Nobody thinks this is funny, Caroline. Karene wouldn't go off without telling us. She's not answering my calls or texts so we're as concerned as you.'

'As concerned as me?'

'That was perhaps the wrong—'

'Are you with Harry? Let me speak to him. Does he know? He's not answering his phone.'

'Harry's not here. I'm at the house with Marcus but Harry left on his own a short while ago and he doesn't have his phone. We didn't want people to track him so we took it when he arrived here.'

Caroline was quiet for a moment. 'A short while ago when?'

'Around an hour.'

'Has he gone to meet Karene? They can't leave the country without my permission. I've got custody.'

'I don't think Harry's meeting them.'

Jameson raised his eyebrows.

'Then what is going on? Where are my children? What have Harry and his bit of stuff got them into?'

Bloom did her best to appease Caroline and promised to let her know if they heard anything. Eventually, Caroline hung up and Bloom exhaled.

'That key I found today,' said Jameson. 'That's not normal, you know? Maybe he is meeting them. Maybe we are blind to what's going on. It wouldn't be the first time.'

She was tempted to say, *For you maybe*, but fought the urge. 'Would he really have it on his keyring if he had something to hide?'

'Perhaps. If he didn't remember he was supposed to hide it.'

Bloom considered that. 'Do you still have it?'

'He never asked for it back. And before you ask, I already have someone checking where it's from.'

Bloom's phone beeped. It was a message from Seraphine.

Today 21:15

Do you think me so crass as to endanger children?

263

Bloom knew Seraphine had no qualms whatsoever when it came to harming teenagers. 'I think we have to assume Seraphine is working with whoever wants Harry.'

Jameson folded his arms. 'And now they have him and the children.'

67

The views and their travel time made him think they were likely somewhere in sub-Saharan Africa. Seraphine was giving nothing away. The woman was an expert at dodging questions and he had grown bored of her verbal games. His head hurt and he wondered if that was just the cabin pressure and air-conditioning or something more sinister.

'Just tell me who Alina Maree is and how I know her,' he said after a long spell of silence.

'It's better you don't know.'

'How is it better? She's the reason all of this has happened to me.'

'Augusta only thinks that because I told her so.'

'So Alina isn't the reason?'

'I didn't say that.'

'Look, Seraphine. You asked me to choose and I did because you said you had answers, so cut the crap and tell me what you know. I'm sick of being in the dark.'

'Being in the dark is the best place to be for this trip.'

'Says who?'

Seraphine swivelled to face him. 'The man I'm taking you to see has been looking for Alina Maree for a long time, and a few months ago he got a big break in his search when your cousin posted a picture on Facebook.'

Harry felt a tightening in his chest. 'You're taking me to the man who murdered Julian?'

'Technically the man who had him murdered.'

'And you think Julian led them to me?'

'I know he did.'

'How? How do you know this?'

Seraphine took a sip of water. 'I have friends in high places, or . . . more accurately, I put my friends in high places.'

'You have a friend in this man's circle?'

'In his organization, yes.'

'And what is his organization?'

'A religious-based freedom movement fighting for the liberation of their people.'

Harry had been in the military long enough to decipher the terminology. 'This guy is a warlord?'

'No, no, not at all.'

Harry felt genuine relief. He had worked for a commander who had been to Sierra Leone and seen the work of Foday Sankoh and his Liberian ally, Charles Taylor, first hand: the child soldiers drugged to their eyeballs, the brutal murders and limb amputations of anyone who dared to resist or question. He had no desire to meet one of those animals.

'But his uncle is,' said Seraphine.

Harry closed his eyes tightly and concentrated on his breathing. He'd always had good control of his emotions, finding it easy enough to manage his fear even in the face of danger. Which is exactly what he was facing now. Had he made the wrong call? Chosen the wrong team? Seraphine had answers and was taking him to the very person who had done all of this, but was that really what he wanted? Of course, it wasn't. All he wanted was to retrieve his memory and find out who had done this to him and why. He didn't want to meet the guy.

The red dusty airfield was nestled within lush green trees. A pristine white SUV awaited them and the driver greeted Seraphine with the politeness of a loyal servant. What was this woman up to?

'Welcome, Sir. I am Abdul,' the man said to Harry with a handshake and a head bow. Despite the reverence, Harry didn't miss the coldness in the man's eyes. He guessed this was Seraphine's man on the inside. They got into the car and drove for around an hour, passing only one small town of low-level huts.

Eventually they arrived at a gated property that was completely at odds with its surroundings. Its smart white façade, complete with three curved balconies framed by elaborate black railings and held up by elegant pillars, would have been more at home in the hills of LA or the vineyards of Italy. This group was well funded. Blood diamonds, Harry guessed.

No going back then. He was entirely in the hands of Seraphine and whatever twisted individual lived behind these doors. Harry thought of his children. He desperately wanted to see them again. Another image came to mind, one he wasn't expecting: Karene. His children were obviously very fond of her – that was clear at yesterday's meeting. And her affection for them made him see her in a different light. Maybe she was important to him after all. He hoped he lived long enough to find out.

Stepping out of the car into the bright morning sun, he took a long, deep breath then followed Seraphine and Abdul inside.

68

'Did you sleep?' said Jameson as he came to join Bloom in the kitchen.

'Not much.' She had been up since four thirty a.m. reviewing the case and incessantly checking for messages from Karene or Seraphine.

Late last night, she had called Detective Superintendent Drummond and asked him to put pressure on the Hertfordshire Constabulary to search for Karene and the children in St Albans. Jameson was likely right that they'd been moved, but she didn't want to make any assumptions. In turn, Jameson had called in every favour he could think of with his old contacts in MI6. But they both knew all of these people had other priorities and other focuses.

'So, we've lost all of them thanks to your interfering mini-me,' he said pouring himself a large coffee.

'I think your man Vic is also at fault. But I wondered how long it would take for me to get the blame. Again.'

'Again? What does that mean?'

'Well, it was all my fault last time, wasn't it? I put you in harm's way. I exposed you to Seraphine. But let's face it, Marcus, I never told you to date the woman or to fall in love with her.'

'I didn't fall in love with her.'

'Who are you kidding?'

'Seriously—'

The gate's buzzer stopped Jameson mid-flow. He stood very still. His eyes locked on Bloom's and he mouthed, 'Stay here.' Then he moved quickly into the hall, collecting his gun from the side table. Bloom held her breath. No one was supposed to know where they were. They'd been so careful coming and going, but obviously someone had been watching. It was either the people after Alina Maree or, if Jameson's theory was correct, some kind of special forces unit bent on shutting Harry up. She had no idea which was the preferred option.

She watched Jameson walk past the door and peek through the adjacent blinds to see what he was dealing with. She imagined a team of black-clad soldiers in body armour and radio mics stalking the perimeter of the building. Or a group of motivated kidnappers tooled up with top-of-the-range weaponry. But then, to her surprise, Jameson pushed the gun into the back of his jeans, unlocked the door and went to open the gate.

Caroline Peterson looked a decade older than she had the last time Bloom had seen her. She was accompanied by a tall man with curly blond hair and glasses. Caroline introduced him as her partner, Robin, but before Bloom and Jameson could say hello, Caroline was on the attack.

'Why the hell has she brought them here? Of all places. I swear to God, I'll bloody kill her. She has no right taking them anywhere without my permission. Where are they, then?'

'They're not here,' said Bloom glancing at Jameson who then shrugged. 'Why would you think that?'

'Oh, you think you're so bloody clever, don't you? Sticking together and pushing me out but I'm not having it. They're my children and I want to see them right now. Sophie? Jake?' She began walking towards the bedroom area.

'Take a look around. They're not here,' said Jameson.

'Why would you think they're here?' asked Bloom again.

'Because I track their phones and my phone tells me that they're here, so you can't hide them from me.' She walked through the rooms followed by Robin, who Bloom suspected was no match for his formidable girlfriend.

'Why would their phones say they were here? They've never even been here,' said Jameson.

Bloom shook her head.

Caroline and her shadow stalked back into the living area. 'Tell me where they are right now or I'm calling the police.'

'Show us where your phone says they are,' said Jameson.

'It. Says. They're. Here.'

'It doesn't make sense,' Bloom said to Jameson.

'You're really going to pretend someone has taken them rather than tell their own mother where my idiot ex and his witch have stolen them to. Who the hell do you think you are?'

'Jake has a smartwatch,' said Robin. Everyone looked at him and he shuffled his feet a little. 'You only have Jake's watch tracked to here. Sophie's phone is switched off or out of range,' he said to Caroline.

'Could Harry have brought the watch back here?' Bloom said to Jameson.

'Or . . . Can I see the tracking app?' he said to Caroline. When she looked reluctant, he said, 'It may be that whoever has them missed the watch. Jake was wearing a long-sleeved hoodie. If he's bright, he'll have kept it hidden.'

Caroline frowned but took her phone from her coat pocket, typed in the access code and opened the app. She handed it to Jameson. He studied the image and then took out his own phone and laid them side by side on the kitchen table. 'Your tracking app shows them to be on this street, but if we take a closer look at where we are on my phone . . .' He typed in the postcode for their location and then zoomed in and converted the image to satellite. 'We are here, just past the school.' He showed everyone then converted back to the map and zoomed out. On Caroline's phone he then zoomed in to the exact location flag for Jake's smartwatch.

'That's further away from the school,' said Bloom.

'Oh, come on. It's on this street. Where else would they be on this street?' said Caroline.

Jameson spoke to Bloom. 'Well they're not here, so I guess somewhere very near. Walking distance.'

'You think someone took them from St Albans and brought them here?' said Bloom.

'Too crazy?' he said.

'Yes,' said Caroline, her patience clearly at its limit.

Bloom thought about it. 'But if Seraphine's involved, then nothing's too crazy.'

'Let's go then,' said Jameson.

69

The interior was overly elaborate, with marble columns, crystal chandeliers and a sweeping staircase. Harry followed Seraphine and Abdul into a room at the rear of the building. Despite the high-backed chairs, no one made a move to sit down and instead the three of them hovered on the thick red and gold rug. According to Seraphine, they were about to meet Antony Bello. His uncle, Jacob Bello, was the founder of God's Liberation Army, a group known to operate in the Central African Republic and the Sudan. Antony was the obvious successor.

Bello arrived wearing crumpled khaki shorts and a faded T-shirt with bare feet. He looked more like a member of staff than the owner of the house. His dark eyes matched his skin and he had a roughly trimmed beard and moustache.

'Sir,' said Abdul. 'Please may I introduce Captain Peterson and Miss Seraphine Walker.'

'You have done well, Abdul.' Bello turned to Seraphine. 'And you have brought him to me. You will be rewarded.'

Harry recognized the accent. It reminded him of the porter with the wheelchair.

'Captain Peterson?' Bello looked at him. 'Do you know why you are here?'

'You believe that I have information. But I don't.'

'Good.' Bello's smile was broad, eager. Harry could sense that there was something strange about him, that he was fanatical and maybe even insane. He approached Harry and stood too close with his hands held behind his back. 'Tell me what you do not know.'

'I don't know where the girl is.'

'Which girl?'

Harry looked at Seraphine and Abdul who looked back without expression. 'Alina Maree?' Harry said tentatively.

'She is alive, yes? And her mother?'

Harry shook his head. 'I have no idea. I have no memory of anything from the past four years.'

'But you know her name?'

'Because Seraphine told me, not because I remember it.'

Bello didn't look at Seraphine. 'Your cousin, Mr Julian Peterson, disagreed.'

'People who are tortured will say anything to make it stop.'

'Maybe so, but your involvement makes sense, yes? Naomi took Alina to the coast for a boat. Your cousin said you were on the ships taking people from the water.'

Harry said nothing. He couldn't disagree. Bloom had told him as much and he didn't question her research, but he still had no recollection of it.

'You will tell me if Naomi is alive and where she and Alina are.'

'How do you expect me to do that? You've wiped my memory.'

'What are you talking about? You are not a computer. Your memory can't be wiped.'

'You did this to me.' Harry placed his hand over the side of his still bandaged head. 'I had surgery.'

'You had a bump on the head and now you expect me to believe that you cannot remember? This is convenient.'

'I did have surgery and I don't remember.'

'This is no good to me.' Bello's eyes widened, more crazed than before. 'These lies are no use. We will make you remember.'

'It won't help. I have no recollections from the last four years of my life.' Harry knew that his protests were in vain. Karene had told him about Julian's injuries; this wasn't a man who took 'no' for an answer.

'We will see. Because I have your children. So if you do not remember then neither will they . . .'

Harry saw a look pass between Seraphine and Abdul. It was the first reaction they'd had to anything which told him that this was news to them too. Was it a bluff? Harry decided that it must be, mainly because the alternative was just too painful to contemplate.

70

'We can't just walk up there and confront these people, Marcus. They're dangerous.'

'Who said anything about confronting them? I'll take a look, see what we're dealing with and then we'll go from there.' Jameson had changed into his running gear, complete with cap, headphones and sunglasses. 'I'll get Vic and some others down here first.'

'Please, Marcus. This is crazy,' said Bloom. 'Let the police check it out.'

Caroline had insisted that they should call 999 and report that her children were in danger near this location, but Jameson had argued that as soon as the kidnappers heard sirens they'd disappear. They would search Karene and the children, find the watch on Jake and then they'd be impossible to find.

'Augusta, trust me. This is what I used to do. I'll be twenty minutes tops. If I'm longer than thirty minutes you can call the police.'

'Be careful.'

Jameson placed his earphones in. 'Careful now, you're starting to sound like you really do care.'

'You know that I do,' she said quietly.

He opened the door and stepped outside. 'Whatever happens,' he said, 'don't come after me without the police.'

Bloom stood at the front door and watched him jog along the pavement and away from her. Her every instinct said that she should not have let him do this.

She turned to Caroline and Robin, both of whom had their arms folded and matching scowls on their faces. Maybe they were well suited after all.

'I need to make a call,' she said. She set her phone timer for twenty minutes and walked to one of the bedrooms. Harry's clothes were stacked on the chair with military neatness. She dialled Seraphine's number. After a short delay, she heard the long beeps that indicated an overseas call. There was no answer and no voicemail. She hung up and sent a text message.

Today 08:16

Call me ASAP.
Marcus in danger.

Her next call was to Detective Superintendent Drummond. 'Matthew, it's Augusta Bloom again. There's been a development.' She explained about Jake Peterson's smartwatch and how they'd tracked it to a house nearby.

'Is the father involved then?' Drummond asked.

'I don't think so,' replied Bloom. It was a good question though. She had assumed that Seraphine was behind the kidnapping. In fact, she was starting to wonder if Seraphine was behind this whole damn thing again. It wasn't impossible. But the other unknown was Harry. They'd no idea what he'd done. And they only had his word that he'd forgotten. He'd been living here for almost a week and now his son and potentially his daughter and girlfriend were hidden down the road. That was too much of a coincidence to ignore. 'But it's worth considering,' she said.

'I'll leave the search going in St Albans just in case and contact the folks nearest to you. Can you give me the postcode?'

Bloom hesitated. Jameson wouldn't thank her for revealing the location of his safe house.

'Dr Bloom?'

'Sorry, yes. It's Southampton. I'm not sure of the exact location.'

'Find out the postcode or the road name,' he said. 'I'll contact the local police and tip them off to potential terrorist activity in the area.'

Bloom wanted to challenge his description of terrorist activity – things had moved on – but she knew it would achieve a prompt response, so she simply thanked him and hung up. She checked the timer. Eight minutes gone.

'I've contacted the police and put them on standby,' she said as she rejoined Caroline and her partner.

'What now?' said Caroline.

Bloom watched the front door. 'We wait.'

71

Bello had left. He'd gone somewhere to find something and offered ominously few details. Harry was pacing the red and gold carpet. 'What the hell is going on?' he hissed at Seraphine. 'Does this guy really have my kids?'

'I'll find out,' said Abdul. 'I'll be back shortly.' He headed towards the front door.

'Can we get out of here?' Harry whispered.

'We've only just arrived,' replied Seraphine. She was moving slowly around the room examining the pictures and ornaments.

'You heard the man. He's going to torture me for information I can't give him.'

'I think leaving now would be premature.'

Harry stopped. 'Why? What are you getting out of this? Why did Jameson call you "the devil"? Are you working with this lunatic?'

'Antony Bello is somewhat . . . too emotional for my tastes.'

'What if he has my kids?'

Seraphine sighed. 'Such sentiment will be your downfall.'

Maybe it was her sense of calm or the slight hint of humour in her tone, or maybe it was the heat, or the headache, or the fear, but Harry couldn't contain his rage any longer. 'I've had enough of this,' he said, his voice rising with each word. 'Of not knowing. Of being attacked. Of being blamed for things I have absolutely no knowledge of. I have nothing to give this man and he can take everything from me. *Everything*. Are you just going to stand there and mock me or are you going to help?'

Seraphine examined her perfectly manicured fingernails. 'Why do you think I brought you here, Harry?'

'To feed me to the lions?' Harry paced again. 'I should have listened to my gut. I should have listened to Jameson.'

'You did listen to your gut. You chose me because something told you I was the best bet. Now, why do you think I brought you here?'

'I have no idea. What I want to know is how you're going to help me.'

'That depends.'

'On what?'

Seraphine tilted her head to one side and lowered her voice to a whisper. 'On what's in it for me?'

72

Today 08.39

Coldeast Mansion. Coldeast Road.
Marcus needs you.
Go now. Alone.

Today 08.39

I mean it, Augusta, ALONE.

Bloom stared at Seraphine's text. Jameson had left the house twenty-four minutes earlier. He'd said he'd be back in twenty minutes, that she should call the police if he wasn't back in thirty, and not to follow him alone.

Caroline Peterson was on the telephone discussing an operation scheduled for later that day, presumably trying to get out of it. Her partner Robin was in Harry's bedroom on his phone, presumably doing the same.

Bloom watched Caroline with a new-found sense of respect. She had disliked the woman initially, but could see now that she cared for her children above all else. Caroline looked up and Bloom held her phone up and then stepped outside as if to make a call. She pulled the door closed behind her and took a deep breath. She had checked the location of Coldeast Mansion. It seemed to be exactly where Jake's smartwatch was: a quarter of a mile down the road. She stood and waited, willing

Jameson to appear jogging towards her with his headphones on, fit and well and safe.

Last time Seraphine had led them both into danger, Bloom had a team of police officers behind her, listening and ready to ensure their safety. But there was no insurance now and they had no idea what kind of people they were up against. She found Detective Superintendent Drummond's number on her phone and held her finger above the call button. But she couldn't do it. She put her phone in her pocket. Seraphine might be a law unto herself, but Bloom knew she was obsessed with Jameson. She wouldn't let anyone harm him.

The leafy, residential road was lined with large detached properties and clusters of smaller low-level dwellings. Bloom passed the deserted school and continued onwards, checking the location on the map on her phone. The entrance to Coldeast Mansion was framed by stone pillars and the building itself sat at the end of a path in a patch of tired lawn. It had probably been an impressive building in its day, but as Bloom approached she could see that it had been neglected in recent years. A few cars were parked out front, and on either side of the large stone porch stood a tree with foliage shaped into a ball and a ribbon-wrapped trunk. She had a look on Google: apparently it was a combination of rentable flats and rooms to hire for parties and weddings.

Her feet crunched on the gravel driveway. She couldn't see anyone outside and all the windows looking out on to the front had open curtains and dark interiors.

A few yards from the entrance she stopped. The large

wooden doors were open and the room behind was dark and shadowed. She sent a text to Seraphine.

Today 08.52

I'm here. Alone
What now?

Bloom waited a few moments and then, when there was no reply, began to walk the perimeter of the house. Is this what Jameson had done? She pictured him ahead of her, possibly still jogging, trying to make his presence as innocent as possible. And then what? Where was he now? Had he found Karene and the children or had someone found him?

Her phone began to ring. It was Caroline. Bloom didn't answer.

The rear of the house was plain with sun-scorched grass and occasional scatterings of confetti. There were floor-to-ceiling windows and, inside, stacks of chairs around wooden tables. On the back wall, there was a makeshift bar with a sign above it that said 'Rufus and Olivia' in an over-fussy font. On the far side of the building, a low annexe jutted out. She could see abandoned stepladders, dust sheets and paint pots surrounding it.

As she rounded the final corner back towards the car park, a man's voice made her jump.

'Dr Bloom?' He stood in front of a smaller side entrance, filling the space with his large frame. 'I've been expecting you.' His expression was welcoming and almost warm but his eyes looked wary. Bloom wondered how Seraphine might have introduced her to these people.

'And you are?' She walked purposefully towards him ensuring her shoulders were square and her back straight.

'You can call me George,' he said as he punched a six-digit code into the security lock on his left and pushed the door wide, holding it so that she could pass. She almost hesitated before entering, but she forced herself to stay strong, to be confident. The only way to help Jameson, Karene and the children was to know who they were dealing with. And this was the only way.

The interior was much smarter than the tired exterior. The corridor was carpeted in cream and the walls were newly painted.

'Telephone.' George held out his palm and Bloom gave him her phone. When he turned and walked away she noticed a gun bulging beneath the back of his shirt. Bloom suppressed her panic and followed him up the wide stairway to the first floor.

'Did you come alone as instructed?' he asked.

'I did.'

George unlocked an apartment door on the rear side of the building and gestured for her to go in. She entered a short hallway with a slim desk along one wall. The surface of the desk was clear apart from a laminated sheet of information about the building. Bloom walked along the hall and at the end, in the room to the left, she found exactly what she was looking for. Karene, Sophie and Jake were sitting side by side on a two-seater sofa. She had been right to come here. She had found them and they were unharmed. She felt a little euphoric. They were staring straight ahead with their hands on their knees. She stepped into the room, trying to catch their attention, wanting them to see her and share her relief. But then she saw what they were looking at.

In the doorway to the kitchen stood a second man dressed in a khaki shirt and combat trousers and holding the biggest gun Bloom had ever seen.

Once more she pushed her panic aside, scanned the kitchen and tried to keep her voice level. 'Where's Jameson?' she asked.

George pushed her further into the room and Karene finally glanced up.

'Oh my God, Augusta,' she said and started to stand up until the man with the machine gun shouted at her to sit back down. She did as she was told, her eyes a mixture of desperation and hope.

George pulled a chair from beneath the table and placed it next to the sofa beside Sophie. He pointed to it. 'Sit,' he said, and so she did.

'Where's Marcus?' she said again.

Karene shook her head. 'We haven't seen him.'

Bloom looked at George. 'What have you done with him? Where is he?' Her heart rate rose as the panic she had been trying to suppress began to take hold.

Jameson ran as fast as he could. He was a cyclist not a runner and, although he was fit, he could feel the lactic acid burning in his muscles. Keep low. Keep moving. It was a good motto for life as well as this specific moment.

Did he have time to call Bloom? It must be nearing the thirty-minute mark now.

How had he let himself get involved in this? Terrorist bombs, mind-altering surgery, torture, kidnap. This was not what he'd expected when he'd signed up to work with Bloom five years earlier. He'd imagined uplifting cases in which they'd provide desperately needed answers to long-standing mysteries. And it had started that way. Their early cases were husbands, wives, daughters, sons, all missing without a trace. He and Bloom had interrogated their lives, their characters, their motives and hunted them down, dead or alive. True, the impact of the resolutions was often mixed – sometimes they brought joy and sometimes despair – but they'd never been the ones in harm's way before. Not until Seraphine.

At the gate, he checked that no one was around and then quickly entered.

Caroline looked up from the kitchen table. Robin sat

beside her working on his laptop. 'Did you find them?' She placed a hand on Robin's arm. He also looked up and placed his own hand over hers.

'Where's Augusta?' Jameson said.

'She left.'

'What do you mean?'

'She went out to make a call and when I checked there was no sign of her. I called her but she didn't pick up.'

Jameson checked his watch. He had left twenty-nine minutes ago so she had no reason to panic yet, and it wasn't like Bloom to jump the gun. 'Why did she go outside to make a call?' He had told them to stay out of sight.

'I don't know,' said Caroline, exasperated. 'Did you find my children?'

Jameson shook his head. 'No sign of them or anyone else for that matter.'

'Is it a house?' said Robin.

'An old stately home converted into apartments. The door had a keypad.'

'So you just gave up and came back?'

'I couldn't wade in there like this.' He gestured towards his running gear. 'I need back-up. When did Augusta go out?'

'Five minutes ago.'

'Call her again. Tell her to get back here.' He'd returned via a different route, looping around the local roads and approaching the house from the south instead. Had she walked north to look for him? What the hell was she thinking?

'Why don't you call her?' said Caroline. Her eyes blazed with anger and her tone was abrupt.

Jameson dialled the number for Harry's boss. 'Because I'm calling someone who I hope can help us get your children back.'

74

Harry accompanied Abdul and Seraphine across the manicured lawn towards a simple wooden outbuilding. Abdul had confirmed that Harry's children and Karene were with Bello's team in the UK and so he had no choice but to comply.

'Dr Bloom is with the others as you requested,' Abdul said reading a message aloud from his phone.

'Well that was easier than I expected,' Seraphine said. 'Where's the fun in that?'

'Who is this Dr Bloom?' said Abdul.

'An investigator. She keeps poking her nose in so it's best that we keep her in check.'

'What's happened to Augusta?' said Harry. 'Is she with Sophie and Jake?'

'Never you mind, my handsome little naval officer.'

'How did you know this woman would be so close?' said Abdul.

'The location I offered to you wasn't selected at random.'

'You deliberately placed our team near her?'

'I like to know where my friends are at all times. It's something of a hobby.'

'You spy on them?' asked Harry.

'I would call it taking a keen interest.'

'So you can help them or hinder them?' said Harry as they reached the door to the outbuilding.

Seraphine looked at Harry and smiled. 'You don't miss much, do you, Captain?'

'Not usually, no.' He looked past her and into the building. 'For instance, I can see pretty clearly that this place is . . . sparse.'

'The significance being?'

Harry let out a long breath. 'Easy clean.'

'In you go then . . . Sir,' said Abdul.

Harry did as instructed.

75

The man in the kitchen was clearly a foot soldier tasked with guarding their little group. He was very young – maybe in his late teens.

Bloom checked that everyone was OK. Sophie had been crying, but they weren't hurt, just afraid.

'Who is this Marcus?' George leaned against the arm-rest of a black leather chair. The apartment was fully furnished. Bloom could only assume this man had rented it.

'He's my partner. He's disappeared.' She didn't want to reveal that Caroline had given them this location. She felt more and more sure that they'd missed him. Perhaps he'd checked it out and returned to the safe house, not bothering to come inside. 'Seraphine was helping me find him.' She knew now that she'd been naive: Seraphine never did anything for anyone. The woman had spotted an opportunity to take revenge. Bloom had to admire her ruthless efficiency. 'Do you know Seraphine?'

George frowned. The foot soldier didn't react.

'What do you hope to achieve by bringing them here?' she said, tilting her head towards Karene and the others. She may as well find out what was going on. 'You know the British military don't take kindly to attacks on their own. They can be swift to retaliate.'

George looked amused.

'What do you need him for?' continued Bloom. 'Captain Peterson? What do you need him to do?'

When George didn't answer, she said, 'Why won't you tell me? I take it none of us are going to walk away from this.' She felt Sophie shift in the seat beside her and Bloom placed a hand on the girl's arm and gave it a squeeze. 'He's clearly important. Or you wouldn't have set off that bomb.'

A flicker of something darted across George's face.

'That was you, was it?' said Bloom. 'It was clever, I'll give you that. If it hadn't been for Karene here, I don't think anyone would have suspected anything. Were you the one to find the young man, the bomber?'

The smallest of smiles reached the left corner of George's mouth.

'I expect the promise of eternal life from a man as charismatic as you would be hard to resist for some.'

'Do you always talk this much?' said George.

'Not at all. Feel free to chip in.' Bloom watched the foot soldier as he watched his boss.

George's phone rang and he answered, listened for a moment and then handed it to Bloom. 'For you,' he said.

Surprised, she held it to her ear. 'Hello?'

'Augusta.' Seraphine's voice was light-hearted and merry. 'How are you?'

'You know how I am. Is this your petty revenge?'

'Revenge for what? Oh . . . you mean the court case? And the charges? And the career in tatters? No. Of course not. I simply know how much you hate a mystery.

So I thought I'd help you . . . again. Put you in a room with some answers. Although I'm feeding you lots of information, so you can't really take credit for this one, you know?'

'And where is Marcus?' asked Bloom.

'I have no idea.'

Bloom didn't say anything. Seraphine had played her. What was there to say?

'Is Mr Selaisse terribly macho?'

Bloom looked at George. 'I'd say so, yes.'

'A bit of a genius by all accounts. It's a shame he's not one of us.'

Bloom bit her tongue. This was not the time to challenge Seraphine.

'I'll leave you to get acquainted.'

'You're too kind.'

'Is that sarcasm? I'm never sure. You know we psychopaths aren't good at spotting sarcasm. But's that why you used it, isn't it? To prove you're not like me? Well, we'll see. Bathroom cabinet. Fake panel at the bottom. Good luck. I do hope we get the chance to work together again.'

Bloom began to hand the phone back when she heard Seraphine say, 'Augusta?'

'Yes?'

'How will Marcus resist me without you there to protect him?'

Bloom cut the call to the sound of Seraphine's laughter.

76

Jameson arrived at the agreed rendezvous point, in the car park outside the local school. A blacked-out Range Rover pulled up behind him. He climbed into the rear and found four Royal Marine SBS officers inside. The Special Boat Service was the naval equivalent of the SAS. These guys did not mess about. Marines were some of the toughest and the SBS were the elite of the elite. He wasn't entirely surprised that Grey had sent these guys: the Navy pulled no punches when it came to looking after their own.

'Morning, gents,' he said closing the door. 'The target building is a quarter of a mile up this road.'

'Roger that,' said the driver, pulling away.

'Who do you think is in there with the family?' said the officer in the front passenger seat.

'That I can't tell you. All I know is that the son is wearing a smartwatch and the mother tracked it to this location. I had a look earlier. There's one entrance with a keypad on the door. I rang the building owner who said there are thirty-seven serviced apartments in total but only four are occupied at the moment, and only one of those by people who arrived in the last twenty-four hours.'

'They just told you that?'

'I can be quite convincing.'

'So I hear. And where is Captain Peterson currently?'

'I can't say.'

'Can't or won't?'

'Actually can't. What's your interest in his location?'

A look passed between the officer and one of his team.

'What was that? That look? What do you boys know? There was a porter that died at Stanford Hall. I think he was there to protect Peterson. Was he one of yours?'

'I can't say,' said the officer in the front seat.

Jameson watched the driver turn left and drive between the stone pillars of the mansion gateway. 'Can't or won't?'

He didn't expect a reply and he didn't get one. But, for Jameson, that was answer enough.

77

George Selaisse stood to answer his phone again.

'Sir?' he said, walking into the hallway and then out of the apartment and into the corridor.

'I need to use the bathroom,' Bloom said.

The foot soldier thought for a moment then gestured with his gun towards the bedroom. She moved slowly and he followed her, pausing in the doorway between the two rooms.

The bedroom was small but light with a large window to the left and a compact en-suite to the right. There was only one double bed, so they clearly weren't planning to stay very long. Was that a good thing? She wasn't sure.

She closed the bathroom door behind her. There wasn't a lock. She knelt on the floor and wedged her right foot against it. The bathroom cabinet was on the far side of the sink. She reached over but its door opened towards her so that she couldn't see inside. She paused to listen. She couldn't hear any movement. She tiptoed towards the narrow cupboard. It was empty. She pushed on the base plate and it didn't budge. She tried to get her nails down the side and prise it up but there wasn't enough of a gap and her nails were trimmed too short. She had no choice but to give it a whack. She turned the tap on, then flushed the toilet before giving the bottom of the cupboard a bang with her fist. The wood tilted in its frame and she darted a finger under the edge and slowly raised it up.

There was a small rectangular box inside. She lifted it out. It was light, too light for a gun, but she knew before she opened the lid that there was a weapon inside. There were two items: a syringe filled with a clear liquid and a yellow pencil with a small red cap and *4B* printed in gold on the side. Bloom stared at the pencil. Seraphine's original murder weapon. As a young girl she had dispatched the school caretaker who had raped her friend with an exact replica. It was an event of particular significance for Seraphine. The moment she realized she was not normal.

More of Seraphine's games. A fresh new test. How had she put these here? As soon as Bloom thought of the question, she knew the answer. Seraphine knew about Jameson's safe house down the road where they'd been hiding Harry. It was why she had orchestrated the use of this apartment. But how could she know these things? How for that matter was she manipulating these people? She was playing chess with every person she met.

Bloom didn't want to take the items – she'd be playing into Seraphine's hands – but she couldn't throw away their one chance at survival. She removed the syringe and placed it in the pocket of her trousers. Then she replaced the box in its hiding place and repositioned the base plate. She returned to the lounge and sat back in her seat.

There had to be another way.

She met the foot soldier's eyes and smiled. 'I'm Augusta. Do you have a name?'

His brow furrowed and he said nothing.

'Your boss is speaking to *the boss*, I take it?'

His expression confirmed that she was right. He was easy to read. That would be helpful.

'I take it the man who died in the rehabilitation centre was your colleague. Did you know him?'

The young man's eyes focused on her.

'Yes. You did. Well, I'm sorry for your loss.' Maybe she could use this. Convince the young man his colleague had been killed by his own people to keep him quiet. Would that work? Possibly. It was worth a shot. 'You know the police think he was shot with his own gun.'

'Do they?' said Karene. 'I thought they shot each other?'

Bloom ignored her. 'He didn't shoot himself. The shot came from too far away, but the bullet was fired by his own gun. Two shots from one gun. Two dead men. And neither committed suicide. How does that happen, do you think?'

'Someone else fired the gun?' said Karene.

Bloom gave a sympathetic smile to the young soldier. 'What do you think? Might he have done something wrong, or questioned what he was asked to do? Or had he outlived his usefulness?'

The young man glanced at her and then refocused his eyes dead ahead.

'Captain Harry Peterson is a decorated military leader,' she continued. 'He's very highly regarded. The disappearance of his family will not be taken lightly. They'll look for anyone involved and they won't stop.'

The soldier squared his shoulders in defiance. 'We have nothing to fear from your soldiers.'

'You may think that. But the British Forces aren't beyond taking out a whole community if they need to, to retaliate against one of their own being injured.' Bloom felt Karene look her way and hoped she wasn't showing any disbelief or judgement. For this to work, the boy needed to believe her. 'What if your leaders need insurance that no one will find out what they've done to us?'

'I'm a loyal servant.'

'I'm sure you are. But if your colleague was shot by his own gun, maybe your biggest threat doesn't come from us, maybe it comes from those who don't want you to say what you've seen.'

The man's eyes narrowed.

'Do they trust you? Does George? The man he's speaking to? Do you trust them?'

When the young man did not respond, she said, 'It might be in your interest that we live as long as possible. Because once you've dispatched us, that gun you're holding might well be turned against you.'

George came back in the room and the young soldier stood taller.

'What are you doing?' said Karene under her breath.

'Oldest trick in the book. Divide and conquer.'

The foot soldier left the apartment, giving George his gun.

'Get up,' said George. 'All of you. Now. We're leaving.'

78

Jameson hung back and let the experts do their thing. The leader approached the caretaker, an elderly man, who was carrying rubbish out to the bins. His eyes widened when he saw the four officers climb down from the blacked-out vehicle in boots and helmets and with headsets and, of course, machine guns. He listened and did little more than nod before leading the team to the side entrance to let them in. One officer peeled off and headed to the rear of the building.

'Morning,' said Jameson to the caretaker. The man's shock had already morphed into excitement. No doubt he'd be dining out on this story for a while.

The men ahead moved stealthily up the stairs and along the corridor to the apartment. The building's owner hadn't been able to offer anything that hinted at who these people might be. She'd said that her apartments were booked online, keys left in envelopes on the desk in the entrance hall, and the side door's access code texted in advance. People could anonymously come and go, she'd said. She rarely saw them.

The team leader gestured for the caretaker who'd accompanied them inside to knock on the door. When there was no answer, he knocked again.

'Caretaker,' said the old man. 'I'm coming in.' He took out a set of keys and held one up to the lock.

The SBS leader placed a hand on the man's arm and shook his head. He took the key and gestured for the elderly man to leave. Once the caretaker had safely passed through the internal door, the team leader tried the door handle. It was locked. He inserted the key and turned it. He pushed the door open and, with their guns raised, the three men rushed inside.

'Armed officer,' shouted the team leader. 'Drop your weapons.'

Jameson stood further along the corridor, outside the next apartment. He didn't want any stray bullets coming his way through the walls.

He heard a different voice.

'Clear.'

And then the team leader walked back out.

'Empty. People have been here but no one's here now.'

'Shit,' said Jameson. He took out his phone and called Caroline. 'Where's the smartwatch now?' he said.

'Why? What's happened?'

'They're not here.'

The line fell silent for a moment. 'It's gone. There's nothing there.'

'I'll find them,' he said, and prayed that he could. 'The smartwatch isn't active,' he said when he'd hung up. 'Either it's out of charge or they found it.'

'Which would explain why they moved.'

Bloom's phone was off. Karene's phone was off. Jake's smartwatch was off.

What now?

79

They were sitting on the floor of a standard transit with a bare metal interior. Bloom hadn't seen the van on her walk around the mansion so they must have hidden it somewhere nearby, probably within the adjacent housing estate.

'Where are we?' asked Karene. 'How did you find us?'

Bloom kept her voice low. There was a partition between them and the front seats but she didn't expect it was particularly soundproof. 'We're down the road from the safe house. Near Fareham Community Hospital.'

'How did you know where we were? Where's Harry?'

Bloom pointed at Jake's wrist. 'That was clever. Well done.'

The boy pulled the sleeve of his hoodie further down to cover his watch.

Bloom leaned close to him and whispered into his ear. 'Can you text on it?' She placed a finger over her mouth to warn him to respond as quietly as possible.

He nodded and then pulled his sleeve up to show her the watch, tapping it a few times to no effect.

'Dead?'

He held his palm to the floor and shifted his hand from side to side.

'Low?' she said.

He nodded.

'I didn't know you had that,' whispered Karene.

'Switch it on,' said Bloom.

Jake did as she asked and the image that appeared was that of a standard watch face. She could see now how their captors had missed it.

The van stopped. Bloom could hear George speaking in the front seat, but not what he was saying. The side door slid wide open and George's large frame filled the space. He pointed at Sophie and beckoned for her to come towards him. Bloom sensed this was a man who knew exactly how to manage a situation and that made her nervous. Sophie climbed out and George motioned for the rest of them to follow.

'No talking. No shouting. Nothing stupid,' he said. He placed his handgun against the small of Sophie's back.

They stepped into a little harbour at one end of a car park. Bloom could smell saltwater and the metallic tang of fish. The foot soldier led them towards a smart-looking yacht. It was over ten metres long with a large enclosed cabin surrounded by a wooden deck and topped with an open flybridge housing the wheel. If they got on that, then what? The foot soldier's weapon was packed away in a holdall slung over his shoulder, but she couldn't do anything, not with George's gun at Sophie's back. She suspected that the syringe was filled with Seraphine's drug of choice – ketamine – and it took time for the effects to kick in. An elderly couple were standing by the memorial monument on the jetty, but other than that they were alone. There was a pub on the corner opposite, but it wasn't yet open.

She tried to think of a solution, willed her mind to find the angle. But nothing came.

They reached the boat. Sophie and George climbed on, followed by Karene and Jake.

'Dr Bloom,' said George. 'Would you untie us, please?'

She looked at the thick rope looped over the bollard and then up at the foot soldier already on the flybridge and starting the engine.

'Dr Bloom, I will not ask you twice.'

She didn't have a choice. Once the rope was free, she looped it over her hand, stepped on to the yacht and watched the harbour wall move slowly away.

80

The outbuilding smelt of wood and cleaning fluid. Harry sat as instructed in the black plastic chair with metal legs. Antony Bello leaned against a small desk in the left-hand corner of the room and Seraphine stood beside Abdul to the right of the door. Harry wondered if she would stay and watch.

'You say that you have no memory of Alina or Naomi,' said Bello.

'That's right.'

'Let's see how right that is.' A phone was lying next to him on the desk. He pressed a few buttons and a male voice came through the speaker. 'Put the boy on,' said Bello.

The voice sounded young and scared but it was unmistakable.

'Jake?' Harry began to stand but Bello pointed at him and he lowered himself down again.

'Dad? Dad? Is that you?'

'Where are you, Jake?' Harry met Bello's amused gaze. 'Who are you with?'

'You may begin,' said Bello.

Jake cried out in pain. Harry ran at Bello. He didn't have a plan; he just wanted to hurt the man. Suddenly he was skidding across the floor on his side. The force of Abdul's punch sent him crashing into the chair.

'Sit down or I will make this worse for your son,' said Bello, still absolutely calm.

Harry wiped blood from his mouth. He had bitten his cheek when the punch landed. He righted the chair and sat in it.

'Dad? Dad?'

'It's OK, Jakey,' said Harry. 'Be brave. I'm going to make it stop.' He stared at Bello. 'I can't remember. And hurting my boy won't change that.'

'What do you know?'

'Only what I've been told. I was working on a search and rescue operation in the Mediterranean in 2015. If these women were there, I may have met them.' He shrugged. 'That's it.'

Bello leaned closer to the phone. 'Again.'

Jake's cry was louder this time.

Harry swallowed his bile. He looked at Seraphine who was watching, almost bemused. She wasn't going to help him. He was on his own. 'Please. Don't hurt him. Hurt me. I'm the one you should be hurting.'

'Oh, don't worry, Captain Harry Peterson. I will hurt you too.'

Harry sagged a little in his chair.

'You took Alina to your cousin. I know that much. Then what?'

Harry shrugged. 'I don't know. I told her to start a new life?'

Bello shook his head. 'Your cousin said you came for her, took her home with you.'

'I don't remember that.'

'Why did you take her?'

Harry shook his head.

'What did you do with her mother?'

Harry said nothing.

'You thought you could take them for yourself?'

'No.'

'You thought you could take my women for yourself?'

'I am a happily married man.' Except he wasn't. He was divorced. Maybe Caroline had moved on because he'd had the affair first. Harry couldn't see it, though. He'd never played around and there'd been plenty of opportunity travelling the world and away from home for months at a time.

'Get the girl,' Bello said into the phone.

Sophie pleaded with them, begging them not to do whatever they'd planned, not to hurt her. Harry couldn't catch his breath and as her scream filled the room, he dug his nails into his palm. It echoed in his brain continuing for much, much too long.

'OK. Stop it. Stop. I'll tell you everything.'

81

The cabin of the yacht was comfortable and spacious, not that any of them were in the right frame of mind or position to appreciate that. They were kneeling on the floor, their wrists fastened in front of them with cable ties. The foot soldier was once again in the doorway, gun in hand and eyes ahead.

'You total bastard,' said Karene, when George re-appeared with Sophie.

'Careful, Karene,' said Bloom. They had no idea what would happen next.

Sophie's hands shook as George forced her to kneel again. She had an angry patch of scorched red skin on the palm of her left hand. Jake had said it was from a lighter, his hand held above it, closer and closer until he screamed.

George didn't respond to Karene. He simply walked out with the phone still held to his ear.

Sophie hung her head and sobbed. Her brother leaned against her in a show of support and Karene reached as far as she could with her bound wrists to touch Sophie's arm.

'What did they want?' asked Bloom. 'What were they asking of your dad?'

'I don't know,' said Jake. 'I heard Dad say that he couldn't remember. That's all.'

Bloom was impressed with the young lad. Not only had he had the wherewithal to hide his watch, but he also seemed to be taking this latest experience in his stride.

'Remember? How can they be asking him to remember when they took his memories away?' said Karene.

'I don't think it was them,' said Bloom.

'What do you mean?'

'Jameson thinks there are two groups after Harry. One want him to talk. The other want to shut him up.'

'Well they should all leave him the fuck alone,' said Karene. 'He's a good man. An amazing man.'

Bloom considered that. What did they really know about Harry? He wasn't an ordinary member of the community, working out his days in a safe little job and raising his two point four kids. He was a worldly-wise military officer who had been to war three times. They didn't know what he'd seen, what he knew, how that might have affected him.

'Did any of you ever go with him when he visited his sister?' asked Bloom.

They shook their heads.

'Why do you ask?' said Karene.

'Just interested.'

'I've known you too long to think you ever ask anything without good reason.'

'Just keeping busy,' Bloom replied. 'A distraction.'

Karene was staring at her. 'I don't buy it,' she said. 'It's too random. Why are you asking about his sister?'

'How long had he been visiting her for?' asked Bloom.

Karene glanced at the teenagers and then said, 'As long as I've known him.'

Sophie and Jake shrugged.

'Did he visit her when you were younger or just more recently?' Bloom said.

'You mean, in the last four years?' said Karene to Bloom.

'I dunno,' said Jake.

'He doesn't talk about Lucy,' said Sophie.

'And yet he spends a full day of every month with her. Don't you think that's strange?'

'What are you getting at?' said Karene.

Bloom wasn't sure how this would go down but Karene deserved to know. 'I asked the police to confirm the visits. It was just out of curiosity and I wasn't sure they'd even do it, but when I spoke to the Detective Superintendent earlier he said there was no record of Harry visiting Lucy at all in the past ten years.'

'That must be a mistake,' said Karene.

'The security in these places tends to be pretty water-tight,' said Bloom.

'Maybe he used a different name?' said Karene.

'To visit his own sister? Why would he do that?'

'I don't know. There could be many reasons.'

'Or maybe Harry's not been as honest with you as you think.'

They sped along the residential streets, nearly three times faster than the speed limit. Jameson braced himself against the door frame. Caroline had called as they left the mansion. Jake's watch had reappeared near Warsash Harbour.

'Where's the last known location?' Grey's voice boomed from the Range Rover's speakers.

'In the River Hamble,' said Jameson. 'Heading towards the Solent. They're on a boat.'

Grey had someone in the room with him talking to the Port Authority. No boats had been logged for departure within the last hour, but that didn't surprise Jameson. These weren't the kind of people who followed the rules. 'Where's the TAPS?' said Grey to his colleague. 'Get me the captain. And I want a Wildcat out searching ASAP.' He spoke back into the microphone: 'You boys let me know what you see when you get there.' And then he hung up.

'TAPS?' asked Jameson.

'Towed Array Patrol Ship,' said the team leader. 'Part of our continuous at sea deterrent, maintained at readiness 365 days a year.'

'Perfect. Let's show these bastards who they're playing with.'

Bello's self-satisfied smile made him look truly evil.

'Tell me then,' he said.

'There was only the girl. I never met her mother. She was alone and I felt sorry for her so I gave her some money when we docked and sent her to Julian. He was a good man. I knew he'd take her in.'

Bello said nothing.

'And then, when the operation was complete, I arranged for her to come to the UK. I took her to the station, gave her more money and told her to go and make a new life. That's the last I saw of her.'

'You expect me to believe that.'

'Well it's the truth, so yes.'

'Which station?'

'London Waterloo.'

'And where can she get to from this London Waterloo?'

'Pretty much anywhere in the country. She could get a train, a bus, the underground or simply walk out on to the street.'

'Why not just tell me that at the start? Why pretend to forget?'

Harry held the man's gaze. 'Because I don't like you very much.'

Bello smiled again. 'I want a list of every city and town she might have gone to.'

'That could be every town and city in the UK.'

'So be it.' Bello looked at Seraphine. 'You are from the UK. Help him.'

Abdul took a notebook from the desk drawer and handed it to Harry along with a pen.

'You're not serious?' said Harry.

'I will find her if it takes the rest of my living days. Alina is mine.'

He left, gesturing at Abdul to follow.

They locked the door behind them and Harry finally looked at Seraphine.

'So you do remember?' she asked.

Harry closed his eyes and tried not to think about what was happening to Sophie and Jake. 'How did this guy get my children? Was that you?' He opened his eyes again.

Seraphine looked at him for longer than was polite. 'I don't think you do remember.'

'No?'

'You lied. Risky. Ballsy.'

'I told him what I think I'd have done.'

She pulled a chair up to the desk. 'I didn't lead him to your children. That was all you.'

'The meeting in the cafe?'

'This man is not to be underestimated.'

84

'Go.' Antony Bello didn't look at Seraphine; he simply ordered her out. Not that she minded. Who cared if an irrelevant person thought you were irrelevant? That just made them even less relevant. She found Abdul on the lawn. He had a bottle of water for her and she thanked him and took a sip.

'Antony is pleased with the progress. He thinks he'll find Alina within the week.'

'And you?'

'I think your man is telling him what he wants to hear.'

Seraphine couldn't help but smile. Abdul was one of her favourite recruits. She wasn't the sort to have friends, but if she had been she'd have picked Abdul. He was polite, sophisticated, attractive and superbly intelligent. A sort of male version of her. Only not as accomplished. 'Who is this girl? Why's he so desperate to find her?'

'It's not Alina. It's more her mother. Naomi was Antony's first wife. He has too many to count now, but back at the start he and Naomi were a normal couple. I didn't know them back then but everyone says it was a good relationship. She took care of him and he, in turn, took in her daughter Alina and raised her as his own. Naomi's first husband died of malaria while she was pregnant. But, over the years, as Antony became more powerful and took on younger and younger lovers, Naomi was punished for her disapproval. He would beat her, humiliate her and rape her. Some here talk about this with admiration but most turned a blind eye because they didn't like what they were seeing.'

'And they couldn't challenge him because of who he was?'

Abdul raised both hands. 'He is protected. He's their leader's nephew and their future leader. Jacob Bello never had children.'

'So Naomi eventually had enough and ran?'

'Like many of these women, I don't think she'd ever have left, but then Antony turned his attention to Alina.'

Seraphine knew this was coming. A man doesn't get as worked up as that about a girl unless there's some sort of sexual motivation. 'How old was Alina?'

'Fourteen. That was when he began showing more than a fatherly interest. Fifteen when they left.'

Seraphine looked back at the outbuilding behind her. It was so quiet. 'We need to get this man out of the picture. What is the situation with his uncle now?'

'Jacob has spent the last few years trying to rewrite history and morph into a legitimate leader. He's frustrated by Antony's immaturity.'

'He wants a more sophisticated successor, someone who can turn his cause from one of resistance to one of genuine political power?'

Abdul smiled. He knew what she was thinking.

85

'Where are you taking us?' said Karene to the foot soldier. The young man didn't reply and so Karene repeated
her question. 'Tell me, where are you taking us?'

Bloom could see through the cabin window that they
were in open water now. They were alone and at the
mercy of two armed men, at least one of whom seemed
happiest when inflicting pain on children. Seraphine had
said that she was disappointed that George wasn't one of
them. But what had she meant? That he wasn't a good
enough psychopath? He certainly possessed the calm,
cold nature and, given he was clearly proud of his bomb
attack, the requisite lack of empathy or remorse. But perhaps he was just an ordinary person who'd experienced
enough trauma to render him detached. Or maybe he
had such a strong belief in his cause that it overrode any
doubt or guilt. It was hard to know. And it was also
a moot point. All she needed to know right now was
that he was prepared to act in a ruthless and self-serving
manner.

She used her elbow to check the position of the syringe
in her trouser pocket. It felt good to have it there, even
though she had no idea how or when she would use it.
She wished she had Jameson here. He had been alone
in inhospitable countries, living a lie, manipulating the

trust of others for his own gain, participating in the destruction of empires and lives. The thought brought a fresh wave of indignation. And, after all that, he had the cheek to judge her for her supposedly psychopathic tendencies? If she ever got out of here, she'd make sure to point that out to him.

'What kind of gun is that?' Jake said to the foot soldier. 'Dad used to take me to the gun range. I was only allowed to fire basic rifles and once a five millimetre.'

The foot soldier didn't respond.

'Have you ever fired an AK-47? I love those. They're really cool. Did you know the guy who invented them wanted to be a poet when he grew up?'

The foot soldier raised an eyebrow.

'Jake?' said Karene in a low voice, a warning.

'Are you a good shooter? I bet you are. You wouldn't have this job otherwise.'

'Jakey,' said Karene again.

The foot soldier was looking at Jake now.

'Is everyone good with guns where you're from?'

The foot soldier smirked.

'That's so cool. Dad would never tell me much about stuff like that. I know he learned to shoot but he wouldn't ever talk about it. How old were you when you learned?'

'Nine,' said the foot soldier.

'What was your first gun?'

Karene went to protest again but Bloom caught her eye and shook her head. This was good. Jake was drawing the young man into conversation and that would only serve to make them more real and thus harder to kill.

'There were many different ones.'

'Which is your favourite?'

'The AK is cool.'

'So you've used one? That's awesome.'

'This isn't one of your stupid video games, Jake,' said Sophie. Her tears had dried and she was sitting upright again.

Jake looked at the soldier and laughed a little as he said, disparagingly, 'Girls.'

The foot soldier laughed too and then set his expression back to serious.

Bloom watched the interaction with interest. 'Is this your first time in the UK?' she said seizing the opportunity to keep the man talking.

He frowned but made a small nodding motion.

'Where's home for you?'

His frown deepened.

'I've travelled all over Africa. There are so many beautiful places to see. Whereabouts did you grow up?'

'A village in South Sudan.'

'Are your parents still there?'

The man shrugged, unwilling or unable to answer. Bloom knew young boys were sometimes taken from their families by resistance movements and turned into soldiers. Learning to shoot at nine years old would certainly fit.

'It must be hard not seeing your mother and father.' She was still convinced this soldier wasn't yet out of his teens. 'So you can understand how Jake and Sophie here must feel?'

The soldier blinked at the wall behind her. If he'd been a child soldier, he'd have been brainwashed with whatever doctrine the men who took him peddled. It was unlikely she'd be able to influence such ingrained thinking. Their only hope was that he might come to see them as real people rather than the enemy.

86

Abdul was speaking to Jacob Bello, Antony's uncle, on the phone. They were still in the garden and Seraphine wanted to know what was happening inside but she also needed to hear this.

'It's not good news, Sir.' Abdul's reverence was impressive. 'He's had the captain brought here and the children taken captive.' Abdul listened to Jacob's response. 'I'm afraid he's already hurt the children.' Abdul paused and then continued. 'He plans to torture him until he gets what he wants, but the man has no memory of the last four years due to the explosion I told you about, so this can only end one way.' Abdul stood perfectly still as he spoke. 'I'm concerned that the implications of this may be severe for you, Sir. The British do not negotiate with those whom they deem to be terrorists and they certainly do not let them sit at the same table.'

Seraphine checked her watch. Antony Bello had been alone with Harry for over six minutes. She needed to get back in there.

'And, in my humble opinion, Sir, I don't think he'll let this go. I'm afraid he's obsessed.'

Seraphine held up her thumb and middle finger in

an 'O' shape and mouthed, 'Keep him talking until I come back.'

There was a shout from behind her. She waited for Abdul to acknowledge her instruction then walked back to the outbuilding.

87

Jameson sat forward in his seat. They'd been to War-sash Harbour and found nothing, and so the Marines had dropped him at the Royal Navy Headquarters on Whale Island in Portsmouth. Jameson was sitting in a poky meeting room awaiting an update from Grey and his team.

He felt helpless and he hated that. There was still no word from Bloom so he'd had to assume she'd followed him to the mansion and somehow been spotted. Which was probably why they'd run. As soon as one person found them, it was only a matter of time before others followed.

By the time Captain Tessa Morrisey arrived, Jameson was pacing around the small table. 'Have they found it?' he said.

'Not yet,' she replied.

'Why the hell not? How hard can it be? It's one bloody boat.'

'Do you know how many boats are in the Channel at any one time, especially during the warm summer months? It's like searching the M1 for a specific car.'

'Which would be found in minutes. There are cameras all the way along. So what's your excuse?'

'We have a needle in a haystack, but no idea what the

needle looks like. It could be a motor boat, a yacht, a sailing boat. They'll find it though. We've confirmed that the target is not in the Solent. They've taken the last known position from the boy's watch and plotted a trajectory into the Channel from there, so it's just a matter of time.'

'As long as they don't change course or come back.'

'Do you want a drink of anything?'

'No, I don't want a drink, I'm not at the bloody cinema. I need something to do. What can I do?'

'There's not really anything to do but wait.'

Jameson's phone beeped. He read the message and then grabbed his jacket. 'There's always something to do, Captain. Can you show me out?' She led him to reception and back through security. 'Call me as soon as you find that boat.'

'I'll let you know as soon as I'm allowed to.'

Jameson walked back towards her. 'I'll tell you the same thing I told Grey. We came to you within days of the bomb and told you it was all about Harry and you chose to do nothing. Now his children, girlfriend and probably my partner are in serious danger. Let's not forget these people killed three and maimed a further eight with that bomb just to cover their kidnapping. So if you do not include and inform me I will have no hesitation in going to the press and telling them that as an ex-secret service agent, who risked his life for the country, I'm appalled with how you people failed to protect one of your own. And before you ask, yes, I will be using names.'

Tessa Morrisey stood a little straighter. 'I will call you, Sir, as soon as we hear.'

88

Harry braced himself for the next punch. The attack had been relentless and he was losing track of time. His mouth tasted of blood and he tried not to think about the head injury and how this might affect it. Perhaps he'd suddenly regain his memories. But probably not.

Their list had been impressive. Harry was pretty sure that Seraphine had enjoyed making it as ridiculously expansive as possible, adding in many obscure and remote towns so that the names filled the entire book. Bello had read the first page with a satisfied smile but then had flicked ahead, each turn of the page more frantic than the last, until the reality of it dawned on him. It would be impossible to use this list to find Alina Maree.

Harry expected a verbal outburst or a demand that they start again, but Bello hadn't said a word. He'd walked up to Harry and punched him hard in the face, probably breaking his nose. After that, he'd grabbed Harry around the neck and pushed him off the chair and on to the floor so that his left cheek was crushed against the coarse wood. The smell of cleaning fluid was stronger down there. Harry had tried to lift his head but Bello had held it down. Silent punch after silent punch; his head, his ribs, his arms. Harry had curled into a foetal position to protect himself and Bello had stamped on his legs and kicked his spine.

And then it stopped, as abruptly as it had begun.

When Harry raised his head, he saw Bello sitting on the edge of the table reading the notebook as though the past few minutes hadn't happened. Harry wondered if he'd had some vivid hallucination, but then he moved and pain screamed from every inch of his body.

'I think the only thing that will convince you to help me is your daughter.' Bello picked up his phone.

Harry tried to protest but his mouth was swollen and the words came out mumbled. He dragged himself on to his knees and leaned against the upturned chair. Bello began speaking, demanding that the children be brought to the phone again. Seraphine opened the door and stepped into the room.

'I thought it was a little too quiet in here.' Seraphine seemed entirely unperturbed by the scene in front of her.

'Wait outside.' Bello pointed at Seraphine. 'You have no business here.'

'I think I'll stay.'

The vein in Bello's forehead protruded like a venomous snake under his skin. 'You. Will. Go.'

'Don't worry about me,' she said. 'I won't interrupt.' She waved her hand in the air as if Bello's activities were frivolous and unimportant.

'You. Will. Go.'

'Mr Bello,' Seraphine took a step towards him. 'Don't forget that I brought this man to you. And I did that because I have my own issues with him and his associates. The least you can do is let me watch.'

Antony Bello's jaw moved from side to side as he studied Seraphine. She was standing with her hands in her trouser pockets, like a woman admiring a thing of beauty rather than one asking to watch a man be tortured. Bello put the phone to his mouth.

'Cut off her hand.'

89

George appeared in the cabin doorway. They'd been sailing steadily into open water. The initial congestion of the Solent and the British Channel had given way to calm blue as far as the eye could see. Bloom guessed that they were being taken to France. Once there, they could hopefully use Jake's watch to notify Caroline and, in turn, Jameson of their location.

But then she realized how quiet it was. George had turned off the engine.

'Everyone out,' he said.

One by one they filed on to the deck. It had a dark blue canvas railing and bench seats on both sides. George instructed them to sit on the longest bench and then fetched the satellite phone from the upper flybridge.

'Sir,' he said. 'We are ready.'

George indicated that the foot soldier should unzip the holdall on the floor. The young man did as he was told, opening the bag and taking a single item from inside.

Bloom squeezed Jake's arm, partly to reassure him and partly to calm herself. She was unfamiliar with firearms and so it had been easy to tell herself that the guns were replicas, there to frighten them and nothing more. But the large wooden-handled knife was glinting in the sunlight, obviously real, obviously intended for one of them.

She'd once seen a similar knife used to slaughter a camel in India. It was an image that had stayed with her for many years.

'You,' said George, pointing at Sophie. 'On the floor.'

The girl shook her head.

'Not a chance in hell,' said Karene.

'On the floor,' he repeated. 'Now.'

'No,' Sophie cried. 'Leave me alone! Please! Leave me alone.'

Karene stood to protect Sophie, her shoulders squared in defiance.

George hit her across the face so hard that she fell to the floor, smacking her head on the wall of the deck and landing hard on her left shoulder.

'If anyone else moves, shoot them,' George said to his colleague.

Bloom could feel Jake's arm shaking.

'Now.' George pointed to the floor at his feet and reached into his pocket to remove a pair of latex gloves.

Bloom checked the syringe in her pocket with her elbow. Could she get to it with her hands tied? If so, would she be able to remove the cap and inject the contents without getting hit or shot? It was unlikely. George had put his gun down behind him, but it was still within easy reach and the foot soldier had his weapon raised and pointed at Karene, who was slowly returning to her seat.

'Use me instead,' Karene said. 'I'm older. Please.'

George paused but then shouted again at Sophie to get on the floor.

This time, she did as he asked. She was still sobbing and pleading for the man not to hurt her, but George just held the phone closer to her mouth.

Bloom's fury with Seraphine reached a new level. How could she put Harry and his kids in this position?

When Sophie was kneeling on the floor, George took a long strap out of his other pocket and tied a tourniquet around her upper left arm.

Bloom realized what was coming.

'Come here, boy,' George said to Jake.

Karene had realized too. 'No!' she said. 'Stop. Why are you doing this? What do you want? I'll help you get whatever you want from Harry.' She looked at Bloom. 'We both will. We're influential women. We know a lot of people. Please don't hurt these children.'

'Boy. Here.'

Jake stood as the foot soldier came closer with his gun.

'You need to hold her hand down,' said George. 'Come this side of me. Hold it down or we'll make it much worse for your sister. Do you understand?' He took the knife and placed it under the cable tie around Jake's wrists.

'Let me do that,' said Bloom.

George looked across at her.

'Don't make the boy do it. He won't be able to hold her still; she's his sister.'

'If he doesn't hold her still, it will be his hand next.'

Sophie began to buck against George.

'Stop it or I'll cut them both off,' he hissed.

Sophie continued to writhe.

'She's panicking,' said Bloom. 'She can't stop and Jake won't be able to hold her. I will. I'm not a relative. I've only just met the girl and I understand that a cleaner cut will be better.'

'I will not hesitate to cut your limbs off.'

'I know. I get it. I'll hold her hand down. You have my word.'

George hesitated and then cut the cable tie around Bloom's wrists. She moved to kneel on the floor next to Sophie. From this position, she could hear the distant, tinny sound of someone shouting from within the phone. She pressed Sophie's hands firmly on to the floor. It struck her that the kindest thing might be to administer the ketamine to Sophie as an anaesthetic to knock her out, but she dismissed the idea quickly. She just needed the right moment. She needed George to focus on his task.

'Sophie,' she said. 'Look at Karene. Karene will help. It's the oldest trick in the book. Distraction.' She hoped Karene was paying attention, that she remembered that the oldest trick was to divide and conquer, that she would know what to do. Their lives depended on it.

90

The sound of Sophie crying and pleading cut through Harry's own pain. He couldn't let these animals lay a finger on his girl. He had to do something. He stood, righted his chair and straightened his back. Karene offered herself in Sophie's place and Harry felt a surge of admiration. He might not remember her, but he didn't doubt that this formidable woman loved him.

'What is this?' Harry shouted. 'Come at me. Real men don't hurt children.'

Bello reached behind his back and produced a hunting knife. He held it above his head. 'You want me to cut you? You think that will stop me cutting her? It won't. Give me Alina's location.'

Harry lunged and the scuffle that followed was nothing like the fight scenes on television. There were no choreographed actions with Harry's blows hitting their target perfectly each time and Bello's repeatedly missing. But Harry managed to avoid the blade, and he felt empowered by adrenaline, or fear, or simply the sound of his daughter needing him, and somehow managed to knock the knife from Bello's grip.

The men ended up on the floor, a mess of flailing arms and legs. Every punch that landed on Bello felt too weak and those Harry received in return felt like freight trains. But he was holding his own and he would not – could not – give in. All he could feel was the bottomless pit of fury within him, fuelled by his love for his children, his anger at being here, and the frustration of having lost precious years of his life.

They continued like that, grappling, trying to gain the upper hand, until Seraphine cleared her throat and said, 'Ahem? I think someone wants you, Antony.' She held out the phone and a voice from the other end said, 'Can you hear me, Sir? We are ready.'

Harry shouted, 'No, don't do it. I'll get you anything you want. Do you hear me? This is Captain Harry Peterson of the Royal Navy and I will get you whatever you want. Don't hurt her.'

Bello took the phone, retrieving his knife from the floor while Harry was momentarily distracted.

'I've told you everything I know,' said Harry. 'This won't change that; don't you see?'

'I will cut off her other hand and then her feet until you understand that you have to comply.'

'You sick bastard.'

Bello brandished the knife at Harry. 'You think it wise to insult me.' He lifted the phone to his ear.

'This is intriguing,' said Seraphine. 'Why do you continue to bully a man who doesn't know anything? All of this time I have been standing here knowing exactly where Alina Maree is.'

Harry and Bello turned to stare.

'All you had to do was ask. But I suppose you assumed that a silly little woman wouldn't know anything.'

Bello lowered the phone and pointed the knife at Seraphine. 'Tell me.'

'Mr Bello, Antony, you may have spotted that Captain Peterson here does not respond well to being threatened. Well, that makes two of us. You can stop waving your little knife in my face and speak to me with respect.'

Bello moved closer, the tip of the blade hovering directly in front of Seraphine's eyes. 'Where is she?' he insisted.

Seraphine tutted and took a few steps backwards. 'Shall we try that again?'

'I will kill you.'

'And how will that get you the information? It makes no sense.' Seraphine smiled; she seemed genuinely amused.

'Are you laughing at me?'

Harry couldn't take his eyes off the phone. He hadn't heard anything; no one was saying anything. Was the man still waiting for the go-ahead?

'Not you specifically.'

'Do you know who I am?' Bello's voice had taken on a deep throaty tone and sweat was glistening on his forehead. 'I can make you disappear like that.' He threw the phone on the desk and clicked his fingers in Seraphine's face. 'Nobody would know where you were.'

Seraphine held the man's gaze. Her sweet smile was fixed but something in her eyes changed. 'Do you know what the real difference is between you and me?' she asked. She waited. 'The world would miss me. The world *needs* me.' She lifted her left hand from her trouser pocket

333

where it had been the whole time. She held a yellow pencil with a red-capped end. 'You on the other hand . . .'

She looked at Harry and winked.

He didn't know what she was planning, but he instinctively knew she was ready to attack. Bello continued to rage at Seraphine, waving his knife, and she was amazingly still, like a scientist studying a rat in a maze. Her head tilted a little one way and then the other. She was watching the man's neck. But why?

Seraphine watched Bello and Harry watched Seraphine. He wasn't sure what he was looking for until he saw it. She tensed and Harry dived forward to clamp his hands around the wrist that held the knife. At that very moment Seraphine plunged the pencil into Bello's neck.

91

Jameson waited for the manager of the Metro Bank in Southampton's West Quay Shopping Centre. He needed to know what the key on Harry's keyring opened. He'd wangled a favour from his MI6 contacts, and they'd eventually confirmed that it was a key for a Metro Bank security box. So he decided to pay their local branch a visit. If he couldn't do anything to help Bloom and Harry, he might at least do something useful. Perhaps he'd discover Harry's secret and be able to pinpoint the perpetrators.

The manager was a young woman with cropped hair and a downturned mouth. She looked like someone you wouldn't mess with.

Jameson offered her his warmest smile. 'Thank you for seeing me at such short notice.'

'You didn't give me much choice, Mr Jameson.' She shook his hand and her grip was disappointingly slack. 'You said that lives depended on it.'

'They do indeed.' He handed her the key. 'Can you confirm if this is one of yours?'

She took the key and examined it. 'Yes,' she said. 'This is one of ours.'

'Any way of knowing which of your branches issued it?'

She frowned. 'You said you work with the police, but you're not police?'

'No, I'm not. There's a number here on the key. Is that an identifier?'

'I can't share any client information with you, Mr Jameson.'

'I'm not asking you to, Miss Rawdon.' He held her gaze.

'Come with me.' She led him through to her office. It was small and the desk was cluttered with papers. 'Is the person who owns the key alive as far as you know?'

Jameson understood the motivation behind her question. If the owner is deceased, the box's contents become part of the individual's estate. 'Very much so.'

'But it's not you.'

'No. It's a client with severe memory loss.'

She raised her eyebrows. 'You need the box number and its branch.'

'Are you telling me you can't reverse engineer that?'

'You need the box number and its branch. And then we need to confirm the identity of the owner.'

'And how do you do that?'

'Using their bank account details. No one can have a security box without a bank account.'

'Fine.' He sat back in the chair and met her gaze. 'I only have one more question for you.'

'Which is?'

'Why bring me back here? If you can't identify the box, why not tell me that out front?'

'Mr Jameson—'

'I'll tell you why. Because you *are* able to identify where the key is from but you wanted to know if I'm worthy of being told. So, tell me, what do you need to know?'

92

The deck was blustery and cold, but when the wind dropped Bloom could feel the summer sun burning her pale skin.

They were all frozen in position, waiting for George to be given the go-ahead. They'd heard Harry shouting, offering George a bribe. But the man didn't seem the type to deviate from his mission. And then the line had fallen quiet. George pressed the phone to his ear and concentrated.

Bloom reviewed their positions. Sophie lay on the floor, face down with her left arm extended. George knelt by her feet, the phone to his right ear and his left hand on his lap holding the knife. Bloom was kneeling by Sophie's head, holding her arm down with one hand and stroking the girl's hair with her other. Karene and Jake sat side by side and in front of them stood the foot soldier and his gun.

Everyone was looking at George, except for Sophie, her cheek flat to the deck.

Bloom heard the distant beat of a helicopter.

This was it. This was the moment.

Bloom scratched her nose with her left hand. No one reacted so she slid her hand down her side and put it in her pocket. Her fingers curled around the syringe and she prised the cap off with her thumb.

Her eyes met Karene's and she knew that her instruction had been received.

'I feel sick,' said Karene to the foot soldier. 'I think I'm going to throw up.'

George nodded to his colleague.

'The lower deck,' said the foot soldier. Karene stood up, stepping past Sophie and Bloom and then climbing down the ladder. The foot soldier followed and ushered Karene along the outer deck behind Jake. Karene leaned over the side and retched.

George watched, his phone still pressed against his ear. His sleeves were rolled up and the skin on his arms was exposed.

Karene retched again. She was a good actress but she wouldn't be able to keep it up for long.

The helicopter was getting nearer now. George raised his eyes to the sky and Bloom seized the moment. She removed the syringe from her pocket, rocked forward on her knees and plunged it into George's arm.

Shocked, he tightened his grip on the knife and spun towards her. She reached for the gun behind him and, realizing what was happening, he shoved it away with the back of his arm. As his muscle tensed, the syringe shot from his forearm. He swung back, aiming the hunting knife at her face.

The foot soldier came running and arrived with his weapon up and also aimed at Bloom.

'Get them inside,' said George. 'Now.'

His colleague hesitated and then followed George's gaze up towards the sky. The helicopter was coming quickly. They couldn't be sure that it was looking for them, but George wouldn't want their group to be seen.

George's eyes met hers. 'What was that?'

The foot soldier ushered Jake, Karene and Sophie into the cabin.

Bloom shook her head. 'I'm not sure. It was given to me.'

'Get inside.'

Bloom was impressed by the man's clarity of mind. He had been injected with some unknown substance and might only have minutes to live, but he was still working.

93

Harry stared at the pool of blood leaking from Antony Bello. It had been pumping from his neck in a wide arc and Bello had been desperately trying to hold it in, but now he was unconscious on the floor and it simply seeped from him.

'Beautiful, isn't it?' Seraphine wiped the blood from her weapon with a tissue. She hadn't a drop on her white top and jacket. 'Thank you for your help. That was quick thinking.'

Harry had worked with some unnervingly calm people before. A close friend was an underwater bomb disposal expert and you didn't get much cooler under pressure than that guy. But Seraphine was in a different league again.

Snapping out of his shock, Harry grabbed the phone from Bello's desk. 'Hello?' The line was dead. How long had it been dead? What had happened to Sophie? He pressed the home button but the phone was locked. 'What about my kids? You couldn't have had them released in exchange for what you know?'

'Oh. Yes. Sorry.' Seraphine twisted the red cap on the end of her modified pencil and its spike retreated inwards. She put it back in her pocket. 'But don't worry. Augusta and Marcus will be on that.'

'What are you on about? What can they do? They're civilians.'

'They look out for each other. That's why I put Augusta in there.'

'What?'

'I sent Augusta to the place Bello had your kids and gave her the means to escape. I can't do much more than that.'

94

The helicopter was deafening. Bloom leaned forward to see out of the window but all she saw was sea.

And then a loud voice announced, 'Civilian vessel. This is Naval Helicopter Blackcat Two. Tune your radio to channel sixteen.' George stood still and did nothing. 'Civilian vessel,' repeated the voice. 'This is Naval Helicopter Blackcat Two. You need to comply. Tune your radio to channel sixteen.'

The foot soldier stepped backwards into the doorway and peeked out and up.

'Attention. Civilian vessel. With the blue hull and white cabin. This is Naval Helicopter Blackcat Two. I will not ask you again. Tune your radio to channel sixteen.'

George moved towards the foot soldier and stumbled a little. He looked dazed. 'If they try to stop us, kill them all,' he said, then disappeared up to the flybridge.

Sophie began to cry loud, desperate sobs. The experience was taking its toll and she was so far past panic now that she was inconsolable. Karene told her to breathe, that everything would be OK, that help was here now, but the sobbing continued.

The blades grew louder and, for the first time, the foot soldier looked scared.

Bloom raised her voice above the noise. 'No one will

hurt you if you don't hurt us. All they want is the four of us safely returned. What will killing us achieve? Other than getting yourself killed too.'

The foot soldier looked out of the side window and his eyes widened.

Bloom followed his gaze. The helicopter had dropped to their level. It hovered above the waves, guns lowered and aimed. The noise of the rotary blades drowned out all other sounds. A sign flashed up in the cockpit that said '16'.

'This is Naval Helicopter Blackcat Two. Drop your weapons and tune your radio to channel sixteen.'

Bloom shouted, 'You can see that helicopter! You know you're outgunned, don't you?'

'It's a Wildcat,' shouted Jake. 'It carries Stingray torpedoes, a door-mounted machine gun and Anti-Surface Guided Weapon missiles. It's a six-foot-two heavyweight boxer. You don't mess.'

Bloom was impressed. Jake had excellent instincts. 'I think that means it's game over.'

The foot soldier raised his weapon at Bloom. There was a dull thud from above. Bloom guessed that George had finally passed out. If she could keep this young lad calm, no one would get hurt.

'I know you're a good person. I see that.' The noise of the helicopter lessened a touch but she still had to shout to be heard. 'You've done nothing to harm us and I'll tell them that. They'll want to know what you know and why you're here, but I'm sure you're trained to handle such interrogations.'

The foot soldier gripped his gun a little more firmly.

'You'll keep calm, stay quiet and they'll send you home. You'll be a hero. Your leaders will be impressed by your loyalty.' She could see that the young man was thinking about it. 'I know George gave you an order, but he's not thinking straight. I gave him a sedative, a strong anaesthetic; do you know what that is?'

The foot soldier looked enraged but nodded.

'I did that to survive. We all want to survive. Jake and Sophie want to see their parents again, Karene wants to see her boyfriend again.' Her throat hurt from the shouting but she persevered. 'We are not bad people. We've done nothing to you. Killing us will achieve nothing, except . . .' She left her point hanging in the air.

'Except what?' he said after a moment.

'If you fire on us now, while George is passed out, they'll blame you for everything.'

95

'I think we're done here, Harry.'

Seraphine opened the door to the outbuilding and stepped into the sunshine. 'Help,' she shouted. 'Help. Someone help. Please!' The distress in her voice sounded genuine.

A metre or two away Abdul finished his call and rushed over. 'What happened?'

Bello's men came running from the house.

She lowered her voice. 'We need to get Captain Peterson out of here before your men discover what he's done.'

'What *I've* done?'

'You were just defending yourself. It's understandable. And his uncle will appreciate that.' She looked at Abdul. 'Won't he?'

Abdul nodded and handed his car keys to Seraphine. 'I'll make sure he understands the situation.' He beckoned to the running men. 'There's been an accident. Quick! Get a doctor.'

Seraphine placed her hand on Harry's bicep. The bruising stung and he winced. 'Can you run?'

'I expect so.' He didn't want to hang around for Bello's followers to clock him as the killer.

'Good,' she said. 'Walk for a moment until they're all

inside. Follow me. Abdul will keep them distracted for as long as possible.'

'How can you be sure? You just murdered his boss.'

'Bello is not Abdul's boss. Now, run.'

Seraphine was fast and Harry did his best to keep up. He could hear one of the men wailing behind them. Would Abdul really be able to stop these men seeking vengeance? Harry could feel his face swelling and the bruising spreading on his arms. It was obvious he'd been in a fight. And they'd all seen him standing outside the outhouse. Even if he and Seraphine made it to the car, Bello's men could chase them down. There'd been plenty of pick-ups parked out front.

They reached Abdul's Toyota and Seraphine climbed into the driver's seat. Harry sat beside her. This vehicle was significantly smarter than the others parked nearby.

'You look worried,' Seraphine said as she reversed.

'How long until they come after us?'

She accelerated down the drive and out of the gates. 'I love a game of cat and mouse, don't you?'

'Who *are* you?'

'Is that really the question you want to ask, Harry?'

'There are lots of questions I want to ask.'

'We have an hour. Go ahead. You can ask. I won't be offended. I see that you're a very observant person.'

'OK. What makes you how you are?'

'Your question is not *who* are you then, but *what* are you?' There was a mischievous glint in her eye.

'I suppose it is. Yes.'

'I'm a high-functioning psychopath.'

Harry's surprise was etched on his swollen face.

'I'd like to say that you shouldn't worry. That I'm not the serial killer kind. But I'm guessing you won't buy that right now.'

'Ha,' he said. It was all he could manage. He'd never met a self-confessed psychopath before. He'd suspected a few, but never known for sure. 'How does a person know that about themselves?' He glanced in the wing mirror. There were no vehicles behind.

'You spot it early on. You normals are pretty intolerable with all those useless emotions swishing about in your brain.'

'I beg to differ. In my experience, emotions are incredibly helpful.'

'Are you picking a fight with a psychopath in an enclosed space?' She laughed at his expression. 'I'm joking. You would say emotions are helpful, being all empathetic and emotionally sensitive.'

'You think I'm sensitive?'

'I've been watching you as much as you've been watching me, Harry. I get what Karene sees in you. You're not dissimilar to my Marcus.'

'Your Marcus? Are you guys a thing?'

'Marcus is my lobster. He just doesn't realize it yet.'

Harry sniggered.

'What?'

'I suppose I've never imagined a psychopath watching *Friends* before. But I suppose your sort must enjoy television as much as the rest of us.'

Seraphine looked bewildered. 'What are you talking about?'

'As in Ross and Rachel. No?'

'I don't recall that. He's my lobster because—'

'Lobsters mate for life. Yeah. That was their point too.' He checked behind again. 'Do you have Marcus's number then? Can I call him about my children?'

'There won't be any signal until we get to the airstrip.' She took a left turn and Harry wondered how she knew where to go. 'See. Your emotions have you all wound up even though you know rationally that there's nothing you can do.'

'But my emotions make me *want* to do something! They drive me to protect the people I love or the people who need help.'

'Like Alina Maree?'

'Do you really know where she is?'

'Yes and no.'

Harry waited.

Seraphine accelerated as the road surface improved. 'I know she's in witness protection.'

'Did I put her there?'

'No.'

'Who did?'

'The secret service.'

'Marcus's gang? MI6?'

Seraphine smiled. 'Neat, isn't it?'

Harry stared out of the window at the dense forest. It wasn't lush and bright like the forests in the UK. The trees were darker, hardier, so that they could withstand the heat and the lack of water. 'So why did Bello come after me? If I wasn't the one who hid her.'

Seraphine said nothing. Maybe she didn't know. Had Marcus known? He must have contacts back in the service. It wasn't a large community. But somehow Harry couldn't see it. Marcus struck him as the straight-as-a-die type. Then again, he was embroiled in a romance with a psychopath. And not just any psychopath. He hadn't missed the undercurrent of her conversations with Abdul. Those two were definitely linked somehow.

Harry's body throbbed. He leaned back against the head rest and closed his eyes. After a few moments, he sat up. 'They didn't hide her until after the bomb.'

'If I wasn't driving I'd give you a round of applause.'

'What's your involvement in this? You asked me what was in it for you, bringing me out here? It was getting in a room with Antony Bello, wasn't it? So that you could kill him. I was nothing more than an in.'

Seraphine licked her lips.

'Are you an assassin then?'

Her laugh was genuine and loud. 'What is it with you boys? Why are we always the nobody, or the secretary, or the hired help? Do you know there are six species of mammal led by females? The orcas and African elephants, whose ladies keep the peace and preserve group knowledge. The lemurs and hyenas whose scrappy little women rarely lose a fight. And then you have the African lion. We call the male the king of the jungle, but it's the lionesses who lead the pride, hunt for the food and defend their young against predators. You know which one is my favourite, though?' Harry shrugged. 'The bonobo ape. Their females resolve arguments by grabbing the genitals of the males, and they're not afraid to severely hurt them in order to protect the group. How cool is that?'

'Very cool,' said Harry.

'Sarcasm?'

'No. Sorry. Headache.'

'Sleep. That will help.' The car hit a pothole and rocked violently to one side. 'Or maybe not.'

Harry tried to focus on what he needed to ask. She had brought him here so she could dispatch Antony Bello and she knew the secret service had hidden Alina. But did she know why his memory had been taken away? 'Who erased my memories then? MI6?'

Seraphine looked perplexed for a split second. 'The staged terrorist attack was George Selaisse. He's one of Bello's men. Impressive.'

Seraphine didn't know about the surgery. She thought the explosion had caused the memory loss. He wanted to tell her that she wasn't in possession of all the facts, but he didn't. He figured Marcus might enjoy doing that and, more importantly, he wasn't sure how she'd take it. He could see that being in the know was something Seraphine took very seriously. 'So how did the secret service get involved?'

'The same way I did. They listen and they pay attention.'

'Listen to Bello's calls?'

'Antony Bello's uncle has been responsible for destabilizing large areas of sub-Saharan Africa for many years.

And now he wants to be taken seriously as a legitimate political power. That puts him and his inner circle on everyone's radar.'

'So you were all listening to Antony and you heard what? Talk of finding some girl. Would that really pique your interest?'

'Not in the slightest. And I'm sorry to say that I didn't bat an eyelid at your cousin's murder either, but after that things got interesting.'

Harry suddenly saw it clearly. Julian had given these men Harry's name. And had probably explained how he had come into contact with Alina – through his profession. 'My job in the Navy was a red flag.'

'Can't have the baddies coming after our good guys, now can we?'

'Who is this Alina?'

'She's the daughter of Antony's first wife, Naomi.'

'What does she know? Why did he want to find her?'

'Nobody seems to know.'

Harry hung his head and shook it a little. 'But I did.'

'Did you?'

Is that why his own countrymen had wiped his memories? To ensure he couldn't reveal whatever he knew about this girl? 'Do you think the secret service knew about the bomb in advance?'

'It's unlikely. There was talk of an attack on you but not when or where.'

'But they'd have been following me?'

'Absolutely. This was their chance to catch Bello with his hand in the cookie jar.'

'Holy crap. I help a kid out and all this happens. That's just—'

Seraphine smiled. 'You thought you were a nobody and then it turns out you're a somebody. You should enjoy that.'

Harry didn't bother to educate her about her flawed logic. Who would ever want to become a somebody under these circumstances?

He must have fallen asleep because when he opened his eyes, Seraphine was out of the car and talking to the pilot of the plane they'd arrived on. *Was this her own private jet?*

He climbed out and walked towards them.

When she saw him approaching, Seraphine ended the conversation and met him halfway. She held out her hand. 'It's been a pleasure meeting you, Harry. You've surprised me and I wish you well.'

It took a moment or two for the truth to dawn on him. 'You're leaving me here. I thought you told Abdul you needed to get me away.'

'I did get you away. But this is where the babysitting ends. Like I said, you people really need to take responsibility for your own survival. You can't keep relying on me.' She dropped her voice and leaned in as if to share a secret. 'Mainly because I'm not that reliable.' She turned and walked away.

Harry followed. 'Wait! What about my passport?'

She stopped at the steps to the plane. 'It's in your home, isn't it?'

'But you had another. You gave the man two at the airport.'

'Did I? Gosh. You do have a good eye for detail. I don't recall. Happy travels.'

She climbed the stairs.

'Seraphine?' Harry shouted. 'How do I get home without a passport?'

'If you managed to smuggle a migrant girl into the UK, I'm sure you can smuggle yourself out of Africa.'

He stepped towards the plane and then thought better of it. She had complimented his quick thinking with Bello and thanked him for his help. Perhaps that was why she was leaving him here. Alive. He took a couple of steps back as the plane began to move. With a woman like Seraphine, he sensed things could have turned out much, much worse.

As the plane took off, Harry walked back to the Toyota. The keys were still in the ignition and on the back seat sat a stack of money.

96

The foot soldier's movements were becoming more and more agitated. The helicopter had moved out of sight. The young man kept checking behind him at the rear deck. He and Bloom were clearly thinking the same thing; their plan was to lower someone down.

'Don't panic,' she said. 'It's going to be fine.'

He aimed his weapon at her again and this time there was something different in his eyes. They were detached. Cold.

'You've been kind to us,' said Jake. 'I'll tell them that.'

'Shut up.'

'He's right,' Bloom said.

'I said to shut up.'

They did as they were told. The boat swayed back and forth. The helicopter blades drummed a rhythmic pulse to match.

Where was Jameson? She imagined he was getting in the face of some unfortunate naval officer and demanding action. She wouldn't be entirely surprised if he boarded their boat right now. He was not beyond pushing his way into an operation. But there was another possible scenario. He might have stayed back, left her to handle things for herself. He hadn't fully forgiven her. And if he really did believe she was a psychopath, he may think her perfectly capable of surviving without his help.

He wouldn't desert Karene and Harry's children, though. He didn't have it in him. That realization brought a fresh wave of optimism.

Ahead of her, on the rear deck, she saw two sets of military boots.

'You're in charge now,' she said to the foot soldier. 'You decide. What sort of man are you going to be? One who lashes out without good cause, or one who's clever and understands that sometimes making friends with the enemy is the best course of action?'

The foot soldier adjusted his gun against his body and for the first time placed his finger on the trigger. 'I told you to shut up.'

Bloom took in so much detail during that final moment. She saw a bead of sweat slide slowly down the foot soldier's forehead. She saw his teeth clamp together in a grimace. She watched the tendons in his hand flex and then flatten. And she saw his finger trembling on the trigger.

She closed her eyes.

The sound of the bullet exploding from the gun silenced every other sound. She could no longer hear the helicopter blades. She braced herself for the impact and prayed it wouldn't hurt.

And then she heard Sophie screaming.

Bloom opened her eyes and looked directly into those

of the foot soldier. They were no longer detached, or cold, or anything at all. They stared unseeingly back as he fell to the floor, an exit wound there in the young man's forehead.

97

Jameson waited in the bank manager's poky little office. He checked his phone. No missed calls. No messages. He sent a quick text to Captain Tessa Morrisey saying, 'Any news?' A few moments later he received a reply, saying, 'Boat located. SBS boarding now.'

He felt a wave of relief even though he knew this wasn't over yet. Not until they had confirmed Karene, the children and Bloom were aboard and alive, and their capturers apprehended or neutralized. He still called Caroline Peterson.

'I just heard they've found the boat and are planning to board it anytime now.'

'Are they on it? Are they OK?'

'I'll let you know the moment I hear. This is good, Caroline. These guys are the best. They'll get your children back.'

The bank manager returned as he hung up the phone. 'OK,' she said taking a seat. It transpired the woman had a brother in the army and as soon as Jameson mentioned the terrorist attack at Devonport Naval Base she proclaimed that she'd seen the story in the press about the officer who'd lost his memory. After that she was more than helpful.

'A security box was leased by Harry Peterson at our Peterborough branch.'

'Peterborough?'

'Is he not from around there?'

'He lives in St Albans and works in London.'

'Well he opened the bank account and the security box on the same day.'

'And which day was that?'

'This is where it's a bit odd, so I had my colleagues check it again, but they say that their records show Mr Peterson visited them on Monday 31st July.'

Jameson moved forward in his seat. 'This year?'

'This year.'

'But that would be—'

'Two days after the bomb, yes,' said the manager.

How could he have opened the bank account after the bomb? He'd been with the kidnappers having his memory surgically wiped.

Jameson thanked the manager and left. In his car he opened his iPad and checked the file on Harry's case. The bomb attack had occurred on Saturday 29th July and Harry had rocked up in Exeter A&E sometime in the late afternoon or early evening of Tuesday 1st August. Jameson looked out on to the shopping centre car park and watched a woman trying to fit a large suitcase in the passenger seat of her sports car. Harry said he had no recollection of the security box key and if that was true that meant his memory was wiped after he visited the bank in Peterborough on Monday morning. That still left thirty-six hours to perform the surgery and get him to Exeter A&E. But how did he get away from them to get to the bank? And more importantly why would he go back to them?

There was only one logical answer. They must have taken him there. Whatever he put in that security box, they wanted him to put it there. They were about to go to extreme lengths to ensure Harry had no memory of his actions over the past few years, and yet they allowed him to put something in a box and keep the key to it.

For the life of him, Jameson could not imagine what that something might be.

98

The helicopter landed on Whale Island in Portsmouth and they were welcomed back by Caroline Peterson, Jameson, Rear Admiral Grey and his right-hand woman Captain Morrisey.

'There's someone here for everyone except me,' said Karene as the helicopter powered down and one of the crew opened the door for them.

Bloom took Karene's hand and squeezed it. 'You've had someone here for you all along.'

'I know. Thank you.'

'You're welcome. I'll send you the bill.'

Karene laughed. Bloom knew it was adrenaline and relief rather than true happiness. She wouldn't truly feel happy until Harry was safe.

Bloom watched Sophie and Jake run to their mother and the three of them folded themselves into a hug. 'Sophie will need some counselling, I think. Jake as well.'

'I'll speak to Caroline,' said Karene.

'And you might too.'

'I'll be fine.'

'Maybe. Maybe not. Think about it.'

'You're the one who had a gun pointed at her head,' Karene said as they headed for Rear Admiral Grey.

Jameson intercepted them and pulled Bloom to one side. 'Your phone,' he said, handing it to her. 'It was left behind in the mansion flat.'

'Thank you,' she said. She gestured to the helicopter. 'And thank you.'

'It was nothing.' They stood for a moment in silence. 'Why did you leave the safe house when I told you not to?'

Jake Peterson joined them. 'You were brilliant,' he said and held his hand out to Bloom.

'I don't know about that. Things could have been very different. But you handled yourself very well. Hiding the watch. Getting that man talking to you. Staying so calm. I was really impressed. Your mum and dad will be very proud.'

The teenager blushed. 'Dad had this story about a friend of his who was taken hostage in the war. He survived by making friends with his guard. I figured it was worth a shot.'

'Smart,' said Jameson.

Jake looked even more delighted to receive praise from Marcus. No doubt he knew that Jameson used to be a secret agent. He rushed back towards his mum and sister who were still coiled together.

'Seraphine sent me a text. She said that you were in danger and that I needed to go alone.'

'And you believed her?'

'I believe she cares about you. So yes. I took it at face value.'

'That woman cares about nothing but her own mile-high ego. So she's behind all this as well, then?'

'I'm not sure.' She found Seraphine's number in her phone and dialled it. 'Let's find out.'

Seraphine answered on the second ring. There was a lot of white noise. 'My favourite psychologist,' she said. 'How are you?'

'Alive. Where are you and is Harry with you?'

'Did you use the pencil? I modified it. Did you work it out?'

'I left your pencil where I found it. I'm not playing games with you any more, Seraphine. Where is Harry?'

'Africa. I think. It's only been a few hours so he must still be on the continent unless he's really resourceful.'

'He's not with you?'

'Why would he be with me?'

'Because you took him away. What did you do with him? Is he in danger?' Her words brought the whole welcoming party a little closer. 'Seraphine?'

'You said you left the pencil. What about the syringe?'

Bloom sighed. This was the nature of conversations with psychopaths. They only talked about what they wanted to talk about. 'Yes,' said Bloom. 'That was useful.' After a moment of silence, she gritted her teeth and said, 'Thank you.'

'Ha. Good. Now why did you call?'

'Stop it, Seraphine. I have the man's family here. They're worried about him. Just tell me where you left him.'

'I told you, Africa.'

'Is Harry involved in whatever it is you and your murder of crows are up to?'

'I like that. Murder of crows. Is Marcus there?'

362

Bloom looked at Jameson. He was standing close. He'd heard the question. When he nodded, she turned the speaker on and passed the phone to him.

'Hello?' His greeting was flat and cool.

'Marcus, my lovely. How are you? Have you solved this little mystery yet?'

'Are you in a plane?'

'Clever little bunny, aren't you?'

'Where did you leave Harry?'

'Well, that's irrelevant because he won't be there any more.'

'So he's alive?'

'Oh, Marcus. I wouldn't hurt your little friend. I liked him actually. He reminded me of you. Another squidgy little action man.'

Bloom saw Jameson take a long, deep breath.

'I expect he'll pop up in the next day or so in one of two locations. So don't you worry.'

Jameson chewed his lip then said loud enough for Grey to hear, 'So in the next twenty-four to thirty-six hours he can get to either a British Embassy or a UN military facility?'

'Oh, I forget how quick you are.'

Jameson held his hand over the phone and said to Grey, 'Check the flight manifests from local airports. Find any charter planes or private jets that flew to Africa, particularly sub-Saharan Africa, in the past twenty-four hours.'

'Consider it done,' said Captain Morrisey.

Jameson closed his eyes and squared his shoulders. He took his hand away from the microphone. 'It's an impressive operation,' he said. 'A kidnap covered by a terrorist attack, two teams competing to help or hinder Harry. I take it you have some deeper purpose.'

'Marcus, Marcus. You're too kind. I would love to take the credit for all of this, but my deeper purpose is a little more, how shall I put it ... sophisticated than bombs and guns. Now, you all take care. I shall see you soon, no doubt.'

'Not if I see you first,' Jameson said as he handed the phone back to Bloom.

'Why do you think Harry's in sub-Saharan Africa?' said Karene.

'Because she said it would take him a day or more to get to an embassy and threatening to cut off people's hands sort of goes with that territory.'

'How did you know they threatened to do that?' said Bloom.

He pointed at Sophie. 'First thing she said to her mum.'

The group headed inside where they were given tea and a selection of sandwiches and cakes. Jake and Sophie demolished the cakes but Bloom noticed Karene ate nothing. Captain Morrisey joined them to say a private jet had taken off from Southampton airport at eight p.m. on Friday evening and its submitted flight plan was to an airstrip in Bakouma in the Central African Republic. 'I've spoken to the Army at the UN hospital in South Sudan to see if we can get some air support to the area. I'm assuming if your contact said Harry can get to an embassy in twenty-four hours he'll be in a vehicle.'

'Thank you,' said Karene.

'It may take some time. And it's a tricky part of the world to be travelling in alone.'

'Do you know where George Selaisse's been taken?' Bloom asked Rear Admiral Grey.

The Rear Admiral had remained very quiet throughout the reunion. He coughed and said, 'Southampton Hospital. Under police guard. I believe the Detective Superintendent who's running the investigation in Plymouth will be speaking to him when he comes round.'

'Detective Superintendent Drummond,' said Bloom. 'They think he'll be OK then?'

Grey and Morrisey exchanged a look. They weren't sure. Captain Morrisey asked to speak to her boss in private about another matter and the two of them left.

'Is that really about another matter?' said Bloom.

'I'll find out.' Jameson finished his third sandwich and then whispered, 'Oh, and by the way, I found the security box. Harry put something in it on the Monday morning, after the bomb but presumably before they wiped his memory. Chew on that.'

99

Harry walked out of RAF Brize Norton to find Karene, Bloom and Jameson waiting for him. After a long flight on a bench seat, courtesy of the RAF's Hercules transport plane, Harry was delighted with the comfortable seats inside the Mercedes.

'Your car?' he said as he climbed into the front passenger seat beside Jameson.

'Good for chucking a bike or a bed in the back. You look great.'

Harry touched his still swollen nose. As he suspected, Bello had broken it and the medics at the field hospital in Bentiu, South Sudan, had needed to reset it. The swelling on his face and lips had reduced, but the bruising had darkened to a deep purple.

'Cheers,' he said. 'I'm feeling good.' He swivelled in his seat as he put on the seatbelt. 'It's not as bad as it looks,' he said to Karene and then he looked at Bloom. 'Thank you. Both of you. For doing what you did to protect Sophie and Jake.'

He had managed to speak to his children and Caroline from the hospital. They'd all been crying by the end of the conversation. As he said goodbye, Caroline had told him to speak to Karene. 'She's worried and deserves to know you're OK.' It felt very odd to have his wife instruct him to call another woman. He knew that things had moved on, but they kept forgetting how new this was to him. He had called Karene eventually, after the nose resetting, a few stitches and as much sleep as he could manage. She had been more sensitive to his memory loss. She was happy to hear from him, he could tell by her tone, but she hadn't said anything that a concerned friend wouldn't, and he appreciated that.

There had been a few hairy moments on his African road trip. He'd managed to find out where he was from the locals working at the airstrip and they'd given him rudimentary directions to get to South Sudan, which was a day's drive away. He knew there were UN military operations there and that without a passport the British Army was his best bet for getting home. But the roads were bad and some impassable. He'd had to retrace his steps twice and felt lost and disorientated for most of the journey. He knew Sudan was to the east so used the sunset and then the stars to guide him, but there were no petrol stations and his fuel was running low. He started to lose hope and considered stopping at the next sign of civilization to get food and sleep and to rethink his next steps when his luck changed. In the early hours of the morning, he came across a group of British Army engineers repairing a road bridge.

After that, he'd just had to wait for authorization to travel home without his passport and the next scheduled trip for the Hercules. All in all, he'd spent over five days in the humid hospital and it felt good to be back in the grey drizzle.

'We're off to Peterborough, then.'

'We figured you'd appreciate another couple of hours' travelling.' Jameson pulled out of the car park on to the road through Brize Norton village and towards the A40.

'I'd certainly appreciate finding out what's in that box and putting this whole mess behind me.'

'What happened out there with Seraphine?' said Bloom.

'We met Antony Bello. He was the man hunting for Alina Maree and her mother, Naomi, who it transpires was his first wife. He was a character. He gave me my makeover.'

'Bello, as in Jacob Bello?' said Jameson.

'Yeah. Antony's uncle is the renowned warlord.'

Jameson grimaced.

'What did he want with these women?' said Karene.

'Not entirely sure. I think he simply regarded them as his.'

'He sounds charming,' said Bloom.

'Not any more,' said Harry. 'Your friend Seraphine saw to that.'

There was a prolonged silence.

'How?' asked Jameson eventually.

'With a spike she'd inserted into a pencil.'

'She stabbed him in the carotid artery?' said Bloom.

'How do you know that?' Harry put the sun visor down and opened the mirror so he could see Bloom behind him.

'It's a thing of hers.'

Harry told them what he'd learned from Seraphine: that the secret service had heard Harry's name and job mentioned in their surveillance of Bello.

'Of course,' said Bloom.

Harry looked at her in the mirror again.

'I'd been wondering why someone was looking for this girl two whole years after you helped her in 2015. And it was that Facebook picture.'

'You think Julian posting the picture of Isobel's party started it?' said Jameson.

'If Bello had people trawling the internet for images of Alina, it's certainly a possibility, don't you think?'

'Anyway,' said Harry. 'Bello's stuff is irrelevant now. He's out of the picture. This girl is free. Apparently she's in witness protection. Put there by your lot after the bomb.'

'MI6?' said Jameson.

'That's what your Seraphine said.'

'She is not *my* Seraphine.'

'Sorry, mate. That's not what she thinks.'

'Do you need something to eat or drink?' said Karene.

Harry liked that she was looking out for him. 'I'm good, thanks.' He smiled back at her then shuffled in his seat to get more comfortable. 'I know this Bello character wouldn't have hesitated to torture and kill me to get what he wanted, but I'm struggling with the fact that our guys did this to me.' He tapped the side of his head with two fingers. 'Surely there was another way.'

'They must have had good reason,' said Bloom.

Jameson overtook a caravan driving ridiculously slowly. 'And hopefully that reason is in this box.'

Jameson insisted on coming in too. He joked that Harry might destroy crucial evidence and Harry knew that it wasn't really a joke. The lady from the bank took them to the vault. Karene had prepared a folder for Harry that included his passport, and they checked his details and credentials. They then inserted their key alongside his and, when the box was unlocked, left Harry and Jameson alone.

It was no bigger than a shoe box. Harry placed it on the table in the middle of the room and sat in the only chair. He looked at Jameson, and then he took a deep breath and opened it.

Inside were four white envelopes. The top one had his name written in his own handwriting. He placed it on the table. The other envelopes were addressed to Jake, Sophie and Karene. Harry held the last one in his hand. He couldn't remember this woman and yet he'd written her name on an envelope and placed it in a locked box in a bank vault. Why? What was he going to learn in here? What was she?

'Do you want me to open it?' Jameson said.

Harry closed the box and picked up the envelope with his name again. Something told him he wasn't going to like what he found in there, but before the idea unnerved him completely, he ripped open the envelope and read the letter within.

Karene tapped her foot incessantly. She couldn't stop. It was like part of her wanted to run.

'You OK?' said Bloom.

'Course.' Karene flicked through the pages of the bank's customer magazine. There was an article on savings and investments.

Harry and Jameson eventually returned to the reception. She wanted to rush over, to ask if he was OK, but something in his expression stopped her. In his hand he held some envelopes. He handed one to her and said, 'I'm sorry. Really. I . . .' He shook his head and walked out of the building.

'So?' Bloom said to Jameson.

'Take her somewhere quiet. Get her a tea. And then let her read it. I'll keep an eye on him.'

Karene didn't understand. Why all the drama? The mystery? Surely this was where they dispensed with all that and found out what was actually going on. She looked down at the envelope. Her name was there in Harry's neat writing. The sight tightened her stomach. He often used to leave her little notes, jokes to make her laugh or to tell her he loved her.

'Come on.' Bloom led her out into the street and around the corner to a nearby cafe. She ordered two teas, as instructed by Jameson, and chose a table in the back corner.

'What are those for?' Karene said, seeing the handful of sugar sachets in Bloom's hand.

'Shock.'

Karene stared at the envelope for a second or two then carefully opened it and unfolded the letter within.

Hey Honey,

This is going to be the hardest letter to write because for you the consequences are so much worse than they are for any of us. You are going to remember what I will forget. You'll remember how much we laugh, how much we support each other and push each other, and you'll remember that neither of us has ever felt like this before. You are my world, Karene. You are unequivocally the love of my life. And I know that if the shoe were on the other foot, I would hate you for doing to us what I'm about to do.

Please understand that my reasons for doing this are about more than just protecting a vulnerable girl and her child. I met Alina when she was fifteen. She and her mum were pulled out of the water off the coast of Italy. She begged us to help her mum, but there was nothing we could do. Alina was so brave. She simply wiped her eyes and asked how she could help with the others. But I noticed that she didn't really belong. She sat apart and wasn't included. People had discovered that she was part of the Bello family and they were either scared or resentful and so, when we docked, I gave her Julian's address and enough money to get there. I wasn't sure she'd make it out of that refugee camp alive.

It was only later that I discovered she was carrying Antony Bello's child. She begged me to hide her from him. Once I'd researched the man and the things he'd done, I couldn't let him find her. I managed to get her set up in the UK and helped as much as I could. She called her son Henry after me and I've been visiting them once a month, when I tell you I'm seeing Lucy. This is a lie, I know, and I'm sorry, but Alina and little Henry are my penance. I'm giving them the life Lucy and Max should have had if it weren't for me.

Karene stopped and closed her eyes. He always brushed away the guilt he felt about his sister's stroke, but clearly it still ate away at him. She should have made him talk about it more, helped him to see it wasn't his fault. Had that been the source of his nightmares?

And now Bello is coming for me. He tortured Julian and I know he'll do the same to me. I can't hide from him without giving up my job and my family and I'm not prepared to do that, so it's only a matter of time before he gets to me. Abraham Lincoln once said, 'No man has a good enough memory to be a successful liar.' I can't risk that I won't be able to lie well enough, that he'll work out where she is or that he has a son, because if he knows that, he'll never stop hunting for her. Hopefully, this way, he'll give up and leave her be. I'll be a dead end.

I know you'll be angry at whoever is making me do this, Karene, but this is my decision, my idea. I want this because I can't be responsible for another young mother losing her child or her life. I just couldn't live with myself.

I hope you can understand and, in time, forgive me for sacrificing us to save them. Just know that the time we've had together has been the happiest of my life. Thank you.

All my love,
Harry.

'He forgot me on purpose.' She screwed the letter into a ball.

Bloom unravelled the paper Karene had thrown on the table and read the letter quickly. 'Karene. Try not to see it as a rejection.' She emptied a sachet of sugar into her friend's tea.

'Of course not. I'm the love of his life, the best thing that ever happened to him, bar his children. Why would I see him deleting me from his brain as a rejection? Why would I think that I was worth consulting before he did this?'

'He didn't have much time and he thought this was the only way.'

'He had time to open a bank account and write a letter. I'm pretty sure that means he had time to call me.'

'Would you have let him do it?'

'Of course not.'

'Well then, Karene. It's done. The only thing left to decide is if you can forgive him.'

The corridors of Whitehall were everything he'd expected, from the grandeur of the entrance to the hushed elegance of the hallways. He stood outside the office of the Secretary of State for Foreign and Commonwealth Affairs. He held a copy of *The Times*, in which was an item on the death of the controversial leader of God's Liberation Army, Jacob Bello, from pancreatic cancer. The article detailed some of Bello's reported atrocities as well as his attempts in later life to transform his organization from one of resistance to one of influence on the world stage. His efforts had largely failed, the article said, but with the appointment of a new leader, an Oxford-educated philosophy and modern languages graduate, there was real potential for change. Abdul had liked the photograph they'd printed of him and sent a short letter of gratitude to the journalist responsible.

His phone began to ring in his pocket. He had a few minutes before his meeting was due to start and so he answered it.

'How was your trip?' asked Seraphine.

'Very pleasant. Thank you.' She had arranged for him to use the private jet.

'I know you have an important meeting and I wanted to wish you luck. Not that you'll need it.'

'You're very kind.'

They spoke for a few moments about his first few weeks as the new leader of God's Liberation Army, as well as his planned rebrand for the organization. He didn't like the current name. It was too religious for the West and the word 'army' too antagonistic. Seraphine had agreed and they were working on a more appropriate title.

'Let me know how it goes,' she said as the conversation came to an end. 'And say hello to the Foreign Secretary for me. Tell him he still owes me one for getting him that job.'

Abdul hung up with a smile as the Foreign Secretary's PA arrived to usher him in.

103

Jameson pulled into the last space in the small car park on the outskirts of Leeds, not far from Harrogate. He had spent the last few days cycling the route of the Tour de France's Grand Départ which had been held nearby in 2014.

Bloom was in the area finalizing the sale of her mother's house. She'd chosen the cafe. It was a homely place with purple-painted windows and a carved wooden sign that swayed in the breeze. When he opened the door, a small bell announced his arrival and the ladies behind the counter greeted him with large smiles and cheery hellos.

Bloom sat at one of the old school desks drinking peppermint tea and writing in her notebook.

'Cute place,' he said, taking a seat. 'Cakes look good.' The counter behind him had an array of home-baked sponges, tray bakes and large fruit scones.

'I thought you'd like that. And it shares its name with a naval vessel that local residents raised money to fund in World War Two, so it seemed a fitting spot for a debrief.'

'They called a ship Bramble Bakehouse?'

Bloom smiled. 'HMS *Bramble*. The bakehouse bit is just for the cafe.' She put aside her notebook as he ordered a coffee and a slice of peanut butter flapjack. 'I spoke to Harry yesterday. He seems to be doing better.'

'Any memories?' asked Jameson.

'Nothing at all. I'm not sure he'll get anything back.'

'How's Karene coping with that?'

'She was angry at first but I think they're meeting for a drink later today.'

'Will that be the first time they've seen each other since letter-gate?'

Bloom nodded. 'He told me something interesting about his visit to Africa with Seraphine.' She reached for the newspaper on the bench beside her, opened it, folded it in half, and placed it on the table between them. 'This man, Abdul Sharif, has just succeeded Jacob Bello as the head of God's Liberation Army.'

'I heard Bello senior had popped his clogs. Good riddance to the sick bastard. Is this guy any better, do we know?'

'Well, that's the thing. Harry swears blind this was Seraphine's contact out there.'

'Oh crap.'

'So, I'm guessing, no, not any better.'

Jameson looked closely at the picture of Sharif. He was slim and attractive with intelligent eyes. 'He looks educated and professional. They'll think he's safer, easier to negotiate with.'

'And yet, if I had to put money on it, I'd say he was a high-functioning psychopath.'

'One of her recruits?'

'I knew she wouldn't have helped us without some gain, but I couldn't see what it was. She made out she wanted time with you, but I suspected there was more to it than that, maybe revenge for the fact I'd outwitted her in the spring. Now, I think she used us to get to Harry and then she used him to get in a room with Antony Bello . . . so that she could kill him.'

'And put her own man in his place. It was common knowledge Jacob Bello was at death's door. What's that woman up to? First she's selecting psychopaths and now she's placing them in positions of power.'

'Indeed she is.'

'But why?' asked Jameson.

'I have my suspicions, but I'm hoping I'm wrong.'

104

Karene arrived at the French restaurant and saw that Harry was already waiting at the bar. Her stomach lurched in a combination of excitement and fear. Why had she suggested the same place they'd met on their first date? It had seemed a sweet idea when she'd first thought of it, but now she realized it would only exacerbate the crushing sadness she felt all the time. It could never be the same. They could not relive the past no matter how much she might want to. Could she make him repeat every date, every trip, every evening curled up in front of a movie, and effectively wipe out the memory loss? In her imagination, absolutely. But she knew that was naive.

'Punctual as ever,' she said, repeating her greeting from back then. That first time, his smile caught her off guard, so warm and open, but today it looked forced and anxious.

Harry ordered without looking at her. He was dressed more casually than the last time. He wasn't trying to impress her.

Karene took the drink and they sat at a table in the centre of the room. She took a sip to drive away the nerves.

'Don't worry,' he said. 'You go ahead. No need to say cheers.'

Karene stared at him over her glass.

'What?' he asked.

'Why did you say that?'

'It's a joke, sorry. You enjoy your drink.'

If this was going to work, she'd need to be honest. 'You said that last time.'

'Last time? Have we been here before?'

'Our first date.'

Harry paused and she couldn't read his expression; irritation, anger, sadness?

'Is that bad? I'm sorry if that's insensitive. I thought it might . . .'

'Jog my memory?'

'Silly, I know.'

'That's not silly. I'm flattered you'd want to after all I've put you through.'

'I don't mean to make you feel uncomfortable or expect you to know what to say. I'm just hoping you might let me be part of your life in some way.'

He held her gaze and it felt a little more sincere. 'I think I'd like that.'

'Have you had any news on Alina and her little boy?'

'I haven't asked. I expect she'll be set up somewhere and hopefully adapting. She's been through enough. I wouldn't want to put her through the trauma of being forgotten.'

'Maybe down the line then?'

Harry shrugged and sipped his drink. 'I've been doing some reading around the migrant crisis. I thought it might help my memory but, well, I think everything's probably gone, if I'm honest. I expect we'll be judged on how we've handled it. It's awful to have people travelling so far with no guarantees.'

'And then to find that the countries they come to for help are turning them and their children away,' said Karene.

'Why are you smiling?' he asked. 'That's not something to smile about. Oh, no. Let me guess. I said something similar last time.'

'Pretty much verbatim.'

'I suppose you can't change a leopard's spots.'

'Or teach an old sea dog new tricks.'

'Less of the old, you.' His laugh was the very best. 'What now? Shall we get something to eat? I'm starving.'

'I'd like to start over,' she said.

He looked up from the menu.

'Do you think we could do that?' Karene added.

His bruises had faded a little and when he smiled he almost looked like her old Harry. 'I don't see why not.'

105

Jameson took a large bite of his flapjack. 'So work this through with me. The Secret Service hear mention of Harry when monitoring Bello's communications.'

'Why didn't they warn Harry straightaway?'

Jameson took a second bite and chewed it quickly. 'They can't have known who this girl was or how Harry was involved. Protocol would be to observe and learn in the first instance. Harry's letter to himself said that when the bomb went off agents on site scrambled to the scene and saw Harry being placed in the ambulance. They followed it, intercepted it and took Harry and the driver in for questioning. The paramedics – or whatever they were – didn't accompany Harry in the ambulance. George Selaisse himself was the bogus sub-lieutenant pictured at the ball. He didn't trust anyone else to make sure Harry was in the right spot and then transferred to their ambulance, I expect.'

'But he wasn't in the ambulance. Was the driver one of his men?'

'No. That guy is smart. The driver was paid in cash. He didn't have anything helpful other than a rendezvous point. This is so good,' he said pointing at the flapjack.

Bloom smiled. Jameson had always been a sugar fiend. 'Presumably the agents grilled Harry and he told them about Alina and her son and requested that they be placed in a witness protection scheme?'

Jameson nodded. 'He was offered one too, but Caroline couldn't join him because of the divorce, so he'd have needed to leave his kids.'

'And that's when he asked them to wipe his memory?' Bloom wondered how Harry had come up with the idea and how long he'd agonized over the decision. 'Is that something you were asked to do often? Erase people's minds?'

Jameson tilted his head from side to side. 'I've had stranger requests. I'm impressed they managed to pull it off though. Things have changed since I left.'

'There's some pretty impressive technology out there these days.'

'They did it at Stanford Hall Rehabilitation Centre.'

'Freddie must have been one of them, then?'

'I'd say so, yeah. And that article in the press. I'd say that was planted by MI6 to try and stop Bello's people coming for Harry again.'

'Broadcasting his memory loss? Clever. It was a brave thing for Harry to do.'

'It was bloody nuts.' Jameson scoffed the last of his cake. 'I was right though. This was all about his job.'

'No. This was all about his character: his guilt at what happened to his sister and her child, his empathy for those in crisis, and his willingness to sacrifice his own happiness to ensure the safety of the people he cares about.'

'But if he wasn't in that job, he wouldn't have been on

that helicopter and he wouldn't have met that girl. None of this happens without the job.'

'But he wasn't the only officer to come across Alina on that mission. His character is the differentiator.'

'Let's agree to disagree then.'

'There's no such thing as reality—'

'Only perceptions of it,' finished Jameson.

'And that's what keeps us in work.'

Jameson sat back and stretched. 'When did Seraphine come into the picture though? That's what I want to know.'

Bloom picked up her notebook and reviewed what she'd written. 'Abdul Sharif wouldn't have been the logical successor to Jacob Bello unless he'd been with them for a while. If Seraphine was involved in putting him there, she'd have known about the search for Alina and then Harry from the beginning. I think when she discovered Karene had asked for our help, she couldn't stop herself interfering, and then she spotted an opportunity to turn it to her advantage. She only took Harry so that she could kill Bello. Harry was lucky she liked him or he might have disappeared too.'

'You shouldn't have invited her in. We gave her access to Harry.'

'Keep your friends close and your enemies closer. As soon as I knew that she was sending Karene emails, I had to speak to her. You can't ignore a woman like Seraphine. If her eyes are on you it's better to find out what she's looking at.'

'She almost got you killed.'

'But she didn't.'

'Well . . .' said Jameson, finishing his coffee. 'Thank you for coming to my rescue when you thought I was in danger.'

'Does that mean I'm forgiven?'

'It means, we should start over.'

Bloom sat back and smiled at him. 'Let's start over then.'

106

They couldn't see her, but she could see them. She watched them through the window while she spoke to Abdul on the phone. She was a pretty good lip-reader so she could follow their conversation easily enough, even though she could only see Augusta's lips. She wished they were sitting the other way around. She liked Marcus's lips better.

She smiled when she saw Augusta show Marcus Abdul's picture in the paper. She knew her old psychologist was one of the few people who would be able to keep up. Augusta placed the paper back on the bench beneath her notebook and pencil. It was yellow with a red-capped end. It was only a matter of time before Dr Augusta Bloom saw the logic of joining them.

Seraphine wished Abdul luck with his meeting and then hung up and watched as Bloom and Jameson discussed Harry's case. She'd done a little digging on the memory loss. She had someone in the secret service and they'd briefed her on the surgery. It made her even fonder of Captain Harry Peterson. Augusta was right: she had intended to make him disappear in Africa. But he'd impressed her with his bravery. Not all 'normals' were disappointing.

As Marcus finished his coffee, he said something that

made Augusta's posture shift, suddenly lighter and freer. Seraphine concentrated on the woman's lips. And then she smiled.

'Yes, Augusta,' she said, putting her hands in her pockets and walking away. 'Let's start over.'

Acknowledgements

The difficult second book. It is a scary thing to look at a blank page and hope you might repeat the magic. Can I impress the publishers again? Can I please the readers again? There were moments of over-confidence and moments of despair. I simply had to keep writing and hold my nerve. Things I could not have done without the help of some truly awesome people.

First and foremost, huge thanks go to my editor Lizzy Goudsmit at Transworld. Along with Sharika Teelwah and copy-editor Sophie Wilson you honed my efforts into a story I feel very proud of. Your constant encouragement has been invaluable. I cannot thank you enough. You and the team at Transworld continue to make the whole publishing experience a pleasure to be part of.

My initial idea for this book – an explosion at a military ball – was based on the most fleeting of insights into the world of the UK's Armed Forces. My challenge was to find an advisor patient enough to help an unknown writer re-create their world. I could not have found better than Lieutenant Commander Jamie Smithson of the Royal Navy. I thank you for your input, your challenge and your constant enthusiasm. You taught me much and I'm forever grateful for your help. I hope I have represented you and your colleagues well.

I also need to thank three awesome medics for their contributions. I wanted the memory loss to be grounded in as much fact as possible and could not have done that without you. Thank you to Dr Daniel Scott at Harrogate Hospital for introducing me to consultant neurologist Dr Rosaria Buccoliero. Our phone call gave me the confidence to write the story in my head. And then there was the wonderful Mr Ian Anderson, neurosurgeon at Leeds General Infirmary. Thank you for taking the time to answer my questions so comprehensively and also for offering ideas on how today's technology could be re-imagined for a fictional world. You are impressive people and any errors made are mine and mine alone.

My wonderful family. Your support is hugely appreciated, as is your sarcasm, which keeps my feet on the ground. I hope I have made you proud.

My Ella. You are my world and you put all this non-sense into perspective. And no, you can't read it until you're older.

Finally, I cannot finish without thanking the brave servicemen and -women of the UK Armed Forces for all the humanitarian work you do for those in need around the world.

Reading Group Questions

The following are just some of the questions you might like to consider:

- In the opening scene of the novel, a bomb is detonated at a military ball. At first, who did you think was responsible? Did your suspicions evolve as the novel progressed?

- At the beginning of the novel, Bloom and Jameson are recovering from the traumatic events that occurred in the first book in this series, *Gone*. To what extent do you think their relationship has been damaged by their difficult past?

- 'No one has a good enough memory to be a successful liar.'
  This is the epigraph at the beginning of the novel. In what ways is it relevant?

- Augusta Bloom is a very private person, and shares very little of her private life with those around her. But at the beginning of *Lost*, we meet Karene, one of Augusta's oldest friends. What do you learn about Augusta through this relationship?

- Leona Deakin, the author of *Lost,* employs flashbacks regularly throughout the novel. How does this movement between past and present affect the reading experience? In what ways does this technique build suspense and tension?

- Many of the characters are struggling with guilt or anger about things that have happened in previous years. How do concerns about the past affect these characters' actions and decisions in the present – thinking about Harry Peterson in particular?

- 'You're quite similar, aren't you?'
    'Karene and I? Not really. I mean, we're both psychologists—'
What are the main similarities and differences between Augusta and Karene? They are both psychologists, but do you think they work in similar ways?

- Towards the end of the novel, we realize that there is a very tangled web of allies and enemies in this story. Did any of these relationships surprise you?

- *Lost* unfolds in a number of international locations. What do the different locales add to the plot?

- 'I always imagined life would be easier with a bit of power and influence but, you know what, it's just dinner with sycophants and self-centred bores.'
The theme of power is constantly at play in this book. Which characters are motivated by power? Do they achieve it?